Cracked Casualty

Lost Royals of Transylvania

Book 2

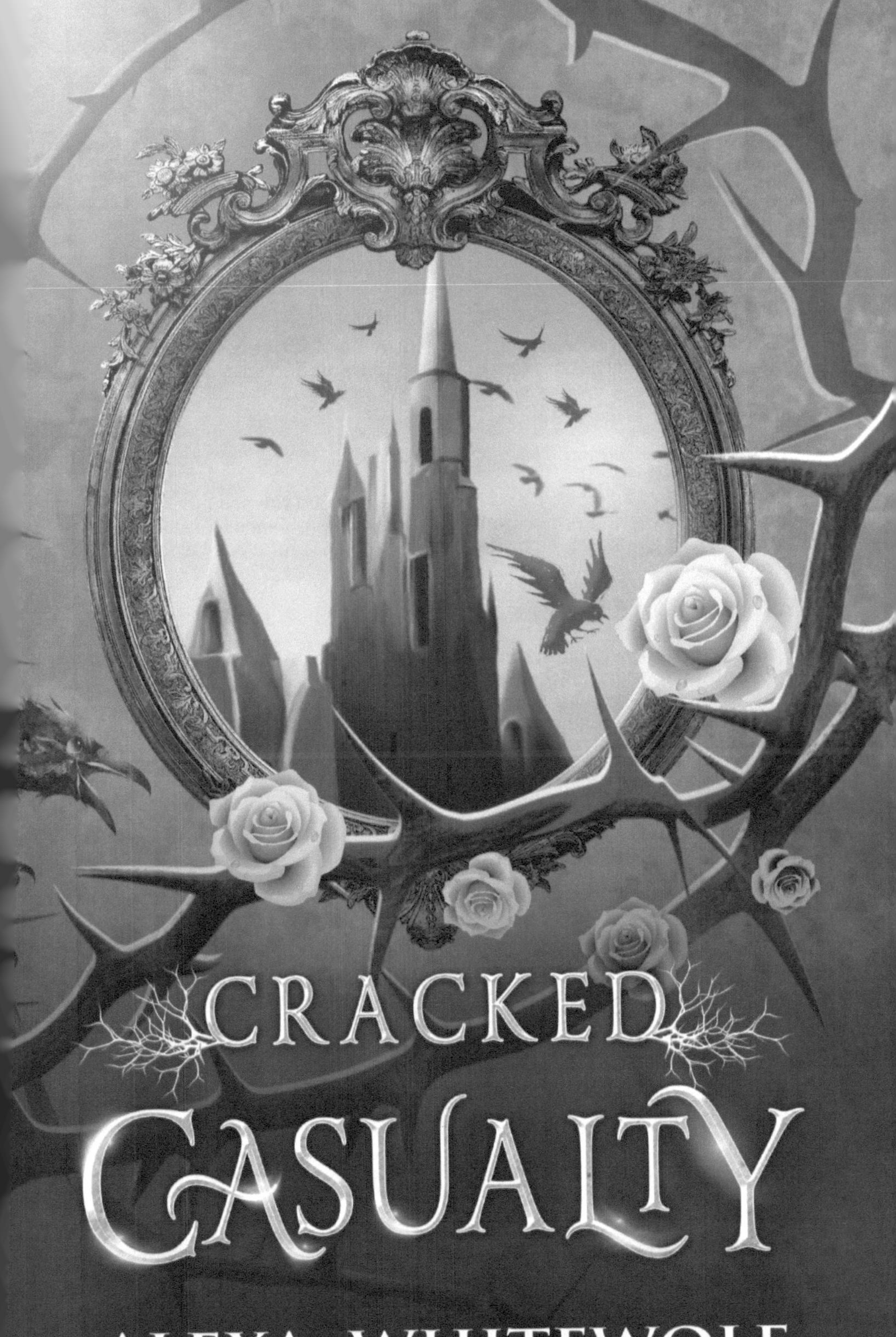
CRACKED
CASUALTY
ALEXA WHITEWOLF

Cracked Casualty
A *Lost Royals of Transylvania* novel

by Alexa Whitewolf

Cover design by Y. Nikolova at **Ammonia Book Covers**
Editing and formatting by Luna Imprints Author Services

ISBN: 978-1-989384-15-2

10 9 8 7 6 5 4 3 2

Rogues Extended Universe – Reading Order

Moonlight Rogues
Flaming Rogues
Immortal Rogues
Lost Royals of Transylvania
Vârcolac Legacy (coming 2022)

Author's Note & Acknowledgements

It's funny... The more time passes by, the more birthdays I celebrate, the more I start appreciating the super small things.

Like the coffee my husband always make sure I have in the morning so I can do my daily writing.

Like the phone calls I get from my mom, checking in to see if I'm still alive and not lost in my writing cave.

Like the friends whose support and every encouraging word help me through the dark times.

Like the doggos who light up my every day with their cuteness and petting demands!

Yes, this series has taken me for another spin. I never would've thought these novels would be so long, so consuming to write, and that the characters would be so impossible to resist! But I prevail, at their mercy, pen at the ready.

I want to give a huge special thanks to my beta and amazing friend Siobhan, for all your patience with the first draft of this mess (and the one before it! And the ones that'll follow!) I can't wait to get those bear shifters of ours out in the world!

An extra special thanks to Annemarie for catching all the embarrassing typos I missed!

To my cover designer, Y. Nikolova at Ammonia Book Covers, for bringing this amazing vision to life!

To the formatting team at Luna Imprints – the jewel you've turned this book into is a work of art!

And as always, to my love: *I wouldn't be where I am without your unconditional support and our lovable furbabies.*

To my readers who stuck by me and all the ones taking a chance on me… I wish you happy readings.

Alexa

GLOSSARY

A few quick things!

Vampir / vampiri – vampire / vampires

Vârcolac / vârcolaci – Romanian werewolf / werewolves (Note: vrykolakas are the *undead* version)

Da / nu – yes/no

Am nevoie de ajutorul tău. – I need your help

Ai grija - be careful

Prinţesa – princess

Nu, nu încă – no, not yet

Imposibil – impossible

Scuze – sorry

Mihai Viteazul – Michael the Brave (a national hero)

Zmeu / zmei – dragon shifters of the Carpathian

Draga mea – my darling

Cozonac – a yummy Romanian dessert popular around Easter/Christmas holidays

Marcus cel Rău – Marcus the Bad One

Pleci? – You're leaving?

Argeş – a river in Romania

Bine – good

Heregie – blue blood

Nu, mersi – no, thank you

Da, prinţul meu – yes, my prince

Chapter 1

Violeta

The sound of laughter draws my attention. Normally, I try to dull these extra senses, in an effort to quiet my own mind. Sometimes I even use human vices—pot being my go-to. Today, nothing has helped.

I've been in the solarium, tending to my plants. A relaxing endeavor, if ever there was one for a vampir of a royal bloodline like myself. Not that it helped much. I'm still restless, still feeling like I'm missing something huge.

Might have something to do with the sword of Damocles hanging over my head and threatening my immortal existence any moment. Or, maybe not. Maybe it's more the fact I'm afflicted by a disease that none of my kind—vampiri—seem to know anything about.

There's a whoosh of air behind me, alerting me to another sibling. This damned disease has taken away some of my senses, making me almost human at times. One massive side effect on worst days is the inability to scent other vampiri. Thus, I'm blind to the identity of said sibling until they speak.

"Again with the plants, Vi?" A long sigh. "You and Nico must be competing for the most boring vampir award."

I let out a strangled chuckle before dropping the leaf of one such plant, and whirling to face my sister.

With her auburn hair, petite stature and hourglass figure, Elizabeth—Liza—could've been an angel. Instead, she's more of a demoness in disguise, using her allure to draw her prey in and use them to her liking.

My eyes are drawn to the scar on her right cheekbone. Her hair is braided today, leaving the angry, red line starkly evident against her pale skin. Out of all of us, she and Alex make no attempt at hiding their true nature.

As always, I shift my gaze to meet hers instead, forcing myself not to linger on the scar. Over the years, I've trained myself to give it less and less attention. It's only a reminder of a past she'd rather forget—not that Liza's the heartwarming, sharing type. The psychotic kind is more up her alley.

"I would hardly call Nico boring these days," I say. "He's been more like himself than I've seen him in ages."

A scowl twists her features. "That goddamned human! I wish she had died and spared us all her presence. Seeing him debase himself like that, with one of *them*! It's—" She trails off, clenching her fists.

I move closer to her, tilting my head to the side. "Don't you think it's time to let go of some of that anger, Liza? It does no one any good."

"No, it's not. It will never be time. The reappearance of the hunters has only reinforced that opinion." Her blue eyes, so similar to mine, blaze red in her anger. "You join him in this stupid human-loving quest. You always have. But don't fucking impose your views onto me."

She's gone in a whirl, before I can even muster the strength to sigh.

"Don't take it to heart," another voice says behind me. "We both know Liza and Alex are...complicated."

I face Vlad, my other brother. "How much did you hear?" When he arches an eyebrow, I roll my eyes. "Right. Everything. Just because I'm losing my senses, doesn't mean everyone else is."

"You never know. For all you know, it'll soon start affecting all of us. We haven't been able to figure out the real root of your disease."

"And maybe we never will." I step back to my plants, caressing some leaves. At least they keep growing and evolving. I'm only stagnant. Soon to be lifeless. "Tassa's cure is temporary and I'm okay with that."

"Are you really?" He touches my shoulder, forcing me to face him. "Violeta, I will find others. Doctors, healers, mages... You just have to ask me."

"We're still in hiding and for good reason. I don't want to risk any of you."

He frowns. "I wouldn't mind. Heaven knows I have enough to make up for."

"As do I. None of us took our turning well, and some could say it was out of our control. But... perhaps this is just another form of punishment."

He sighs. Giggles float to us again, and he glances in their direction. Amusement dances in his eyes when a darker, male chuckle answers.

"It's nice to *see* Nico again," I whisper. "The real him."

Vlad meets my gaze. "It is. I know it's been driving Liza and Alex crazy seeing them being so loving towards each other—a *lot*—lately, but it gives me hope. That some of us may find happiness, after all."

I nod. "Even if it is temporary."

Vlad kisses the side of my temple. "Don't give up just yet, Vi. Father didn't turn us into immortal beings for no reason." He's gone the moment after, too.

The laughter rings clearly again, and a smile stretches my lips as I recognize the voice. I leave the solarium, making my way to the library a few halls over. When I peek my head through the large oak door, I find Tassa and my brother, Nicolae.

They're both staring at a map laid out over the massive mahogany table. He's behind her, his arms wrapped around her waist and peppering kisses under her earlobe. Giggles escape her as she leans into his embrace.

Unseen and unheard, I take a moment to soak in the picture. It has been centuries since I've seen my brother show emotion. After losing his best friend over two hundred years ago to an unfortunate set of circumstances, he closed himself off and refused to care for anything or anyone. Even us, his siblings. Blood of his blood, created by the same man. For the longest time, all he knew was the emptiness of this immortality we've been blessed—and cursed—with.

Then Tassa burst into his life, and it was full-color again. It took some time, and a lot of coaxing them, but I knew from the beginning her love was not something Nico could turn his back on. Consorts—in other lores called mates—for vampiri don't come often. Ever, in fact, according to Father. It's why he was so broken when he lost his one and only.

Because of our souls—or lack thereof—we don't get second chances at love. It happens only once that someone will balance out the Darkness in us, complete us. And the longer we live, the rarer it is.

But when it comes to these two? I knew the moment I saw them in the same room that they were destined to be together.

Nico, well, it took him a little bit longer to reach the same conclusion. I had to remind him of Father's loss to finally knock some sense into him. After all, Vlad Țepeș never would have been the man we'd grown around if he hadn't lost his first wife. And I, amongst all my siblings, am probably the most aware of the pain he carried with him, day in and day out until he couldn't handle it anymore and took his own life.

Memories of our chats whisper through my mind like a soft breeze carried through an empty land. My consciousness is so vast, filled with so many centuries of remembering, that sometimes the heaviest shroud falls on my shoulders. This life I've lived, is it truly a life? Or merely an existence spent experiencing things left and right?

I've travelled the world. Before we all went into hiding, before Father died, I travelled. I was worshiped and admired and loved. I found human lovers and vampiri lovers and savored life. Having been a sickly child only made immortality that much more precious, more of a forbidden fruit.

And still, now, knowing I have an expiration date, it makes me wonder if I've truly *lived.* What relationships do I have, aside from my siblings? What legacy will I leave behind, besides their broken bonds?

I force my thoughts back to Nico and Tassa. Seeing them together, his cheek resting against hers, his arms wrapped around her midsection, warms a part of my soul I'd thought dormant. One that craves that same intimacy for myself. And it reminds me there are other things, beyond this castle and my sickness. Things that I've limited myself from experiencing these last two years, suffering in silence as I feared being on my deathbed.

Thanks to Tassa, that's no longer the case. She bought me time. My five siblings, with their centuries of knowledge, couldn't figure out the reasons behind my disease. And they couldn't ask for help, since our entire royal bloodline is threatened by other vampiri clans. But this human who'd lost her father was able to dig into my disease and figure out a solution.

We're still blind to the cause of this disease that makes me more human than vampir, but at least the concoction with muroni—cave-dwelling vampiri—blood she created for me has been working.

At least enough to temporarily make me feel like myself, if I consume it regularly. How long that'll last for... Who knows?

I knock on the open door, drawing Nico's gaze to me. He smiles, and Tassa waves me over.

"Did we wake you?" she asks.

I chuckle. "No. I was in the solarium, remembering what it's like to move around without feeling like I'm dying."

Her smile falters a bit. "Is the muroni concoction—"

"Still working, da, don't worry. I didn't mean to rain on your giggle parade." I glance at the map. "What are you looking at?"

"Travel," Nico says. "I've bribed Tassa to come with me to Marea Neagră."

The Black Sea is our version of Mediterranean heaven, though it's a body of water that's, well, land-locked—and also the world's largest. Most people think it got its name because of the aquatic life that looks dead. Given there's plenty of marine life in it, it's not quite the case. More to the point is the fact its name refers to an old system of cardinal directions based on colors. Black was for north, red for south, white for west and green or light blue was east. Marea Neagră, thus, was north.

But it's easier to explain to anyone that'll listen that its name derives from the color of the water or its climatic conditions.

"But we can postpone," Tassa adds quickly, breaking me from my thoughts. "If you need me here, I mean."

I shake my head, reaching over to tug on one of her dark brown locks. It doesn't escape my notice that this human has shown me more compassion than some of my own siblings—but then again, she hasn't lived centuries. Such an existence would be long enough to lose even *her* kindness.

"Don't even think about it," I say. "You've been living back in the village for, what, two weeks now? And I haven't croaked and died. Believe me, I'll survive while you go on a honeymoon."

Her cheeks pinken adorably, and I turn my gaze to Nico again so she doesn't see the envy I'm trying hard to conceal. "Smart choice, too. There are no clans who've claimed the territory there. Ergo, no one to worry about."

"My thoughts precisely." He tilts his head to the side. "We're leaving tomorrow, but if you need me, call Tassa's cellphone."

He never did like electronics, but at least now he has a human with him who's perfectly used to them. And since Tassa made sure I know her number by heart, it means I'll be able to reach him whenever—not that I plan to interrupt.

I grin. "Will do. Enjoy the trip, lovebirds!"

Before tears can escape my eyes, I turn on my heels and walk out. And out. And out, until I'm under fresh air and surrounded by woods, and leaning against a tree trunk.

I am happy for my brother. He deserves this, he really does, and I've done everything possible to ensure Tassa and him end up together. But seeing them together also fills me with...loneliness. Because the last time I had someone, he was snatched away from me harshly. Elizabeta—my slightly psychotic sister—didn't like that he was with me and tried to rob us. A stupid plan for a human, really. But I'd cared for him, for a time.

And before that?

I can't remember a single time I've had something as pure as these two do.

And while the rest of our siblings mutter and scoff in distaste—Alexandru and Mirabela don't particularly enjoy having a human around—I can feel myself staring at them with longing.

Since this disease hit me two years ago, I thought I was done for. A walking carcass. Now, I have another chance, albeit a temporary one. Maybe it's time I take my destiny in my own hands, break with the routine and find out what else is out there for me to sample...before I turn to dust.

Sighing, I face my home once more. The castle extends larger than life to the skies. It's been our home for only a few weeks, and has none of the luxuries we've been used to. But it's close enough to a human village for hunting and far enough from vampiri strongholds to keep us hidden...for now.

Perhaps it really is time to take a step off the beaten path and find out what lies beyond it.

When I wake up from sleep this time, it's to a new beat. The hunger for blood that normally accompanies my awakening isn't quite there, not anymore. On the contrary. *Real* hunger has taken its place, and it's thus I find myself in the castle's kitchen, munching on food perfectly suited for Tassa, and no one else.

This has become the latest development of my disease. Eating human food, instead of humans *as* food. I gulp down some meatloaf and potatoes Tassa must've brought in, barely bothering to breathe. The first time this manifested, around a week ago, I'd taken the time to savor each bite. Now? I'm consumed by a need to fill my stomach before I'm only back to being able to do so with blood.

It's the oddest paradox. When I was turned, I lost myself. High on immortality, on all it could give me, I had no limits. Nico helped me find those limits. And I learned I'd forever miss the taste of human food, but the scent could still be just as appealing as before.

Now that I'm able to have it again? The enjoyment is bittersweet from the knowledge it's because I'm losing my immortal self.

Thoughts of earlier still jump around in my mind, making me feel more and more restless. Before, it was a single thought, but now it's a cacophony demanding that I take what I can while I am still able to do so.

Father instilled in us a certain independence, but also a family mentality. We were turned to be ruthless, to rule over the other vampiri in the area. To be his legacy.

We might've not realized it at the time, but in retrospect I think he'd always planned to take his own life. He'd loved his consort so much, speaking her name was akin to tossing holy water on him. Losing her broke him in a way I don't think he understood. None of us did, really. We were all too busy dealing with our newfound immortality.

The shame of those days fills me, cutting off my appetite. How many lives I'd taken, when I'd been unable to control myself. How the bloodlust was all-consuming, even more so than this food I've been ingesting. How nothing else mattered, except life after life snuffed under my lethal fangs. If it hadn't been for Nico helping me control it, I would've become the next Bloody Countess of these parts.

And therein lies the crux of the problem. Anything I do, anything I suffer now, my siblings will feel responsible to fix for me.

I gulp and set the food away.

This castle, my siblings—I need to be away from them. They will do whatever they can to stop this plague that has descended on me, but in so doing will rob me of my freedom. They're dysfunctional and slightly psychotic, but when it comes to us and having each other's back, they've always been there. Sometimes too much.

And while my disease has been the talk of the last few weeks, there's more beyond that. The vampir clans who'll hunt us when they find our new hideout. The hunters who seem to have made it their life's mission to exterminate each and every single one of us. And the new wolves who've settled here. Their allegiance isn't yet certain.

On their own, these elements would lead us to be more cautious.

Coupled with my disease, it will soon send my siblings into a frenzy, one determined to protect me at all costs since I'm the weakest of the family.

And I cannot allow that. I've fought too hard for my freedom, only to have it snatched away.

It's either now, when Nico leaves and no one will think to look for me right away, or never.

I rush back to my room. At least vampir speed is still mine to control, but for how long, I don't know.

As quickly and quietly as I can, I shove some items in a backpack. Clothes, an old notebook, the leftover muroni concoction—there should be enough there for a few weeks—and scribble a note with Nico's name, then head back out. He'll find it when he's back from his vacation, which means I'll have plenty of time to enjoy some unrestrained fun.

On the edge of the castle grounds, I look back. Dark towers reach for the sky. Moonlight reflects off arched windows, both ethereal and ominous. Its imposing structure is formidable and ominous, as if warning me I'm about to undertake a path all by my lonesome.

One I'm nowhere ready for.

Yet despite the warning echoing in the rustling of leaves, I move into the woods, and disappear as the morning sun rises.

I make sure to stay off the beaten track and stick to the woods. The sun won't kill me, but it will make me move slower, potentially weakening me. When my body's already running on empty, I'd rather not add more burden onto it.

Luckily, I've always had a great sense of direction, and it doesn't seem to elude me now. It's more potent than ever as I make my way through woods, streams, valleys and more, all in a matter of a few hours.

By the time I pause for a quick rest, the sun is nearing its zenith. It's normally a time I need to spend indoors, or have had to since my disease. Today, none of that crippling weakness hits me, and I throw my head back and enjoy the warmth of the rays on my skin, breathe in the fresh moss smell and the mustiness in the air.

For a moment, a bare moment, I just *am*. A willow in the breeze, swaying back and forth.

It's been a while since I was able to enjoy such.... peace. No wonder humans like it.

My siblings can't understand. They've become too jaded with immortality. Unable to relate to things, let alone the living creatures that still exist in this world.

Nico is only now starting to change his mind. And that's all thanks to Tassa, for pulling him out of his indifferent state. I'd worried for him, for so, so long. Alex and Liza are lost in a different way, something that won't stop until someone yanks them out. A force of nature colliding with theirs, teaching them a lesson it's taken me a while to grasp.

It will be harder for them, that's for sure. They're so set in their psychotic ways, in their malice, that some days I doubt there's light left in them at all. But I've seen it, and I know it's there, perhaps just buried under eons of... well, living.

Vlad... Out of all of them, he's the soul more kindred to mine. And I know he struggles just as I do, with when to interfere and when not to. When to let the others bash their heads, and when not to.

And Mirabela... Until recently, I thought she had no saving. But after witnessing the change in Nico, perhaps there is hope for her, too. If something can happen to get her caring for someone other than us, that is. She is vicious when she has to be to protect us, that part is for sure.

I blink, aware of the sudden darkness. Somehow I've gotten lost in my thoughts, and night has descended unawares. Hmm. I close my eyes, inhaling the fresh air, picking the various scents... No human blood. No gut-wrenching craving for it, either.

It's the duality of this disease. When I have my vampir attributes, my speed, it seems my thirst for human blood is gone. But when these attributes disappear, my hunger comes back tenfold, and I have no speed to rely on, only weakness. Unbearing weakness.

With renewed vigor, I cover more ground. Until my body finally says enough, and I drop under a little hillside, using my backpack as a pillow. Before my head even hits it, I pass out.

A dull thudding in my ears.

Pasty mouth.

And my limbs...

A pained moan escapes me. What the fuck happened while I slept? Why does it feel like my entire body was run over by a train, or worse, a tank?

I blink, the sun's rays hitting me repetitively. Ow. *OW.* I move my hand, bringing it up to my face, and trying to ignore the shooting pain all through my body. And my skull. As if thousands of knives have decided to pierce my eyelids and go straight to the brain hidden beneath.

Then my lungs clench, my breathing becomes heavy, and I jerk upright, panting. That weakness I'd been dreading, it's hitting me tenfold. Horribly. Gasping for air I *need*, I fumble with the backpack, the vial with muroni concoction. I finally seize it, but in my haste, it slips out of my hands and rolls away, smashing into a rock and shattering into a myriad of pieces.

Panic seizes me—I've lost the only thing keeping me sane, and I have no one around to help me. No one.

No...one...

The lack of air finally becomes too much and darkness welcomes me once more in its embrace.

Marcus

"You've got nothing to fear."

I catch the doe's eye, keeping myself fully immobile. Her ears twitch—fear for herself, or for her little one? Smiling reassuringly is as useless as dangling a carrot, so I keep doing what I've been doing and not move.

We're surrounded by thick woods. The smell of imminent snow is in the air, and a chilly wind whips at my cheeks. For now, we're alone. But it won't be forever.

"You may want to move," I whisper just as softly, jerking my head away. "I'm not the worst thing in these woods, believe me."

She stares at me another beat, then prances away, gone in one swift kick of the legs, and her little one with her. I let out a heavy breath, one I didn't realize I'd been holding.

Air. Wind. Hunt.

This is what I'd come here for, this is what I exited my cabin for. Nightly, dark, cool air, whipping at my cheeks and my body, carrying the smells of the mountains, the freedom they offer, and the oblivion.

I run through the woods, enjoying the crunch of the frost-bitten leaves under my feet. It reminds me of the crunch of bones on a battlefield—*You're no longer that person.* No, I've gone and reinvented myself into something much, much softer. A teddy bear.

The bitter chuckle stays lodged in my throat as I continue my progress onwards. My steps lead me to the top of the mountain, and I stop, enjoying the dead quiet. Nothing moves. Nothing breathes. Outside these woods, the sun is setting. Within them, darkness has already descended as their foliage blocks out the last remnants of the light.

Not that it matters, as I can see perfectly well. But it's not for the view that I've come here. It's not even for the hunt, though I could've hit bullseye a thousand times over.

It's for the silence. The dead quiet encompassing me is loud enough to drown out my own thoughts. My own shame. My own regrets.

I've been used as a weapon, and I willingly listened. I've hunted and killed and maimed, all for an upper echelon that was quick to discard me when I started disobeying orders. Or, they would've been. Except I had enough sense left in me to find the leverage I needed to buy my own freedom.

And when I did, when I broke from those who'd used me, I was lost.

Until I found my home again, my peace and quiet, and learned to live away from others. To enjoy the small things in life. To breathe life into an otherwise empty existence.

Does the loneliness get to me? Sometimes. But being alone isn't always a bad thing, when compared to being around others who'd only use you.

I toss my head back and close my eyes, soaking in the darkness.

I've travelled the world, been in capitals and cities of empires and tsars, and the only place that ever makes me feel like this is...here. Home. On the border with Hungary, nestled in the last of the Carpathians, *this* is where I've always belonged.

Away from the world.

Away from anything I could ever harm again.

And I would have it no other way.

Chapter 2

Violeta

When I next wake up, it's night again. I lie very still, trying to figure out if that same debilitating pain is still in my body. My mind lingers on every muscle, every tendon, every dead organ within me and...

Nothing.

As if it never was.

Slowly, still wary, I stand. Once I make sure my legs can hold me, I grab my backpack. My gaze lingers on the broken vial of the muroni concoction. The cool night air has frozen most of it, but I move closer to it and let my fingers linger on it, then bring them to my lips for a taste of what's left.

What had Tassa said, in terms of dosages? Was it every week or every two weeks? I'd been taking the blood every day at the castle, more as a prevention. *Whatever the right dosage is, maybe I just have to find some muroni and get it straight from the source. It would lack the rest of the ingredients Tassa used, but surely it would be enough?*

Problem is, muroni never travel alone. As cave-dwellers, they're always in packs, and can be rabid and dangerous. There's a reason my siblings always insisted we hunt them together, rather than alone. Meaning, unless I want to put myself in danger and risk having one of my fainting episodes while fighting them, I'm out of luck. And to top it off, I've gotten so far away from home using vampir speed that heading back on foot—walking as a human—would take me weeks.

No matter. I've come this far, I might as well keep going. It was freedom I wished for, in the end. A chance to find new experiences and enjoy life so I feel I actually have lived it. And if that means living it weakened of my vampir strengths, and more fully human than I'd like, well, I'll just have to survive it. If there's anything immortality has taught me, it's that erasing bad choices isn't as easy as one would like. Not even when you have eternity ahead of you.

Best I start by moving. I never should have stayed here as long as I have. Not with my pedigree, not with my disease. Vampiri clans are still hunting us and I'd make the perfect prey. A quick glance around confirms what I already knew even as I put distance between the castle and me—I'm no longer under my siblings' protection.

For a moment, my gaze lingers on the path I travelled here. I haven't even been gone that long, and I miss the comfort of having my siblings around me. And it would be easy, albeit painfully long, to go back.

Only, I can't. I left for a reason. And if my fate is to die alone, far away from everything I hold dear, then... so be it. At least I'll have died enjoying the rest of my life instead of being cooped into hiding.

I straighten the backpack on my shoulders, then pull on my leftover vampir speed and move.

In retrospect, I should have been more careful.

But hunting as a trio, always with my siblings, meant I'd always been protected. I never had to worry about watching my back, or being fully aware of my surroundings, especially the last few times.

Which is why I don't think twice about the darkness of the woods, or where, exactly, I've landed. I just keep running, thinking I can make my way through the rest of the land unencumbered.

That was my second mistake. I don't have time for a third one.

Something slams into me from the right, with the entire force of a boulder, and crashes me into a tree. We—the tree and I—go toppling down, then roll down the hill. I lose my backpack halfway, and the tree nearly crushes me. I'm only saved by a boulder that acts as a deflector, sending the trunk flying in the air and landing a few feet farther down.

Gasping, I get up. My limbs are wobbly, my arms painfully sore from the hit.

But I know I'm in danger. My instincts kick in...a tad late.

When my attacker moves from the shadows, I recoil backwards at the ferocious look on his features. A twig snaps behind me. I glance over my shoulder, noticing another one coming out of the woodwork.

And, yes, a third one to my left. And a last one to my right.

I'm surrounded, practically boxed in. Woods, a ravine underneath me, or climbing the mountain are my three options. *Great job, Vi. Really.*

The situation is even more dangerous because of who's surrounding me, moving at incredible speed. They're not human, nor are they muroni. They're regular vampiri. And since most vampiri in these regions belong to a clan, it means they're probably bound to one as well. Probably one that has been hunting us.

The one thing that saves me is most vampiri nowadays don't remember what we look like. The old ones would, but the new ones? To them, we're myths. Fables. It's not like we have a vampir World Wide Web where our faces are plastered on *Wanted* posters.

And these four, judging by their cocky attitude and skin tone that's closer to human than vampir, have been recently turned—as in, somewhere in the last decade. If it hadn't been for their fast movements and protruding fangs, I wouldn't have pegged them as vampiri in the first place.

Still. Not knowing who I am will only get me so far. Even new vampiri would know of our existence, if not necessarily our looks. They would've been told to watch out for vampiri that are oddly strong with eyes of intense blue. Which means if they realize who I am... That I'm heir to a legacy that supersedes them...

"Look what I found here," one says, brandishing my backpack.

Oh, I'm so fucked.

He ruffles through it, then comes out with a notebook. Because out of all the notebooks in my bedroom, I'd been stupid enough to grab the one with our House of Dracul crest all over it.

His sharp inhale tells me he recognizes it. But he takes his time, putting it back where it was, before looking at me. "Must be our lucky night, boys. And here I thought we'd just caught ourselves a regular bite to eat. Instead, turns out we're graced by the presence of a princess."

I let my upper lip curl over my teeth in a snarl. "Get your shit right. The correct title you're looking for is Your Highness, you uncultured twats."

"Only a vampir of the House of Dracul would call us uncultured," the leader laughs. "What brings you to these parts, *Your Highness*?"

I ignore his sarcasm. "Just passing through. And unless memory serves me incorrectly, you and whatever clan you belong to are bound to let me pass, freely, through your territory."

They share a look and a laugh.

Shivers of foreboding crawl up my spine. We've known for a while that the vampiri in these regions, are, for lack of a better word, disloyal to us. Father's death caused a domino effect that affected us all, whether we wanted to or not. And it wasn't just his death.

Lately, after Tassa was kidnapped, we found out there had been letters sent by humans to all clans in the area. Letters that clamored we were alive, and in hiding—as well as our location. Most of those were intercepted by Mira and Liza, but we've been worried some have gotten through.

Still, knowing about said clan disloyalty and seeing it, hearing it, being faced with it, are completely different things. Especially when I'm alone, weakened, and there's four of them.

"I'm afraid it's not that easy," the leader says. "See, you trespassed. Didn't inform us you were coming."

Centuries of training have me straighten my spine and level a cool-headed glare his way. Despite the sweat trickling down my back, and the tingling in my legs warning I'm getting close to that weakened state. "Trespass? Either you're joking or you forget who you're talking to. We own these lands and every vampir lives here by our grace alone."

"By your grace alone?" Another's lips curl. "You've lost the right to rule us when you showed your cowardly true colors. We don't need royals. We don't need a goddamned monarchy. This is free land—*our* free land."

"Wrong." I clench my fists, filled with a rage that gives me a second burst of energy. "It belongs to the House of Dracul. *My*. House."

Laughter rises from all of them. "There are six clans in this area who would argue against that."

Six? We thought there were twelve... Just how out of date is our information, anyway?

The one who'd spoken takes another step closer. "You think you're so *majestic*." He spits towards me, but luckily it lands far away. "Where were you when hunters started coming after us? Where were you during the wars? Nowhere!"

"Nah, they were somewhere," another says. "Probably enjoying all their richness while we were left to deal with the mess they left behind."

I have no defense to that. We did pull back, and went into hiding, specifically because clans fought the idea of what we represented. I'm starting to think Liza and Alex were right, and we never should've backed down.

Hiding my confusion, I lift my chin in the air and level my gaze on them. When I try to reach for some glamour inside me, I fall flat. No way I can sneak my way out of this, then.

"Write a damned complaint," I mutter to them. "Bottom line is, we're royals for a reason. Now get the fuck out of my way."

"Tsk, tsk. Not such great language to use for a royal."

I glare at him. "Fuck off. Do you want my siblings to rain hell on your clan?"

"Well, see, that's assuming they know where you are. Which, judging by the fact you left in the middle of the night, tells me that's not the case."

Ah, shit. They'd *followed* me? And I hadn't even noticed? My senses are completely off, and I'm about to pay for it.

"Doesn't mean they won't come. I left instructions with where I was going."

"See, that's what I thought. But then, you seem to have been following a completely random path." He tosses my backpack and its contents at my feet and taps his temple. "I'm not just a pretty face, you know. So cut the lies, Highness."

They've been staking us out. Meaning they know where we are. Meaning they know where my siblings are. Meaning...

Nico and Tassa left today for their vacation. Were they being followed, too?

I force myself not to show any of the panic slowly threatening to consume me. Clearing my throat, I ask, "Why, exactly, were you stalking my family?"

"Stalking? No, no. We merely wanted to pay our respects. After all, it's been well over four hundred years since any of you have been *seen*. Or so we've been told. And, we were curious. A royal family meant to rule us all, yet one that's been, hmm, lacking in leadership, shall we say."

"I'd like to see you do better."

A rumble of laughter runs through them and they step in tune closer to me, tightening the circle. I need to leave, and I need to leave *soon.* If they come any closer, there's no way I can take them all on. At least, not if my body gives way again to...

Nu. Don't think that way. Can't think that way.

I spread my legs wider, putting weight equally on my feet, so the next hit doesn't take me by surprise. The first vampir speeds towards me, and his punch strikes my gut. I double over, gasping—thankfully the pain eases off from one breath to the next.

They're definitely not playing around. Judging by the determined glints in their eyes, these guys are not here just to apprehend me. No, they're here to execute me. Which, granted, is a capital offense by our laws, not that they seem to care.

Hiding was a mistake. Liza and Alex were right—we never should've given up our stronghold. If we hadn't, we'd still be top of their food chain.

I move, ducking under his second punch, twirling to the side, kicking blindly—I make contact, hear an oomph of surprise—then moving yet again. I need to stay out of their grasps, it's my one way out. Then another punches me from behind, this time hitting something sensitive. Blood spurts out of my mouth, leading to a racking cough.

I fall to the ground, more coughs escaping me. Out of the corner of my eye, I see his feet coming towards me, and manage to roll away. Nico once told me if ever I can avoid a fight, to do so. Which is why with the last of my strength, I take the coward's way out, grab my backpack, and run off.

Their shouts echo behind long after the trees have swallowed me.

Marcus

The hares bang against my back as I make my way downhill, heading back home. Where I can once again be alone, far away from the world and all its treacheries.

I'm halfway down the hill when I catch the change in the woods. Like the deer not that long ago, I stop and perk my ears, listening for the faintest trace of danger.

There it is—someone's hurtling through the trees. Leaves are hitting their body, branches leaving scratches, and... I swing the hares off my shoulder and onto a low branch, turning to face the dense woods I'd just left.

What was that?

Listening to instincts that have never steered me wrong, I move out of the way and into the shadows, letting a massive tree trunk hide me. Between my camouflage clothing, and the many changes in the foliage, there's no way I will be seen unless someone is looking for me. And whoever this running person is, they're in too much of a rush to do so.

The sounds increase. My ears continue to pick up on them. My fists clench in muted response to whatever this threat—this derangement of the woods—is.

This deep in is not a place you'd normally see visitors. Hikers will occasionally venture this far but the closeness to the border can make the land volatile. The only ones who'd be in these woods are Dmitri's vampiri, but there's no way they'd make this much noise.

A moment later, a form bursts through the trees, then runs down the path. I only catch a glimpse of raven-black, shoulder-length hair, a pale face, and she's gone. Leaving behind the scent of blood—*her* blood, I realize with a jolt.

The scent is intoxicating. Sweet. Like vanilla and fresh valleys mixed together. I take a step closer, unconsciously wanting to take another whiff, and almost miss the reason she's running. Or rather, *four* reasons.

A quartet emerges out of the trees, and this time I only catch flashes of dark clothing. They're moving way too damn fast.

What the hell would four vampiri want with a human, I wonder?

They fill these parts, belonging to one of the ruling clans. Not *the* clan, but nonetheless a powerful one. Although they sometimes roam as if they're masters, they're only pawns under their ruler—Dmitri. And even so, he's not the scariest one. There are others...

I've kept myself informed, despite living far away from everything, if only because I know how much misinformation has already cost me. I refuse to go through that again.

Then I tell myself to stop wondering. It's not my business, none of this is. I'd sworn as much when I left the Guards. And I don't intend to go back on that promise. Those I served don't deserve it, and humanity even less.

So I wait a beat, then another, and step back onto the path. Hares over my shoulder, I follow behind the vampiri—but only until the path leads me home. No more.

That's what I tell myself, at least. But once I reach the fork in the road, the one that if I take left, I'll be home within the hour, I hesitate.

Why *were* four vampiri chasing that girl? Curiosity gnaws at me, and I should be master enough of my emotions by now to shove it away. But, I can't. I reason that if her body is found on my territory, it'll be me who has to answer for it, which would go against my whole living peacefully new mentality.

A darker thought rises. What if that's the intent? What if this is Dmitri's latest attempt to draw me back into the fold?

Vampiri aren't meant to hunt humans, at least not in the open like they're wild cattle ready for slaughter. Even if these woods are far removed from general society, the consensus is there *is* such a society out there. One with smart phones and TVs and cameras that can put an end to an otherwise seamless existence.

And, da, a human body would also put an end to that. It would also put an end to my peaceful existence.

A weak reasoning, but once the thought takes root in my mind, I find it harder and harder to ignore it. So I move closer to a tree and perch my hares on it, away from any predators. I'll come back for them soon as I figure this shit out.

Then I move down the path, unencumbered and completely focused on anything I might hear. Which, is a whole lot of nothing. Unlike before, there's only complete and utter silence. Hmm. My better trained instincts tell me that's just as concerning. I remind myself they were part of a rigid military structure I have since disavowed, so maybe I'm better off ignoring them, after all.

I advance in a crouch, careful not to step on anything that might make an unwanted noise. As I round a tree, I finally catch the first sound. Barely.

A faint moan—a sound of pain.

Moments later, I emerge into a tiny enclosure between trees, and stare at the carnage before me.

The four vampiri I'd seen, they're in various states of decomposition, suggesting they've been killed at different times. Normally, it takes them a day to become full dust, but in the meantime they excrete as much gore as regular human bodies. The ground is wet with their blood, and their guts, and more than that for some.

I turn in a slow circle, assessing the entire scene for any leftover threats—there are none. And then my gaze lands on *her*.

The woman who'd been running earlier.

She's curled up under a massive tree root, her body hunched over. I don't have to move closer to smell the blood on her.

Did she do all this? Overpower four vampiri?

I take in the carnage once more, before inching another step towards her.

My foot lands on a twig—stupid mistake. Her head jerks up, and her unfocused gaze lands on me. Eyes of the brightest blue catch mine, and then her eyelashes flutter and she crumbles, as if the last of her energy has escaped her.

I hesitate. If I leave her here, she'll die. I could return tomorrow and burn the entire place down, her body included.

And then you'll forever wonder how she did what she did.

Well, that settles it, then.

I move closer, and my brain decides to point out then and there that I haven't been around a female for a long time. Too long. Guess I'll just have to get over the awkwardness real fast, then.

Once I reach her, I make sure she's still unconscious, before turning her over. Her clothes are soaked with blood, and it's hard to tell which is hers and which is theirs. A glance at her cheek shows me she's been punched—more than once, judging by the forming bruises. Anger unfurls within me, low and grumbling. Men attacking women, isn't that just fucking...

I let out a sigh. I can't just carry her to my cabin if she's bleeding all over the place, she'll leave enough scent for anyone—including animals—to follow.

So I remove my backpack and pull out a blanket, planning to wrap her in it. Then I gently run my hands over her legs, trying to see if they come away with any fresh blood. A gash by her thigh—I rip a piece of my t-shirt and tie it around the wound. Nothing else. I then move on to her mid-section. There's too much blood, so to be safe, I grab the entire blanket and securely wrap it around her, hoping to staunch whatever is cut and bleeding.

Finally, I pull out one more blanket and wrap her entire upper body in it, before hoisting my backpack again and then picking her up in my arms. Once I do, I notice a small bag that had been hidden behind her and the tree. I pick that up, too, and turn away.

For better or worse, I've now made a choice I'll have to live with.

Chapter 3

Violeta

I'm back in that forest, with them taunting me. Telling me how they'll kill my family, soon as they kill me. I know it's them or me, there is no other choice in this moment. I pull deep within my core for the strength that's failing me, and launch myself at them with all the remaining force I can muster.

Our royal lineage gives us extra strength and power, coupled with a glamouring ability that will take over even the strongest mind. My strength was waning, I could practically feel it slip out of me, replaced by that odd weakness of the human pull. So I acted fast.

I might've been alone, and scared, but giving up was not what

Father taught me.

Alex and Liza would've been proud. By the time I was done, none of them were left standing, and their blood coated the ground in a red river. I'd managed to do exactly what I've been avoiding for centuries, which is shed blood. Lots and *lots* of blood.

Tears leave my closed lids, running down the sides of my face. I've broken a promise I held so dear to my heart. A sworn oath to myself that I'd never take another life, after I woke up next to a child's dead body. It was the most despicable crime I ever could've committed, and I've never forgiven my nature for carrying it out.

Granted, this particular situation was out of self-preservation and it was vampiri I'd killed, not humans. But...

"Hey, hey."

I jerk awake at the voice. Blink in the darkness.

"You're all right, you're not—*OW!*"

I reach out blindly, punching in the darkness. Not sure who or what has spoken, I'm not about to take any chances. Then I try to move off the bed, at least what I'm assuming is a bed, but only succeed in falling.

The thud of hardwood floors against my bare knees makes me wince and release a hiss of pain. But I push through it, hating the weakness coursing through my body, and take off in a run.

And soon realize what a bad idea that is. My nightly sight is gone, instead I'm hitting things. Clashes echo everywhere. Completely unable to orient myself, panic rises in my throat.

"Wait, I'm not going to hurt you!"

I don't care what he says – the deep, masculine voice is unfamiliar, thus no reason to trust it. Especially after the last four men I've run across, and the fact they tried to kill me. Whoever he is,

I'm not interested to find out more.

A faint light from the outside catches my eye—a door! I run for it, stumbling and swaying, my legs refusing to take me as fast as I wish them to. And then I topple sideways and—

"I got you."

He does. Unfortunately.

Silently cursing my own limbs, I force my eyes to open once more. Two strong hands have gripped my waist in what I would like to describe as a very clinical hold. Unfortunately, the heat perusing through the clothes only makes me aware of the strength in said hold, and thus makes whatever blood's left over in my body warm up...considerably.

There's a light on now. I don't know when he turned it on, but the dimness of the bulb is enough to show me his face. A strong jaw, filled with a few days' worth of stubble. Thick eyebrows, full lips, pressed tightly. Eyes the color of the woods I've just escaped, narrowed in confusion on me. A strong nose, nostrils flaring as if holding back an onslaught of emotions. And further down...

A strong neck, tendons corded. Muscles equally taut, holding my weight. Biceps, showcased by a gray shirt that's seen better days.

My knees wobble, from a different kind of weakness now. Why is the sight of him hitting me so hard? Granted, in two years I haven't taken another lover thanks to this unknown thing hanging over my head, but I have centuries under my belt. This—he—should be just as inconsequential as others have been before him.

I force my gaze back up to his face. And when I speak, I'm thankful for all the years of my royal education drilled into me. "Unhand me. Now."

He blinks at the order in my voice, but slowly stands, lifting me from my half-crouch. Once he's assured I'm steady on my feet and not a moment before, he lets me go. I feel the loss of his hands on my waist, and instead hug my own around me.

"Who are you?"

"My name is Marcus." He lifts his palms up, showing me he is unarmed. "I was out in the woods, found you hurt. Brought you here, thinking you needed help."

His words make sense, but takes my brain longer to process. I remember the vampiri, and being chased. Then the rage consuming me, demanding I act as my maker would wish and take over. The bloodlust.

"Are you all right?'

Without even realizing it, I've started shaking. My trembling only stops when Marcus speaks, as I become aware of it. I can't let him see how shaken I am, how easily I can fall apart at the seams. For all I know, he could be one of those hunters after us. He has the bulk of a mercenary, that's for sure.

Who *is* this guy? Who even goes around rescuing girls in woods?

I clear my throat. "Da. Just...shaken. At the attack."

He nods, as if we're talking about something completely normal. "It must have been horrifying. What's your name?"

We're dancing around the topic. If he saw me, he must've seen the dead guys. Were they already decomposing or did their bodies still seem human? Does he know they were vampiri or is he pegging me for some lunatic?

"Violeta," I answer softly.

I take a closer look at him. Is *he* a vampir?

Normally, I'd be able to tell. I can always recognize my own kin. But not this time around. There's no scent that gives it away, no stark pallor in his olive skin. His eyes are a regular color, nothing intense, and he doesn't seem affected by the smell of the blood around us.

And not for the first time, it hits me that I'm alone. Unable to rely on my siblings or anyone else.

I made a choice. Can't go back on it now.

While I may not have them to rely on, I do still have a great instinct. And something about the wariness in his expression tells me he's not a bad guy. Of course, I always did trust too easily.

Marcus clears his throat. "I saw. The vampiri."

I jerk back, second-guessing my initial reaction. "You know..."

"Of course." He hesitates, then gestures to the table. "Sit, please. You look like you're going to fall over."

I glance at the table he pointed to, then at him. After a beat, I move over and perch myself on a chair. When the cool wood hits the back of my bare legs, I glance down, startled. "My clothes—"

"You were soaked in blood, and I couldn't see your wounds. I had to clean you up."

The shirt I'm wearing comes to my knees, and it's definitely not one of mine. His, then. The cotton feels worn. It's unlike the expensive things I've been used to my whole life, but infinitely more comfortable. Huh.

"I also found this in the woods." He points to a corner, drawing my eye to my backpack.

Relief spreads through me—at least something survived. I'll have clean clothes in there, and...a lot of other things.

I gulp, trying to force my gaze away. "Thank you."

"You're welcome."

He moves to the small kitchen, which is really just a sink and an ice freezer, and goes about boiling water. Then he pours something in it—tea?—followed by a dash of liquid. When the steaming mug lands in front of me, I smell alcohol and chamomile.

"It'll restore your senses," he says, shifting on his feet.

Something about his gruff, awkward demeanor is infinitely endearing, like he's not used to having company. Yet he can't be much older than me—the human version me, that is.

And to think this guy saw me naked, cleaned me up...

I glance around, assessing the rest of the space. A bed in a corner, a worn armchair in another, some lamps thrown about. A bathtub under a window, perfect for seeing the full moon. The tiny kitchenette on the other side of the house. Three dead hares are perched on the counter.

Minimalistic, for the most part.

I clear my throat. "Thank you. For the tea, and for saving me. And not thinking I'm a lunatic who goes on a killing spree for no reason. Most men would've left me there."

He jerks his head. "I'm not most men."

"No, you're not." I take a sip of the tea, the hot brew nearly burning my tongue. The fact I can taste it tells me I'm fully drained. Which means I'll need muroni blood, and soon, lest I get as sick as I was a few weeks ago.

I glance around the house again. It may be fairly sparse, but it's homey. Warm. My bare feet are on the wooden floor, but it's warm. A fire burns in the corner.

"I'm sorry, for how I reacted when I woke up. I think I was still in shock."

"It's only natural."

I tilt my head to the side. "You speak as if you have knowledge of it? Being in life-or-death situations."

He gets up from the table, as if unable to sit down. I recognize a restless energy in him, perhaps one that's been in me, as well, for longer than I realized. Most definitely since I've been bedridden.

"I have been," he finally says, his voice soft, shoulders turned inwards and away from me. "A long time ago."

My eyes roam over the wide expanse of his back, his rigid stature, and I know the truth before he even speaks it. "Army?"

A surprised gaze is levelled my way. But behind that gaze is a whole other story. Instead of elaborating, he simply nods. "Yeah."

"It's none of my business, then. But... thank you."

A corner of his mouth lifts in a quirky smile. "That's the third time you've thanked me. I think once is more than enough."

I shrug. "It's not every day knights in shining armor prove their existence."

The smile falls. "I'm no knight. And you didn't need saving, you had it all under control." He sits again, eyes narrowed on me. "Which begs the question of how you survived that. Most humans wouldn't."

Hu— He thinks I'm *human.*

I bite down my knee-jerk reaction to correct him. Instead, I take another sip of hot tea to pretend to calm my senses.

It makes sense, I suppose. What else would a human think when finding someone like me in the woods? He has no reason to think otherwise. And it's not like he can hear my heartbeat—or lack of one.

How he knows about vampiri, that's a different story. Our world is meant to be hidden. Living this far away from civilization, he must've seen things, I suppose. But... "How, exactly, do you know about vampiri and...?"

His expression darkens. "Let's just say I have had one too many close encounters. In these parts, when you live alone, it's hard not to."

"And they leave you alone?" I have a hard time believing that. Vampiri are known for going off track and hunting humans in the woods. Especially the stronger clans.

Marcus shrugs. "For the most part. Let me refill your cup."

I hand it over, and in the brief second our fingers touch, a zap of warmth runs through my arm. I bite my lip to hold back the gasp threatening. *Cliché as ever, Violeta... Get over yourself.*

I can't admit what I am. Not if he's had encounters with the vampiri, and especially not when I'm this weakened. It's in my best interest he keeps thinking I'm human, if it means he'll feel like he has to protect me.

A moment later, Marcus returns with another cup of tea, equally strengthened with alcohol.

I take another sip, then whisper, "To answer your question, it was a stroke of luck that I survived. Nothing more."

He arches an eyebrow. "I'd wager it was a lot more than that."

"Fine. My father trained me to fight, when I was young." All true—I'd learned a long time ago that successful lies are based on truth. "And it came in handy."

He watches me a moment longer, his green gaze darker still. I resist the urge to squirm under his perusal. I'll have to leave here, and soon, before he realizes exactly who he saved and brought into his home. Before more of those vampiri come looking for me. Because they will come, soon as this group doesn't return to the rest of the clan.

"I see," Marcus finally says. "Well, you're more than welcome to stay here until your wound heals."

"Wound?" I don't get wounds. Not any that last, anyway.

He gestures to my midsection. I drop my hand to it, wincing at the tenderness. I press more and Marcus winces, getting out of the chair.

"Don't do that, you'll open the wound again and the bleeding was hard enough to stop the first time around. Hey, hey can you hear me?"

I'm stumbling backwards, my horrified gaze on the blood on my hand. What the hell is going on? Why haven't I healed properly? Even before, when the disease hit, I was still able to heal. I might've lost other vampir senses here and there but *not* my healing.

Worse still, my knees buckle under me, and there's nothing I can hold on to before toppling over...to be swallowed by darkness once more.

Marcus

I catch her as she falls, then pick her up in my arms and carry her over to the bed again. The wound on her stomach is bleeding again, so I slowly lift the shirt up and re-bandage it. I've done it before, bandaging comrades—male and female—in battle. They healed faster, and this one doesn't, but still.

The first time, when I was cleaning her up, I hadn't yet heard her voice. Or her story—as riddled with holes as it is. She wasn't a person, just a stray I'd picked up. Now, I avert my eyes of her body unless absolutely necessary. When I have to lift her up to wrap the bandage around her midsection, I try to ignore the softness of her skin. The coolness worries me, and I sure hope she's not about to die on me.

It's with a sigh of relief I drop the shirt back to her knees and pull the covers to her chin, then settle back in a chair to watch over her. Her features should be relaxed in unconsciousness, but they're tight with a burden only she's aware of.

My gaze drops to the backpack in a corner, but I dismiss the thought the moment it comes in my mind. She deserves her privacy. So long as it doesn't mess with my life, she'll have all the rights to it.

The axe hits the chunk of wood, splitting it in two with a satisfying *crack*. The pieces fall to the ground and I repeat the action with another, then another. Mid-cut, I sense eyes on me. I glance back to the cabin, noticing the curtain fall back. Violeta must be awake, then. She's slept for two days on and off, in fitful rests with fever. I'll have to find her something to eat soon. Hmm.

That problem is soon relegated to secondary when I catch another scent on the wind. I move to the edge of my woods, then farther in. I don't want *them* anywhere near my home, especially not with a human inside it.

It's only two who come to meet me. Dark clothing, cropped hairs, a gold raven pin on their left breast pocket. I recognize one of them—Grigore. I didn't serve with him, but I've seen him around here and now. Last time he'd come on my property, he didn't really enjoy the feel of my axe cutting into his leg.

I smirk. "Long time no see. How's the leg, Grigore? All healed up?"

"Can't even feel it," he mutters. "And it's not like I spend my time thinking of one measly fight with a hermit in the woods."

"Hmm." I shift my wrist slightly. Their eyes narrow, taking in the axe in my hands. I make no move to set it aside. "I suppose so. Bigger fish to fry and all?" When he doesn't answer, I drop all pretenses. "What do you want?"

"You should watch your tone, Marcus. Some may think you inhospitable."

"*Some* can get the fuck off my property."

"Hmm, testy."

I force myself to breathe. "*What* do you want?"

"Looking for a stray," Grigore says. The other's too busy surveying the surroundings. "Seen one?"

"Nu."

"That was a quick no." He moves fast, until he's in my face. "You sure about that? Female, tiny. Probably bleeding to death somewhere."

I tighten my grip on the axe. "I said no."

He stares at me a moment longer, plainly not believing me.

His companion clears his throat. "Let's go, we have more ground to cover."

"Mm. Well, if she lands on your doorstep, do send her our way, won't you?"

"Sure will." Not.

Grigore walks away, then glances over his shoulder towards me. "Say, how about hunters? Heard anything about *them* in your neck of the woods?"

My grip on the axe becomes white-knuckled. "Nu."

His back to me, Grigore says, "Of course. You don't know much these days at all, do you? It really is sad what you've become, you know. I remember the stories. *Marcus cel Rău*. Marcus the Bad One. Such a perfect soldier, a perfect mercenary. And now, what a waste!" He slowly faces me, inspecting my worn clothes and appearance.

"Not that you'd care, but vampir hunters have invaded these woods. Dmitri's had issues with them—entire squadrons going missing—and we're on high alert. They're pests and getting smarter, using all kinds of poisons that seem to work against even our elders. Other clans have reported the same. Suffice to say, their guerilla-like attacks have put a dampen on our leader's plans to move against the royals, including having to cancel the recent meeting with the other clans—again, not that you care. I mention this only in case you see or hear anything in these woods, you're to *tell us.*" A glimmer of amusement enters his expression. "After all, we wouldn't want those poor orphans of yours to...suffer."

It takes all my strength not to toss the axe at his head in a perfect bullseye.

Instead, I watch Grigore and his companion walk away, waiting until they're gone. And then I wait a little longer, making sure they're not coming back. Only once I'm fully sure do I return home, wondering what the hell I've gotten myself into by protecting Violeta.

Back home, the smell of chocolate and cinnamon assails my senses, making me pause long enough to wonder if I've entered some parallel universe. No, not the way of things, that's for sure.

"What are you doing?"

Violeta glances at me from the stove. She's now wearing her own clothes, a pair of fitted jeans with a loose, off-the-shoulder sweater that shows more of that creamy skin I'd been trying to ignore. Her hair is wet, too.

"Did you shower? The bandage—"

"I saw the outside shower and couldn't resist, even with the chill in the air. I was careful with the bandage and found a spare one and used that to redo it. I think I managed." She gives me a tentative smile. "And, I saw you working with the wood so I thought I'd make some hot chocolate in case you're hungry."

I sniff. "Doesn't smell like any hot chocolate I've ever tasted."

"It's sweet-loaded."

She hands me a mug and I take it, inhaling deeply. I won't taste anything, but it's the least I can do to pretend. So I do, under her watchful eye, and groan in appreciation. "That's really good." She doesn't have to know it's the smell of it alone that I can taste.

The smile widens. "Thanks."

I gulp some more of the beverage, then gesture for her to turn around. "Let me see the bandage. I don't want you to get an infection."

She sighs and listens, letting me pull the sweater just enough to make sure the bandage is secure and neither wet nor filled with blood.

"Hmm. Good. Seems the wound stopped bleeding."

She turns to me, a faint reddish tinge to her cheeks. I try to ignore it, and the answering hunger it arouses inside me. I can't afford to get entangled, least of all with a human, least of all with my own history and the burden I carry.

No matter how tempting this particular human is, nor how her sweet scent makes me wonder if her blood would be just as sweet.

"Thank you, again. For watching over me."

"You're welcome."

She hesitates, her eyes meeting mine. Does she remember me in the middle of the night, wiping her brow and holding her as she moaned in pain? I don't know if she recalls the odd rambles of the fever, but I doubt it. For my part, I'd been selfish, hoping she'd reveal something about her real purpose in these woods. I was sadly mistaken.

"I've probably overstayed my welcome," she says.

"No, you haven't." I gesture for her to sit, waiting until she does so I can lean over her. Her eyes widen at my aggressive stance, at the fact I've boxed her in. This close, I can smell my shampoo on her hair, and shake off the weird stirrings. I need to jostle some kind of truth out of her. "But I think I'm done with the half-truths, precious. What were you doing in these woods, and why did I just get a visit from a vampir clan on my doorstep asking about you?"

Chapter 4

Violeta

Shit.

Shit, shit, shit.

Marcus is leaning over me, way in my space, and judging by the determined glint in his eyes and the clenching of his jaw, he's not going to let up unless he gets some answers.

But what can I tell him?

How much can I trust him?

He saved my life, sure. And he's taken care of me for the last two days, when he could've left me in the woods, to my death. Covered in blood as I'd been, and surrounded by the decaying bodies of the vampiri, I would've either been discovered by their comrades or torn apart by animals. Whether I want to admit it or not, I *owe him.*

Yet I know so little about him. And he seems perfectly familiar with vampiri and the inner workings of our society.

Is the fact that I owe him for saving my life enough for me to open up, knowing what that can cost me? And not just myself. I think of my siblings, of Nico and Tassa who've just found love and peace. Of a sort. They can protect themselves, I'd hope, but I still need to find a way to reach out to them and warn them the vampiri had been staking us out.

In the end, that's what decides me. I can take the risk for myself, but not for them. I won't risk them, not even Liza and Alex, who couldn't care more about humans and all this other shit. I've spent too many centuries fighting to defend my family and keep us from falling apart, for me to stop doing so now.

He believes I'm human. Maybe I can start there.

And thinking of Tassa gives me another idea, albeit a complicated one.

"I'm sorry."

Marcus arches an eyebrow at my whisper. I only give him a moment, then throw my head forward, and head-butt him.

Marcus swears and stumbles backward, out of my way. I lunge for my backpack, then run out the door, hoping my play works.

If I'd given in and told him straight up my fake story, he wouldn't believe me. This way, if I at least struggle, maybe he'll believe me more. I hope so, at least.

It's a good thing I'm still weak and vampir speed doesn't come as easily to me. Makes it easier to match my pace to be more similar to that of a human. Even so, the speed at which he catches up to me throws me off balance. Even more so when he tackles me, and we roll on the cold, hard ground. There aren't enough leaves to break my fall, only the frost of a chilly day and the hardness of the ground.

My backpack flies out of my hand, and we roll until he's over me. Panting hard, holding my wrists, and pinning me to the ground. His dark gaze is no longer understanding, it's flat-out blazing. And his hard body presses against mine, completely immobilizing me.

I try not to think of it, but my flesh is too sensitive to his, and to the power he exudes. There's a hum of electricity that feels like it started where his hands grip mine and runs all over my body. *Shit.* This need unfurling in me is not a good thing, and a complication I don't need right now. Later, maybe, but not right now.

I buck under him, and he grits his teeth, leaning over me some more. "Violeta—"

Before he can continue, I knee him in the back, and roll us over again. He seems surprised at my strength, and it's another reminder to be more vulnerable. Weaker. I grit my teeth against the word, even as I pin him under me.

"How do I know I can trust you?"

He blinks, stopping his struggle. I do, too—a mistake. The moment after, I'm on my back again. This time, Marcus straddles my hips and grips my wrists, making sure I can't move. Every inch of him is pressed against every inch of me. This time, it's more than electricity that courses through me—and damn him, but he seems completely unaffected!

He leans into me, his lips mere inches from mine. "You don't. But what other choice do you have?"

He stares at me a beat, and another. I can't escape that gaze, and I wonder what else he sees. At a loss, I whisper, "All right. I'll tell you."

He doesn't move off me.

I scowl. "Get off me first."

"Nu. You either talk, or we can stay here until night falls. And believe me, these woods aren't kind at night."

"Argh!" My struggles are futile, though very real at this point. In the end, I give in. I've dug this hole, now I have to be convincing enough. "Fine. My father died, or rather was killed. By some vampiri. And I ran away, but they...followed."

He frowns. "Why would vampiri kill your father?"

"Because he worked with them. As a doctor. Only, he was both a doctor to humans and to vampiri." That part is true. Only it's not my father I'm talking about, but Tassa's.

"Hmm." Marcus lets go of my wrists, then stands. He holds out a hand to me. "Come inside. Your lips are turning blue."

I let him pull me up, then dust myself off and pick up my bag under his watchful gaze, before following him back into the cabin. I take a seat on the same chair as before. Marcus places a glass of red wine in front of me, and I take a deep swallow, grateful at the warmth seeping into my bones again.

Not that long ago, red wine would've rejuvenated my vampir body. Now, all it does is make me lightheaded like a regular human. I've forgotten what it's like to be this cold, but this weakened body is quick to remind me.

"So these vampiri that came here, that's why they were after you? Because of your father?"

"I suppose so." I look into the glass, holding it with both hands to hide their trembling. "Did you tell them I was here?"

If he did, I'm screwed. In more ways than one.

"Nu."

I gulp, trying to stay as nonchalant as I can. "But you know them?"

Marcus runs a hand over his face and nods. "Da, I do. They're from Dmitri's clan."

I rack my brain, trying to match the name with the clans I was aware of. "Dmitri Ardelean?" My eyes narrow. "His clan was based in Transylvania, not this far out." *And it's part of the ones we flagged as probably making a move against us.*

Marcus freezes, staring at me. "How do you know that?"

"I—" Shit. "My dad. He, um, there was a job he had to complete there." I think back to the map in our library, the painstaking layout Vlad had gone to the trouble of producing. And what the vampiri in the woods had told me, about six clans instead of twelve. And my worried thought returns. *Just how out of date is our information?*

"How long ago was this job?" Marcus asks.

"I'm not sure. All I remember is the name, not the details."

He watches me a second longer and I fight the urge to squirm. Then, he nods. "Da, that's him. Ardelean. His clan was based in the Transylvanian region but they migrated about twenty years ago." A scowl twists his lips. "Thought I'd been rid of them, and yet they followed."

It's my turn to be confused. "What do you mean? Why would a clan follow a human?"

The expression on his features changes too fast for me to read it. Surprise? Can't be sure.

But then he turns his back on me and starts pacing. "Same as your father, I was involved with the vampiri. I had...certain skills. Skills they wanted."

"Soldier skills?"

He gives me a tight nod. "It took a while to convince them to end our arrangement and when they did, I moved far away."

"Here. Away from civilization."

Another nod. "I didn't feel the need to be around...people. Except for some monthly trips into the closest town, I still don't interact with them." Under his breath he adds, "Better off this way."

There's a rawness in his words that guts me. "But Ardelean... How did he migrate? Aren't there....laws?" At his sharp gaze, I add, "Dad said there was a hierarchy."

Marcus snorts, then nods. "Da. But that hierarchy no longer matters. Ardelean's vampir clan isn't the only one doing as they see fit. Romania used to have twenty-some odd clans. After 1945 —the last war— they were forcefully amalgamated into larger ones." He purses his lips. "Six now exist, from what I'm told. In this country. Hungary and Ukraine have their own groups, but they're half a dozen or less as well."

The tension in my gut coils. "You're saying they've....joined forces?"

That gaze lands on mine again. "Of course. Which is why Dmitri's land now extends to here."

"And you're back to having to follow his rules?"

His only answer is a clenching of the jaw.

"But you didn't tell his people about me?"

"Nu. I've got enough problems with them as it is."

"What kind of problems?"

Marcus hesitates. We stare at each other like two boxers in a ring. I'm reminded of one particularly vicious fight I'd seen in an underground club... Only to then run into those same two fighters sharing a pint of beer at a pub later that same night. Will that be us, perhaps? Becoming buddies at the end of this?

Not like I'll have enough time to find out. With my body getting weaker and weaker, it won't be long before I'm fully human, and the rest of my presumably too long existence catches up to me. Then I'll be ashes in the ground, same as every other human.

And is it fair, then, to ask Marcus to take these risks? Trained to be selfish and thinking only of my safety since the moment of my turning, I didn't bother considering the implications. But he's a human, with vampiri knocking on his door. When all is said and done and I'm gone, that problem won't leave for him. It might even get worse.

Can I handle having another death on my conscience? Because those vampiri I'd killed didn't seem like they followed a code of honor.

"Never mind," I whisper, and drink the rest of the wine before standing. "Maybe I should go. I feel like I'm causing more issues than I'd intended. I thank you, truly, for helping me, but you've done enough." And if these vampires have joined in larger clans... I need to warn my siblings.

I pick my bag up again, and head towards the door.

"Where will you go?" Marcus asks.

"Away. Cross the border if I can, maybe take off to Western Europe." *Right after I find a way to warn my siblings.*

It hadn't been my plan, but now it sounds saner than staying in the woods with someone who's obviously got the weight of the world on his shoulders. Too many humans have already paid for their association to us, and Marcus doesn't deserve this kind of trouble.

His hoarse voice comes behind me. "Don't. I... Stay."

I turn to him, trying to understand his reasoning. "Why?"

"Because..." He runs a hand over his head, then seems to remember his hair is cropped short and he can't run his hands through it. "Because I'm not sure if those vampiri are gone. And, I know them. I..." He works his jaw, then adds, "They won't give up just yet, but they also won't come back here."

"Why not?"

Another muscle ticks in his jaw. "Because we have a deal, them and me."

I mull that over for a second. His protection would be nice, and I wouldn't lie by saying I found him attractive. Because I do. I have ever since he turned on the light and moved his hands off me. A part of me wants nothing more than to climb that body and remember what it's like to *feel*. It's been so goddamned long...

"Violeta?"

I snap to, blinking at him. I'd been staring like an idiot. "Sorry. It's just... If they do come back, it'll mean trouble for you."

"I can defend myself."

I hesitate. *This* had been my plan, to secure a spot where I can catch my breath, before running into those vampiri again. But looking at Marcus, at the honesty in his gaze, makes the first inklings of guilt rise within me.

"Are you sure?"

"Yes. Stay."

Marcus

I must be losing my mind. The last time I played Good Samaritan didn't end up well for me, and yet here I am, making the same mistakes all over again. Not to mention this is putting my pact with

Dmitri's clan into question.

He'd agreed to let me off the hook, what with the leverage I had on him. And despite the years of taunts, and Grigore's last one, he hasn't crossed the line to make me persona non grata. But something tells me if he finds out I've willingly hidden someone he's hunting from him, things could turn ugly, fast.

As I sip from my glass and watch Violeta sleep that same night, I wonder over and over again why I didn't just let her go.

My gaze lingers on the soft features, the dark lashes, her full lips, and hair that looks as soft as silk. I've given her my bed again, while I'm sleeping on the couch like all the other nights. But despite my best efforts, no force of nature can make me look away from her.

And still, the answer to my question remains as elusive as ever.

When dawn comes, I get up from a restless night, pick the dead hares up off my counter, and head outside. Violeta should still be sleeping by the time I return, but I can't delay my trip any longer else the kills will be useless.

The ground crunches under my feet, and there's a windy tinge in the air that hints of winter being too damn near. Small flurries already cover the leaves.

Once I'm hidden by the woods, I shift to vampir speed and zig-zag in the trees towards my destination. I wouldn't put it past Grigore to have someone keep an eye on me, but at least they'll see my routine hasn't changed.

Trees speed past me, but I've done this too many times to count.

Within less than twenty minutes, I'm in the ravine leading to their camp. And then I'm on the edge.

A scrawny kid half my size pops out of the woods, a crossbow trained on me. When his chocolate eyes realize who it is, a wide grin spreads his lips and he launches himself in my arms.

"Marcus!"

I chuckle and hug him back, and before long I'm surrounded by another dozen kids.

If I try to pinpoint when, exactly, they've become my only tether to humanity, I wouldn't be able to. All I know is I've hunted in these woods for decades and decades, and ran away from Dmitri's goons and traps more times than I can count. A lot of times, that meant I'd stay away from home.

In one such instance, I ran across this little camp. The kids—orphans—all banded together to protect each other, running from the foster system in their respective villages. They'd all suffered countless abuses, and found they were better on their own, hidden in the woods, than in the villages where they'll be at the mercy of adults.

I've tried to return them to their families—they have none. I've tried explaining that adults could help out—they won't hear of it. So the best I can do is hunt for them once a week. They're more than capable of doing it, but I help out as I can and bring food, supplies, and whatever else they need from towns.

My only interactions with humans are centered around these little humans. Does it make me a knight in shining armor, like Violeta said? Nu. Not even a little bad. Just a broken person who takes care of other broken ones.

I settle Ramon on the ground, ruffling his hair, and face the rest of them. Thin faces look up at me, with dark eyes that have seen too much. But they're all happy, and well-adjusted. And if I have to spend the rest of my years watching over them, I will.

My gaze automatically sweeps their little camp. Two trailers that have been stuck in the woods since time immemorial, an area for food, another for fire.

I hand the hares over to Ramon and he follows behind me, suddenly serious as we all take a seat around the dimming flames. After the usual chatter of what they've been up to, I get down to the important stuff.

"Are you running out of wood?" I ask.

Ramon shakes his head, too serious for a fourteen-year-old. "Leana got some the other day, dry and perfect."

I glance at the blonde child with her shy smile. "Good girl. What about anything else? Any other supplies?"

Ramon pulls out a folded piece of paper from his worn jeans and hands it to me. "We've been writing things down. That should cover it, I think? Unless it's too much, we—"

"I'll get it," I say, without even looking at the list. I know he hates to beg, and I'm not about to make this embarrassing for him. "But I need to talk to you guys about something."

Ramon pulls out a knife and starts skinning the hares, but I can tell his attention is focused on me by the tense set of his shoulders.

"Pleci?" Leana asks.

I smile at her. "No, darling angel." I reach over and tuck a strand of dirty hair away from her eyes. "I'm not going anywhere. But I need you guys to."

Ramon's gaze snaps to mine, and his hand lowers the knife. "Why?"

"The vampiri."

Silence descends on the group. Some shiver, others look away in fear. I feel bad for bringing them this news, but they need to know.

"Hunters?" Ramon asks, matter-of-factly.

My chest constricts. No child should have to know the pain he has, but then again, life is never fair.

"Both," I whisper. "I know you all lost your parents either at hunter hands or vampiri hands. They're equally dangerous, and it seems a war is on the brink of starting. I don't want you caught in it."

"So you're asking us to leave." Ramon frowns. "We can help you. We can fight."

I reach over and clasp my hand on his thin shoulder. "I would never ask you to. But I *am* asking you to protect everyone else here."

He stares at me for a long moment, then nods. "Where should we go?"

Relief spreads through me. At least they'll be safe, away from whatever Grigore has planned, and from hunters stumbling upon their little camp. It's the least I can do, since it's quite probable that my choice of helping Violeta is what's putting them in even more danger.

Chapter 5

Marcus

Instead of heading straight back home after seeing the kids, I take a detour by the closest village and grab the supplies they need. *Then* I head back.

Violeta's wide awake on my return, but looking worse for wear. Yesterday, her hair had been lustrous and shining, and her cheeks had color in them, despite her wound. Today, she seems clammy, and she's shivering even as she's moving around the kitchenette making herself tea and toast.

I set the supplies aside and touch her shoulder. "Are you feeling okay?"

“Hmm?” She looks at me, her eyes glazed. Then she blinks and smiles faintly. “Yeah, fine. Just feeling under the weather. I’ll be all right.”

I’d been planning to ask her more about the vampiri hunting her, to find out what exactly the reason was—besides her father—but somehow I can’t bring myself to. Instead, I help her back to the bed after she’s had her tea, and watch as she falls back asleep.

My gaze shifts again to the backpack. And, once more, I shove the thought away from my mind. I won’t invade her privacy.

Once I’m sure she’s fully asleep, I grab the supplies and head out again.

Violeta

The grogginess and aches all over my body wake me up. I need the muroni concoction—or at least muroni blood. I need...

In a daze, I get off Marcus’ bed. Dimly, I’m aware of having to keep the pretense of being human, but he’s nowhere to be seen. *Even better.*

Stumbling more than walking, I head to the door, and step outside. The sun is almost setting. Nighttime. Muroni love hunting at nighttime. *If ever I have a chance of finding a lonesome one, now’s the time.*

I’m not sure how long I walk for. The bone-numbing cold soon gets through my clothes, freezing me. Still, I continue on, blindly seeking what’s sure to be my salvation or my death.

“The o-one t-time I n-need a m-muroni...” I mutter through chattering teeth.

I escape from the thick woods into a small, clear field. Glancing behind me, I realize I have no idea which way Marcus' house is. So much for my sense of direction.

Sighing, I sink to my knees and let the coolness of the ground seep into me. Maybe the cold will make do with me. Would it be so bad?

It would be. I haven't yet tasted Marcus' kiss.

The thought is jarring enough to make me chuckle. About to freeze to death, and what I'm thinking about is as unattainable as health is to me right now.

I close my eyes, lying on the ground and wanting nothing more than to sleep. I image if I'd been truly human, my heartbeat would slow down, and I would soon...drift...into...

"Help!"

...sleep.

A moment goes by, and another. Had I imagined that cry?

"Help!"

Even more groggily than before, I get up, barely able to hold myself up. It sounded like a young child.

"*Help!*"

I stumble to my feet this time, blinking at the darkness. "H-hello? Is s-someone t-there?" The chattering of my teeth has returned full-force, and I wrap my arms around myself in a futile attempt to instill some warmth in my frozen body.

I move onwards. And onwards. Back in the woods, losing my footing ever so often. I hear cries in the distance, still.

And then I see it. A misshapen form, bent over a child's wrist. The child has her face turned away, tears streaming down her cheeks as the muroni drinks from her.

Muroni are the scum of our society. While vampiri have more or less managed their impulses, muroni have no such control. They've given in to Darkness fully and enjoy the cruelty they can inflict with additional powers—and weaknesses. They also hunt hikers and any human who dares enter the woods. Because they dwell in caves, they're extremely sensitive to sunlight. But the worst is their shape-shifting abilities. They can blend in with the night or darkness in a heartbeat, something we've lost over time. Bottom line is, they're the danger no one sees coming.

And this poor human child definitely didn't.

A burst of rage slams into my ribcage, giving me that much-needed energy I'd craved. And then I'm rushing at the muroni, slamming into him and tackling him away from the child. We roll on the ground, and I come up above it. I register a gaunt face, saggy skin, claws that try to get to my throat.

Grunting, I push those hands away and get a punch in—then his strength overpowers me, and I'm tossed off him. I hit a tree and fall to the ground, groaning in pain. The child is frozen, a few feet away from me.

I meet her chocolate eyes and whisper, "Run. Save yourself."

She scrambles to her feet, at the same time as the muroni. He shakes his head, then glances at us. I grin, beckoning him closer.

"It's me you want, fucker." I lift my wrist. "Fancy a taste of royal blood?"

That's all it takes, and then he's walking towards me, ignoring the child who's escaping.

And then, right before he can kill me, it jerks. My blurry gaze drops to his chest, and the point of an axe embedded in it. The muroni stumbles forward, then falls on me. Its blood sprays me all over, getting into my eyes, my mouth, and all over my clothes.

I swallow, pushed by some instinct of survival. And then I swallow some more.

Someone grabs the muroni off me, shoving it away. Then Marcus is there, cupping my cheeks and trying to wipe as much of the blood off me as possible.

"Violeta! What the—How did you—Violeta!"

I'm too dazed to try to comprehend any of it, and I pass out.

When I next wake up, it's under the bright starry sky, and with the smell of a fire burning nearby. I'm feeling better. Not quite perfect, but it seems the small taste of blood I'd had was enough to, well, rejuvenate me. But where the hell am I?

I push off the ground and the blanket I'd been lying on, and glance around.

Marcus is tossing things into the fire—including the limbs of the dead muroni, by the looks of it. I guess if he knows about the vampir world, it only makes sense he'd know about these creatures, too.

"You're awake," he says and walks over to me, crouching so he's eye level. "What are you doing in the woods?"

"I..." *I needed blood. Nope. Can't say that.* "Sleepwalking? I don't..." I shake my head, doing my best impression of confusion. "I'm not too sure."

Marcus wipes his hands on his jeans and reaches to the side, handing me a bottle of water. "Here, drink. I'll take you back to the cabin soon."

As I drink, I glance around again. "There was a girl. The muroni..."

"She's fine," he says and tosses the empty bottle I hand him in the fire. "They all are."

"*All*?"

Marcus purses his lips, then shakes his head. "I don't understand how you land yourself in these situations. That thing could've killed you! And yet, here you are, as unharmed as ever."

He reaches for me, and the touch of his hand on my cheek is fire. I tremble, closing my eyes. He must misread my reaction as he pulls his hand away.

"*All*," he whispers, and I open my eyes again. "A group of orphans I've been helping out. They choose to live here, because they don't trust adults. Not after their parents were killed by vampiri and hunters alike."

I gasp. "Hunters?"

Marcus nods. "There have been more attacks in the area, and not just here. Sometimes I travel to other villages, and rumors abound of weird happenings." He shakes his head. "It doesn't matter. To me, anyway, since I live far away from anything. Point is, the kids weren't safe here anymore. I've made sure they're away, now, and will be protected." He gets up and holds his hand out to me. "Let's go back to the cabin, da?"

I look at his hand, then at him. This man is so full of layers, I can't even wrap my head around it. And every single one that's peeled away intrigues me more and more.

Better be careful, Vi. Else you're going to fall in love with this one, and it'll hurt.

Gulping, I take his hand and let him pull me to my feet. In the most clichéd of all actions, I stumble and land against his chest, splaying my hands over his broad muscles to balance myself.

Marcus freezes against me. When I look up into his features, his green eyes are a darker hue, reflecting the light of the fire. His jaw is tight, his lips pressed together, and his nostrils are flaring like he's running a marathon.

We stay like that, suspended, for a long moment. The crackling of the flames is the only background noise as we stare at each other. Searching for...I don't know. Nor do we find it.

When he gently sets me away, I can't help the disappointment coursing through me. *Guess I won't get that kiss, after all.*

Marcus

A week goes by and we settle into a rhythm. While I hunt and ensure the perimeter is always clear of vampiri, Violeta tries out new baking recipes and slowly tries to fatten me up. I humor her, and deal with the after-effects of her cooking when she's asleep.

She hasn't said anything about my orphan wards since that night, but she stares at me, when she thinks I'm not noticing. I can never tell if it's admiration or consternation, but I feel her gaze like the hottest of touches on my body.

She also hasn't spoken more about her father, but more than once I catch her staring out the window, lost in thought, and it makes me wonder if that's where her thoughts lie. Or if they're with an ex-lover, someone she left behind to protect.

Aside from what she told me, I still don't know much about her. Other than her being on the run, and there being a price on her head.

Not that it makes a difference.

With each passing day, my body makes it harder and harder for me to ignore the fact she's a full-bodied woman living in my house, wearing my clothes when hers are being washed, and leaving her scent all over my home. All over my *bed.* And when I close my eyes, all I can remember is her, bathed in the firelight, staring at me as if begging for my lips on hers.

More and more, urges rise within me. And with each day that I ignore them, I get crankier. Until one day I snap at her over something, and storm outside in search of food. Not *human* food, not this once. But I can't afford to be this low on actual sustenance and still be around her, unable to control my primal urges.

The poor hiker I run across, way at the bottom of the mountain, gets the brunt of my attack. I take just enough blood to sustain myself for a while, then leave him with the wound healed. When he wakes up, he'll be able to return to his life as if nothing happened.

Unlike me.

Taking blood, after what I've done when under the clan's employ, is something I loathe. It makes me loathe my entire being, if I'm entirely honest. So I always hold off until the last possible moment, until I know there will be consequences if I don't feed. I wait until my vampir senses are so haywire, that if I don't feed, I know I won't hear the others coming after me, nor will I be able to defend myself.

It basically means I'm only half-operational as a vampir most of the time, except for the days when I feed. Then, my senses are in full span, and I'm at my best.

This time around, the need wasn't out of a desire to protect myself. It was more to make sure I don't try to feed on Violeta. Because more and more, her presence disturbs me in my deepest core, awakening thoughts and desires I'd long since buried.

When I return home that night, she's asleep.

I head to the couch, where I've been sleeping for the past week and some, and try to get some shut eye. The moment I'm close to passing out, Violeta gets off the bed and moves around the house. She must think I'm asleep, because she tiptoes more than usual. In the light of the fire, I see her warming a pot.

It takes me a few confused moments to realize she's warming the water for the tub. My entire body feels electrocuted at the realization. *No. She can't be seriously drawing herself a bath. Fuck, if ever there is a deity out there who can take pity on my poor, nonexistent soul...*

Such is not the case.

But there, in the firelight, Violeta sheds her clothes, then steps in the water. Her soft, pleasurable sigh makes my body tighten in all the wrong ways. Or right ways, depending. I try to ignore the sounds she's making, but it's no use. There's a splash of the water, over and over. The smell of vanilla and fresh valleys gets more intense.

And when she moves in the water, rising like Aphrodite herself, I can't help my gaze landing on her. Water drips down her body, droplets caressing her skin in a way I've been yearning to since I first saw her. The firelight gives her a golden hue, and her pert nipples stand to attention as she bends over, retrieving a towel from the side of the bathtub and giving me a perfect view of her heart-shaped ass.

I must've made a sound, because she freezes, then turns to face me. Catches my gaze before I can look away. Her features are bathed in shadows, so I'm unable to figure out if she's about to yell at me or not. All I can see are her blue eyes, staring at me as if lit by an inner light.

And then she steps out of the tub, the towel wrapped around her body. Never once leaving my gaze, she inches closer and closer to me, until I can smell the vanilla off her body.

"How long have you been awake?" she asks softly.

I gulp. "Since before you stepped in the tub."

She inhales sharply, and again I wonder if she's about to yell at me. She'd have every reason to—just because she lives in my home doesn't mean she doesn't deserve her privacy.

But instead, she comes closer still, and lowers herself on the sofa, straddling me. I can feel the heat of the water come off her, and some droplets still cling to her skin.

Violeta leans in, her wet hair tickling my face. "Then, maybe we can stop dancing around this, hmm?"

"What?"

For an answer, she kisses me. Her soft lips brush against me once, twice, and I remain unresponsive. The third time, I give in with a groan, like I give my entire soul. I dig a hand into her scalp, the other around her waist, and rise up on the sofa, enough to have her plastered against me.

Violeta sighs against my mouth, and then she moves against me. Pulls my shirt off, and her hands are roaming my chest and I'm reminded just how fucking long it's been since I've had a woman's hands on me.

I grip her wrists, trying to find a way to explain myself. "Slow down, precious. Otherwise this'll be over before I've even gotten started." One hand releases her, to travel between her spread thighs. "And I very much want to get things started properly."

She sighs, sinking onto my fingers and letting her head drop back. She undulates above me, her breasts rising and falling, tantalizing me. I add a third finger inside her, and this time she groans. Her eyelashes flutter, eyes seeking mine, pleading...

I haven't been this close to a woman in years. *Too many years.*

Since I landed in this forgotten corner of the woods. I couldn't afford to, not with Dmitri willing to use anything against me to regain control.

My body is keen to remind me of my needs. Brutally. With a scorching heat in my veins, in my groin, that has me gritting my teeth. All that is completely secondary to her reactions right now. But I also don't know how much longer I can hold back before I sink myself in her heat.

My thumb moves to her clit, gently, slowly caressing it, watching as she sinks faster on me. Her hands move to her breasts, toying with them, pulling on her nipples. I want to take over, but all I can do is watch her features, her parted lips, soak in her sounds.

I don't remember feeling this good when I've given a woman orgasms before. I don't remember this electricity running across my skin, turning me so goddamn sensitive everywhere.

And then Violeta tightens around my fingers, and I curl them deep in her, and she gasps her surrender, my name on her lips. I remove my fingers and lick them clean—fuck, she still tastes like cinnamon—and then my hand's at her nape, pulling her closer, kissing her again as she returns from her high.

Violeta's hands find my chest again, and my cheek drops against her chest.

And then I freeze.

Because she just climaxed. And her heartbeat should be out of control.

But instead of a heart beating, all I hear is silence.

My full vampir senses kick in, giving me everything I've missed before. The coolness of her body. The faint scent underneath that sweetness, marking her as a—

Her hands are still roaming over me, but it's like I've been doused in holy water. And before I can stop myself, I toss her to the other side of the couch and move away. Too fast. Vampir fast.

She stares at me, stunned. Then her fangs come out as she hisses. "What the fu—"

I stare at this woman, the one I've just helped climax, at the rosy hue of her cheeks, the shine in her eyes, now turned to ice. And the fangs—glinting in the light.

"You're a *vampir!*"

And just like that, we're no longer two lovers.

Instead, we're two predators in a crouch, fangs out and metaphorical claws extended, hissing and snarling to see who'll give up first.

Chapter 6

Violeta

My entire body's trembling as the reality of the situation hits me.

Marcus is a vampir. He's just like me. And I've been living with him for days without realizing it. Not only that, but he knows the vampiri who are hunting me. What if...

His story runs through my head fast. Knowing of vampiri. Leaving them. Being followed. Not being left alone.

I tighten the towel around my naked body, trying to push aside both my annoyance and my fear, not to mention my arousal. He'd played my body like an instrument, knowing what buttons to press and watching me as I came apart. I don't remember the last time I've had a lover who was so dedicated to my pleasure first, let alone one who didn't immediately jump to satisfy his own needs after.

And for a few blissful moments, I forgot everything. My lineage, my purpose, my disease, all of it was gone. Evaporated in the wake of an all-consuming desire. The same craving that's been humming in my core since I've met him. And damn him, but I want to finish this!

But all that is gone, a blip on the radar now when compared to what my eyes land on. Which is Marcus, crouched a few feet away from me, his fangs extended and staring at me with equal measures of shock and distaste.

No. He doesn't get to do that. Not when he lied to me just as much. I know what my reasoning was and why I did what I did. But him? He has no excuse, not even if his past is half as dark as he's alluded to.

"You lied," I accuse first, straightening from my crouch. I *can* and *will* have this conversation with him as an adult. No matter how much I want to strangle him right now for allowing things to get so out of control.

"As did you," he points out, mimicking my movement.

And just like that, the rush of desire we'd felt is set aside. Instead, it's replaced by wariness, and a healthy dose of distrust. I turn my back to him and head to the bed, pulling on a pair of sweatpants and a sweater. I ignore his comfortable shirt that I'd tossed off me when going for my bath, and instead reach for my own clothes.

I need their safety, especially now.

Finally, all dressed and semi-pulled back together, I walk back to him. Marcus is by the window, staring out, avoiding my gaze. But he's definitely not avoiding the subject.

"Why did you lie?"

"You first," I mutter.

He turns to me, eyes narrowed. "You don't *smell* like a vampir. I didn't know. And I wasn't about to reveal my existence to a human, right? Or did you forget that little unspoken rule in our lives?"

I hadn't. Because my family had instilled said rule. *No humans are to know of our existence. Without exceptions.* Father had been clear about the implications if such a thing got out. And over the centuries, as we've witnessed human technology evolve, we've only become more wary. Evidently, at least some measure of that same wariness continued to be touted in the vampir clans. Even if they hate us now.

But I'm not about to admit any of that to Marcus, not when he's this defensive. What got up his ass, that he thinks he's in the right here? Just because he saved my life twice doesn't put him in the right, here.

"So because I didn't smell right, you figured it was best to stay quiet."

"Da." His eyes narrow on me. "And you didn't see fit to correct me, might I add."

"I'll get to that in a second. What about the vampiri looking for me?"

"What about them?"

"Were you truthful, in that you told them I wasn't here?"

"Of course!" He takes a step closer, then stops himself. "I wasn't... I'm not stupid. I know how they hunt, and I realized early on they had only the worst of intentions for you. I just couldn't figure out why they were after you."

"Hmm."

He shakes his head, scoffing. "Wow, you really do have trust issues. Been alone for too long?"

I hold back a scowl at his implication. Vampiri are not solitary creatures. When alone, we tend to let the other part of immortality—the craziness—take over and lose our minds. In a way, it's what contributed to the creation of the muroni. The fact Marcus seems to think my loneliness affected my brain capacity shouldn't be surprising, but I ignore the question anyway.

Instead, I ask, "Why aren't you with Dmitri's clan?"

"Personal choice."

I tilt my head to the side. His stance changed as he spoke the words. I shouldn't be so aware of him to notice it, but I am—and dammit, can he not put on a shirt already?

There's got to be more to his story.

"Is it because of the orphans? You obviously care for them... Enough to make sure they're protected now."

Marcus scowls. "It has nothing to do with them. I walked away from the Ardelean clan seventy years ago, and haven't looked back since. They've tried to get me back. At first, they were happy to allow my whims. When they noticed I was for real, they did everything possible. From taunts, to destroying my house multiple times, to attacking me when I least expected it. They got tired of losing people...And then they got preoccupied with other things."

"Such as?"

His expression darkens further. "Politics. Vampir hunters."

The short answers are enough warning to drop it, but I don't. "Vampiri wouldn't let you be alone. It's a risk, to lose your mind. Immortality consumes us, we need to be with others and not on our own."

Something shifts behind his eyes, and he slowly nods. "Da, all true. And I had enough leverage to buy out my freedom."

Buy out his... It's my turn to frown. "I don't understand."

He leans against the kitchen counter, crossing his arms over his chest. "Neither do I. Why lie about your history, and that your father supposedly died? Why *are* those vampiri hunting you, if not because of that?"

Shit. It only makes sense the interrogation would go both ways, but I'm not ready to reveal anything. Especially not where I come from, or where I'm going. So what can I say, so he'll believe me? And do I even want him to? Wouldn't it be much simpler to just...leave?

"And above all," Marcus adds, "tell me why the hell you don't smell like the rest of our kin."

Ah. That. At least that's an easy explanation, one that might distract him from the rest. I hope.

"I'm sick." I clear my throat, and glance at my sweatpants, picking off invisible lint. "I haven't been feeling well for years, and it came to a standstill a few weeks ago. That's why you can't smell me properly."

Marcus frowns. His body language is even tenser now. "How sick? What do you mean, *sick*? Our kind don't get sick."

I shrug. "Apparently, I do. I must be unlucky."

"But..."

A sigh escapes me. "I know you have questions, but I have little answers. All I know is it's not going away, and somehow it's making me... almost human. I don't know how to explain it. I still have some vampir strength, but sooner or later that will be gone, too."

"Almost human? Like it's reversing the turning?"

"Da. I've...seen people. Asked around. There's nothing to be done, in as much as I've found out. Best I got was a tincture that was supposed to help me, and it did...until it got shattered in the woods." I tuck a strand of hair behind my ear, then shrug. "Anyway, it is what it is."

More of Marcus' defensiveness leaves him, confusing me further. What is it about me that's making him so interested, when he should still be mad? And what is it about him that's drawing me in so much, to the point I feel I could talk to him for ages?

I clear my throat, breaking contact with his green eyes. "I'll probably find my end by someone's hands, eventually. Weakened as I am, it won't be long."

He uncrosses his arms then and stomps to me, gripping my shoulders with a firmness that surprises me. "I'm not going to allow that to happen."

A startled chuckle escapes me. "It's not like you have an obligation towards me, Marcus." He only stares at me with that unsettling gaze, so I continue, "Really. You don't. So whatever hero complex is ruling you right now, you can get over it."

I remove his hands off my shoulders and walk to the sink, pouring myself a glass of water. The coolness hits my throat, and I close my eyes as I drink it all. It alleviates some of the dizziness in my head, but not all.

Marcus seems to shake off whatever's come over him, and turns to me. "When you say this sickness is making you human..."

"It's not contagious, not that I know of."

"That's not what I meant." The exasperation in his tone has me turn to him.

I don't understand his reaction. He should be annoyed, pushy, and yet he's acting like all of a sudden I'm his to protect. Which is not the case, and the sooner he gets that through his head, the better it'll be for both of us. I'd only meant to scratch an itch with what I initiated, not create emotional complications for either of us.

A brief flash of Tassa and Nico runs through my head, interrupted by the stirrings of envy I'd felt when watching them. Fairy tales and happily ever afters don't come true for the likes of us, and I'd best let go of those notions.

Marcus draws my attention, grabbing my wrist again. "How long do you have?"

"Why do you care, Marcus?"

A muscle ticks in his jaw. "Because I do. Because I saw you running for your life, and then I came upon a carnage you left behind. Because I cleaned up said carnage and lied to very dangerous people."

If only he knew how dangerous I could be…

"And because I've been here for you these last weeks. And you've seen you can trust me. So the least you owe me is an explanation about this *disease*. Just tell me everything you know about it."

I roll my eyes. "What's the point?"

"The point is, has anyone found a cure?" He clenches his jaw. "I don't think so, not judging by your eagerness to give up. But I've travelled the world, and if anyone can help you out, it's me."

"You really do think highly of yourself, don't you?"

He leans against the counter again, his expression determined. "I do. So, will you tell me?"

I sigh and pour myself another glass of water. What's the worst it'll do, if I tell him what he wants to know? It won't be everything, but it's a start.

Marcus

The crunch of leaves under my boots draws me out of my thoughts. I've been so involved with what Violeta revealed, I wasn't really paying much attention to what I was doing. After she told me everything about her sickness, I offered to go hunt something for food. Especially now that I know she definitely needs to eat.

According to her, the muroni blood I'd cleaned off her a few days ago was actually helping, but it had to be taken in a certain concoction. For the most part now, she eats human food when she's weak—something I can't wrap my head around.

My departure was also an attempt to get away from her, her body, and those damn eyes. Once I get my head screwed on straight, I can return and actually be of use. I'd meant the words I'd said—that I wanted to help. Despite her lies and half-truths, I...*need* to help her.

She's sick.

How can she be sick?

Our kind never gets sick. I've heard of injuries and poisons—there was even a string of them in the region a few weeks back when Dmitri's guys came to me—but this is something completely different.

And despite my best efforts, all I can think of is I need to save this woman. Why in hell am I not pissed off at all her lies? Or the fact she still hasn't told me why the vampiri are after her?

I lean against a tree, resting my forehead on the rough bark. Why, why, why?

So many questions. All rounding up to one answer. And it's that I now feel responsible for her. I have ever since I picked her up in my arms and carried her to my home. Even more so when I helped her heal, and the last nail in my proverbial coffin was when I lied to the clan.

Years might have passed by and the vampir world might've

changed. But to me, handing out my protection still means something. Violeta is under my protection now, and like it or not, I need to hold up my end of the bargain. Even if she's determined not to get any help from me.

I see a hare in the distance, and within seconds it's in my hands, neck cracked. A loud exhale later, I move back to the cabin, and the woman within.

I know the moment I step in that she's gone. Mainly because I can't sense her presence or her scent, but also because my spot isn't that big, anyway. Cursing under my breath, I drop the hare to the ground and run back out.

Where would she have gone?

The sun is close to setting, and the temperature is dropping. Even if she's on a good day, with her vampir senses more on point than not, she's vulnerable. Especially at night.

"Dammit, Violeta!"

A few curses later, I'm speeding through the trees, trying to find any inkling of her scent. And then I catch it—the sweetness of it. I take off even faster, pushed by an urge I don't quite understand to be back in her presence. Trees blur past me, nothing but a vague landscape, until I finally find her.

She's leaning against a tree, trying to catch her breath. I could leave, let her go, and she'd never be the wiser. Even thinking that makes me nauseous.

"Violeta?"

She turns to me and at the same plasters herself to the tree by default. Her gaze is unfocused, and her fangs are extended. It's the first time I've seen her like this—the way I am, when I'm hunting for food.

And god*damn*, but my body stirs, answering to a call that's even more primal than our hunting self.

"What is it?"

She shakes her head. "You need to leave."

"Why?"

"Because—" She inhales deeply, and then her eyes open again and land on me. The blue irises glow, otherworldly. "You smell too damn good."

"I... what?"

I don't get a chance to register her words. She's on me—moving at vampir speed—the second after, her legs wrapped around my waist, arms around my neck, holding onto me like a monkey. The force of the contact sends us barreling into another tree, and still she doesn't let go of me. With surprising force, she tilts my head to the side, gripping my hair as anchor, and sinks her fangs in my neck.

I freeze, shocked at the attack. A vampir attacking a vampir is unheard of—

And then something akin to molten lava spreads through me. A mix of agony and pleasure, the sensation takes hold until a groan escapes me, and instead of pushing her away, I find my hands going to her ass, pulling her closer. So much closer. My own fangs extend, wanting nothing more than to sink into her—but she's not a human. I don't understand the urge, nor can I be bothered to try.

Violeta moans against my neck and tightens her hold on my hair and waist. I dig my fingers in her flesh. If she'd been human, I might've worried about leaving bruises on her ass, but I can't even think of that. Not when my hardness is rubbing against her, and she's moaning while sucking my blood, my very essence, and all I can do is groan and silently offer more.

I've never felt this ecstasy. This... need. I should be weakened, but it's the exact opposite. With each slurp of my blood, she infuses energy into me, while simultaneously taking it out. There's no rhyme or reason to it, only a dark, primal urge, fueled by both of our predatory natures.

I try to shift her at some point, wanting my mouth on hers instead, but she only growls and rubs against me some more. And I forget my intention, instead letting the haze of pleasure take me farther down a never-ending tunnel.

Whatever sorcery this is, whatever's going on with Violeta, it's more than either of us understand. It's definitely more than I do.

She sinks her teeth more into me, and I slide to the ground, pulling her with me. She doesn't realize she's rocking against me, but if she doesn't stop soon I'm going to embarrass myself in the worst way possible. It's been seventy years since I've had a woman like her in my arms, and I'm already on edge from the earlier incident at the cabin. This is nothing but part two of the same event, but on steroids.

I grip her hips, trying to hold her steady, but she lets loose another growl. And then she grinds on me more, and I find myself pulling her hips closer, encouraging her, instead of stopping her. The friction drives us both insane, and before long she comes, moaning against my neck, and the suction plus this craziness between us pushes me over the brink.

I'm left panting, my head leaning against the tree, and Violeta plastered to every inch of my body. Slowly, the haze of whatever-the-fuck that was lifts off me, and she releases my neck. There's an audible pop as her lips disconnect from my flesh, and then she rises above me, her cheeks flushed, her gaze brilliant, and sated.

"I'm so sor—"

I lift a finger to her lips. Still under the daze of what just happened, all I can say is, "Believe me, I'm only sorry you stopped."

She leans towards me, brushing her lips against mine, and I'm equally aware of the need to thrust my aching hardness inside her, as well as the urge to pull her closer and hold her until I recover. Before I can do either, Violeta pushes off me, turning her back to me.

"Wait, Vi—"

She freezes, but not because of my plea. Something else has her attention. Something worse. Something I would've heard, were it not for our passionate...whatever that was.

Because the forest is quiet, aside from us. The air is thick with tension. And underneath it all, it doesn't feel like we're alone anymore.

And when they speak, I realize why Violeta's now positioned as if to defend me.

"Vi, is it? And here I thought you didn't know her."

The voice makes my blood freeze. It's Grigore and the other one, and some friends. Have they been tracking us? How could I have not heard them coming? How did Violeta...?

I shoot to my feet, but dizziness threatens to drop me back down. I can't allow it to. Although it sends me stumbling into the tree, I use it to hold myself up. I clench my fists, refusing to be the weaker party.

I won't allow them to hurt her.

But before I can do or say anything, Violeta turns her profile to me, regret in her eyes. "It's my turn to protect you."

Chapter 7

Violeta

My body's still humming from the orgasm. Second one within a few hours. When was the last time I've had something so explosive? Not in the last centuries, not even with Cristian—the toy boy turned robber, as Liza called him. Definitely not.

It only makes me wonder what it would be like without any clothes on, and that's a bad, bad thing to wonder.

Especially when I'm faced with half a dozen vampiri, each more determined to see me dead than the last. And judging by the look in their eyes, they're well aware of who I am. Shit.

"Violeta—"

I force myself not to look at Marcus. If I take my eyes off them, they *will* attack. And given it's my fault we're in this, the least I can do is protect Marcus. Especially as he's weakened because of me.

A shudder runs through me—a deeper part of me wants to turn to him and continue tasting his blood. It had been so *good*. Flavorful, better than any wine I'd drunk when I was human, and sure as hell better than any blood I've had as a vampir.

How can that be possible? It's unnatural, craving one of my own kind like this. How can—

I forcefully put a stop to the thoughts and shove them in the *I'll-deal-with-you-later* box in my head. Over my shoulder, I say, "I've got this."

I spread my stance, leaning just that little bit more forward. My eyes take in the vampiri, trying to determine their pattern of attack. If they're well-trained, they'll try to box me in. That's something easy to predict, easier still to counteract by myself. But if they're untrained and raw, then I'm in shit.

When I'd first been turned, Nico spent years teaching me the finer points of control. The bloodlust was stronger than any teachings, until the day I woke up to the corpse of a child. That had been the wake-up call I'd needed. But I still remember those days, if I choose to dig into the memories. And not only was I reckless, I was also powerful because of that recklessness. *I'll have to tap right back into that.*

It takes me seconds to assess them, to notice their straight stances and the way they prepare to move. As a unit. *Thank goodness. Well-trained, then. More so than the others who attacked me, but they're wearing the same uniform.* The gold raven pin glints at me, warning me I'm facing off against a squadron of extremely focused soldiers.

It's more than I can say for myself. What the hell was I thinking? Getting hot and heavy in the middle of the woods, when I'm being hunted, when my entire family's being hunted! And what was I even doing, sucking Marcus' blood? He's a vampir, not a human! Yet his blood had tasted so—fucking—good. It's enough to make me salivate, just thinking of the richness, the...

"Disgusting," says one vampir, staring from me to him. "Is this what it has come to, then? Vampir upon vampir?"

I need to shut him up before he says more than I want him to. Like the fact I'm a royal. Marcus doesn't need to know that. Regardless of what happened between us, I remember Father's teachings all too well. *Say the least possible about yourself. Always listen. Make sure not to give them ammunition against you.*

Marcus might react well to my lineage, but then again, he might not. There's no way to predict it, and I don't want to take the chance and upset the fragile balance we have.

I'll have enough to explain as it is with the sucking of his blood.

That's enough of that. First things first.

I allow my vampiric speed to take over and rush towards the one who'd spoken. To my surprise, I slam into him hard, and fast. There's no hesitation in me, no weakness, none of that crippling haze that had descended upon me mere minutes before Marcus had found me. The strength in my veins is even more than regular. It's...enhanced. I haven't felt this good since my first turning when I'd been a new vampir.

We topple into a tree that cracks, and I let the vampir go so I don't get dragged down with him. He rolls downhill, much as I did when the others had tracked me.

Then I whirl on the other five. Marcus is still using the tree to hold his weight up, but I can tell by the clenching of his jaw he wants to help. His nostrils flare, surveying the vampiri as he, too, looks for weaknesses. Stubborn man. The soldier in him won't stay put for long.

I grab the closest vampir, my nails dig into his throat, and I pull it out. His vocal cords are mush in my hands, and blood splatters everywhere. The sight of it has me mesmerized, for a moment, as the same blood lust that I'd dealt with ages ago tries to make a comeback.

"Violeta, ai grija!" Marcus yells.

I duck in time, narrowly avoiding another vampir who'd tried to put me in a chokehold. On a growl, I whirl, knee him, then shove my fist into his stomach. I'd wanted to punch him only, but the force of my movement results in my hand cutting through him like butter, and soon enough I find myself wrist-deep in his intestines.

I yank my hand out as he falls to his knees, and crack his neck, then rip his head off for good measure. Then I'm turning on the last two.

No crippling weakness. No debilitating dizziness.

What the hell is going on?

How is this possible?

I'm moving faster, stronger, deadlier than I have in years. And the only explanation is that Marcus' blood did this to me.

The thought makes bile rise in my throat, but I can't be complacent. I have no time to waste on being disgusted with myself. I need to make sure we'll be fine, and that he'll be safe. And then I need to disappear. Because if his blood has this power over me, there's no saying what I'll do when we're alone again.

By the time I glance around me, there's blood everywhere. Without even thinking about it, I've ripped apart the other two vampiri. Panting, I glance at my hands. Their whiteness is fully coated by the burgundy hue of their blood, as is the frozen ground.

Marcus is stepping towards me, his gaze wide on what I've caused. As is mine. I'm in such shock, I don't pay attention to my back. The first vampir I'd slammed into—the one who'd rolled downhill—drives a stake through me. Luckily, he misses my heart by inches.

"Grigore!"

With a roar, Marcus tackles the guy. He's still weak from the blood I've taken but something else entirely seems to motivate him. Once he's pushed the vampir off me, he balances his stance on both feet and slowly advanced towards the vampir.

My attacks had been reckless, careless. A mess. Marcus is something else entirely.

The vampir tries to feint and duck around him, still aiming for me. Marcus blocks him at every turn as if he can guess his moves. And still he advances while dancing out of his reach. On one such attack, the vampir shoves the stake blindly forward—Marcus swings out of the way, then grabs his wrist and rips the stake out of his hand, along with a few fingers. The man falls to the ground, howling in pain. It's abruptly cut off by the stake shoved in his throat.

Marcus pulls it out then, same as I had, tears the vampir's head off and tosses it on the others. The rest of his body acts as if it's being burned from the inside out, and he shrivels.

I gulp at the sight. For a second, it becomes superimposed by another memory—Father. Equally shriveled up, like a mummy.

Don't think about it.

His loss had hurt all of us, but it had torn me apart for years. He'd been more of a father to me than my own, and without his guidance I wouldn't have turned into the strong, compassionate immortal being I am now. Why he couldn't turn some of that wisdom onto himself, I'm not sure.

"They must've been old," Marcus says, unaware of my thoughts. "At least this one. The others are losing too much blood to be that old."

I take in the sight, nodding. Normally when a vampir is killed with a stake to the heart, their body automatically reverts back to the decomposed form it should've been in all along. Like death catches up with a vengeance. But when vampiri are killed otherwise—head ripped out, dismembered—those limbs need to be burned to avoid humans finding them. A vampir's dead body, if not fully destroyed, has the potential to turn the leftover soul into a stafie—an evil spirit prone to possession. Last thing we need is to deal with any of that shit.

I turn to Marcus, holding my side. The wound from the stake is already healing, I can *feel* the flesh tying back together. That, too, is faster than it has ever been. I'm not even remotely dizzy at the attack, the loss of blood, or anything.

On the other hand, Marcus looks even worse for wear. He sways on his feet, then drops. I catch him before he hits the ground. And without worrying about what else is out there, I use my newfound vampir strength to drag him back to the cabin.

It takes Marcus a good half a day to wake up. And despite my desire to run off, to leave him as I'd planned, now I feel responsible enough to stick around. At least for the time being.

While he rests, I go back to the clearing and burn the remainder of the bodies, trying to remove all trace of what I'd done. Hard, when the ground is frozen and the blood has nowhere to soak. But as I go about my business, the temperature drops and the skies cloud over. With a bit of luck, it'll snow tonight and the last traces of the fight will be hidden. In the meantime, the burn of the woodfire covers the area with more ash.

I can't even imagine what Marcus saw or what he'll think when he wakes up, but I know we can't risk another Ardelean squadron landing on their dead bodies and realizing what happened.

When I return to the cabin, Marcus is still asleep. My gaze gets drawn to his phone, tucked in a faraway forgotten corner of the kitchen counter. I'd noticed it before, when I'd made hot chocolate. And I shouldn't. The last thing I should do is actually call them, but after what just happened...

Without giving it much more thought, I grab the phone and dial the number Tassa made sure I know by heart.

"Da?" The clipped tone is unmistakably Nico's.

I pause, hesitating, before saying, "It's me."

There's a long exhale on the other end. "Violeta? What's going on? Why are you calling from a weird number?"

"I'm not home."

"You're breaking up. Say that again?"

I glance over my shoulder, making sure Marcus is still asleep, then clear my throat and raise my voice. "I'm not calling from home. I left."

"You *what*? Why would you—"

"You know why, Nico. We both know why. I can't be sitting down and doing nothing while life ebbs out of me. So I went away, wanting to live what's left of it."

"You could have told us."

"I did. I left a letter. For you."

I can almost see him scowling as he lets out an exasperated sound. "A letter? One I wouldn't have found until I returned from vacation? We deserve more than that. We would have understood."

"Would you really? Or would you have made it harder for me?"

He sighs, knowing I've got a point. We're not known for listening to each other—well, except for Vlad. He's the greatest listener of us all. Probably because his demons are worse than mine.

"How are you feeling?"

Nico's tone is softer. I can't help smiling, knowing it's Tassa who brought this change in him. I'm glad of it, because he's back to being the brother I knew, the one before all our centuries of existence. Then the smile slips when I recall the purpose of my call.

"That's why I'm calling, actually."

He knows me well enough to notice the catch in my voice. "What's going on?"

"I, um, something happened."

He waits.

"You have to warn the others somehow," I start. "We're being staked out by a clan."

"A vampir clan? Or muroni?"

"Vampir."

He sighs in the phone, not sounding too bothered. "We knew they would find us."

"But this... Nico. They followed me. They waited until I was alone and then they attacked me."

"Fuck," he mutters and I can hear noise in the background now. "Are you hurt?"

"No, no. I escaped those ones. Um, defended myself."

"Do you know which clan?"

"I didn't initially, but I met someone and he.... he said it's the Ardelean clan."

Nico cusses under his breath, then adds, "So you're in Transylvania?"

"That's the thing... I'm not. I'm farther south, near the border with Hungary, I think."

"That far off? Violeta—" He bites his tongue. "It has to be another clan. Vlad's map was pretty encompassing."

I gulp. "I don't think it is. My source says they... amalgamated. Grown bigger. They're coming after us, Nico. Have been building up to it for decades."

"Where are you? We'll pack up and come to you."

I turn to Marcus and his sleepy form. "No, that's not necessary. Please. I don't want this to ruin your vacation, and it's not like your presence here would change anything."

"Vi—"

"Just hear me out." I take a deep breath. "I, um, fed on a vampir."

There's a stunned silence on the other end. It comes across through the distance.

"You...*what*?"

In short, concise terms, I explain as best as I can what happened. Leaving out the part about how arousing it was. The silence only lengthens.

"Hold on a moment." He fumbles around the phone and then he's back, but he sounds a bit farther away. "You're on speaker,

Tassa's here. Mind repeating all that?"

I do again, and listen to the same stunned silence. I can clearly picture them sharing a long look, trying to figure out what the hell is going on with me. They're not alone. I've been trying to figure out the same thing.

"Vi, I want to say this gives us more of an idea," Tassa says, "but the truth is it's even more confusing. It could be tied in to the muroni blood concoction. I mean, they *are* a breed of vampir... Maybe the blood within it has the side effect of making you crave more vampir blood."

I lower my voice. "But wouldn't that have shown up while I was at home, with other vampiri?"

She mutters something then, louder, says, "I'm not sure. Delayed reaction? I can have a look at Daddy's notebooks, I brought them here for more light reading." Nico makes a noise in the background that sounds suspiciously like he's laughing at her, but she ignores him. "I'll let you know if I find anything. We were planning to follow a lead here, too. Another potential cure. Where can I contact you?"

"Umm.... I'll call back."

"Okay, but try to do so soon. And in the meantime, maybe stay away from vampiri and humans alike. If you can, I mean."

I nod, my gaze turning to the bed. Marcus is awake, staring at me.

Shit. How long has he been awake for, and what did he hear?

Marcus

Violeta stares at me, and I'm having the hardest time combining this doe-eyed beauty with the monster who coldly killed those vampiri. I shouldn't talk, after all I'm a monster, too. And I've done much worse things than I can admit to.

But I've spent the better part of the last two weeks thinking she was human, and now that I know she's not, the idea is enough to drive me to the brink of craziness.

The way she'd moved, no hesitation, no inch of remorse, like she'd done this before… It's awe-inspiring, and a little scary. Never mind the fact she protected my ass when it needed saving. That means more to me than anything else. It's the kind of act that gets her unbridled loyalty from me. And it's been a hell of a long time since I've given that to anyone of my own free will.

I stand a little in bed, running a hand over my face. "Who were you calling?"

She hesitates, then says, "My brother. I…" She takes a step closer, then stops, as if thinking better of it. "What happened, me drinking from you, I know it's not normal. I was hoping he might have some insights."

I take in the way she's fumbling with my phone, the slight tremble of her fingers. This unknown makes her agitated, but does she even realize it? I'm getting the feeling Violeta's a woman of many facets, many of them unknown even to herself. *Especially* to herself.

"Did he?" I finally ask. "Have insights, I mean."

"Not yet, no."

I'd heard a female voice on the line, too. Will she tell me about that?

When she doesn't, I add, "Who was the woman on the line?"

Violeta gulps. I don't understand her uneasiness, especially when her answer is so very normal. "His girlfriend."

"Ah." I try to stand, but the room spins around me. "Woah. It's been a while since I've felt like this." A chuckle leaves me, followed by a full-blown laugh.

"Are you okay?"

I shake my head, then stop abruptly. There's more in my mind than her brother and that phone call. A hell of a lot more. And I'm not planning on keeping it all inside. "No, I'm not. I've had the hottest connection with you, and all I want is you, here, with me. To finish that. You're in my head, in my goddamned veins, Violeta."

She bites her lip, and the movement goes straight to my groin. I close my eyes, then force them open again.

"But there's this whole other thing that I don't understand."

"Neither do I."

I get up, this time able to stand. At least I'm slowly getting better. It feels like I've got the world's worst hangover. My limbs are heavy, my head is pounding, and my entire body, really, feels like it's been put through the wringer.

And through it all, despite the fact she's the cause of it, I desperately want to touch her.

So I do. I tug on her wrist, pulling her against my chest, and unceremoniously crush my mouth against hers. Violeta doesn't resist, on the contrary. She clings to me, welcoming my kiss like it's the breath she needs, pressing herself against me in a way that has me remembering *everything* from before.

Before things get too hot and heavy, I pause, step back. "I want to help you, Vi. Not just have a fuck. Whatever this is, whatever you're dealing with, let me help you."

Tears fill her eyes. Monster, this one? Not in the least. And I was a fool for even thinking it.

"Haven't you done enough? Your entire life is now threatened because of what happened. What'll take place once the Ardelean clan realizes those vampiri are missing? They'll come after you."

I cup her cheek, resting my forehead against hers. "And I will deny involvement. They have no way to prove it."

"But—"

"I want to help."

She shakes her head in weak denial. "My brother's looking into it. That concoction I mentioned before? I didn't tell you, but it had muroni blood in it. The doctor's—my dad's—writings had notes about how it could help, and it has."

I jerk back from her. Blue eyes, shiny with unshed tears, meet mine in confusion, and wariness that I'll be repulsed by the idea. But that's not what had me moving so briskly. Rather, it's hope.

"Muroni blood? You should have said earlier. I may know someone."

Chapter 8

Violeta

"I don't understand. Who, exactly, are we seeing?"

After his cryptic statement, Marcus refused to listen to my pleas for rest. Mainly for him, as I still feel oddly rejuvenated. Instead, he insisted we go see this person right away. And in typical fashion, the storm clouds I'd seen gathering earlier have now morphed into heavy flakes falling all around us as we nearly fly at vampir speed through the trees.

Marcus pauses in his rush and turns to me, a flicker of uncertainty in his green gaze. "I need you to keep an open mind."

"Why wouldn't I?"

He drags me farther, until we're on the edge of an abruptly-ending cliff. Marcus grabs my wrist just in time to stop me from slipping off it. I stare below.

The ground curves deep, deep down, as if it's been scooped up by a giant hand. There's no easy way to get to my destination other than jump. All I see below are rotten tree trunks, and the opening of a small cave. Its entrance is blocked by massive tree branches that, at first glance, I think are natural. Then I realize they've been placed there strategically to cover up a much larger entrance.

"Because it's a muroni I'm bringing you to see."

I move backwards, shaking my head. "A muroni?"

"I know after the last incident you're probably traumatized by them, but they're not all alike."

"Not all alike? That one attacked a child! They're dangerous—"

I bite my bottom lip in an effort to stop the outpour of words. It won't help my case, and Marcus is looking at me as if having expected this.

"They're not that different from you and I," Marcus says softly.

I hold back a scoff. He thinks my reaction is because of the one incident, but I've run into them before. Father hated their kind, but was also paradoxically interested in them. So much so, that he captured one of the first muroni and tortured him until he found out how he'd regained his shapeshifting abilities. Then he'd killed him...and found another to satisfy his curiosity.

It's one of his actions I'm less proud of, but they were also necessary. Because thanks to his acts, we found out everything we needed to know about these pests. And why they have some of the weaknesses we don't, but also strengths we no longer are privy to.

And, now, we hunt them. Every area we've ever hidden in, there's been some kind of muroni coven. The moment they know we're around—it's like they sense the House of Dracul, perhaps because of Father's attacks on them—they either try to attack or they leave. More often than not, it's attack. And we can't afford to allow them.

So, we kill them. Alex has been taking savage pleasure in the hunts. I don't agree with it, but I do agree with survival. And if nothing else, our survival instincts are above reproach.

I shake my head. "I don't understand. How did you come to be on speaking terms with one? They're not exactly rational."

A flash of pain crosses his expression. "Long ago, I made a lot of mistakes. And the clan I belonged to—Dmitri's—had a lot of infighting. One such fight led to me being extremely injured and…she was there."

"She?"

He nods, his expression blank. I don't know what to make of the revelation. There's no special way he talks about her, but a muroni? Helping out a regular vampir? It seems…odd.

"And what, if anything, can she do to help me?"

"She's been around for a long time, and she's…different. She *sees* things. I'm hoping she'll have seen this disease or have a different kind of insight. Maybe. It's worth a shot, rather than being in the dark, no?"

There's hope in his voice, and I don't want to be the one trampling all over it. Not when he's making such an obvious effort to help me out.

So I nod. "All right."

He turns his head to the gap below and whistles low. One time, two times, three times. Then he waits. A moment later, a similar whistle echoes back.

"Follow me," he says, "but stay behind a little until I explain."

I do as he asks, and the moment we're down in the ravine, he nears the mouth of the cave. "Kalla, am nevoie de ajutorul tău."

It's a simple plea. *I need your help.*

There's silence, then a hoarse voice. "Who did you bring with you? I can smell her."

"A friend of mine. She...needs help."

"Then let her come and tell me herself."

I hide my surprise as best as I can. Muroni, in general, are notorious for being territorial. Females more so than males. Should I be even more wary of this one, then?

Marcus steps out of the way and touches my shoulder, then puts a distance between us. It's my turn to head closer to the cave, and the person hiding within it.

My first impression is of a tall, willowy tree that could be easily swept away by the faintest storm. She stands against the far wall, but there's enough light coming from the cave itself to see her features. A long, oval face, dark eyes, sharp nose, pouty mouth. The dress she's wearing has seen better days.

"So, what is it you're suffering from?"

I move into the shadows closer to her, unafraid. "What makes you think I'm suffering?"

"Your scent isn't that of a vampir, though you are one. Marcus wouldn't be stupid enough to bring me a human."

I get closer still. Her hair is dirty, her nails are caked in mud, and she shies away from the light like it'll kill her. Because it probably will.

"To answer your question... I think I'm turning human."

She comes closer, sniffs, and snorts. "Nu, nu încă."

"*Not yet*? Then...what's happening to me? Have you seen this before?"

She tilts her head to the side. "Maybe. Maybe not. Or maybe it's a curse completely tied to your bloodline, prinţesa."

I step backwards—*princess*. "How do you... How do you know who I am?"

Another laugh. "Everyone does. Whispers are in the trees and earth itself, darling. Whispers of the return of the House of Dracul, and everything they stand for. The clans you fear? They *all* know. They're all mobilizing to come after you. Everyone, that is, except for poor Marcus. But you'll be hurting him soon enough, won't you?"

"I... No, that's not my intention."

Her eyes glitter menacingly. "Isn't it?"

Before I can do anything, she advances on me, gripping my wrist. I tense, ready for an attack, but that's not what happens. In fact, Kalla only freezes. Then her eyes roll at the back of her head, until only the whites remain.

In a lower, hoarser voice, she says, "*The seven will pay for the sins of their father. Within the monsters will rise, tearing at their insides, at those around them. Their blood will taint the Carpathians until the bloodline of Dracul is no more.*"

I've been around long enough to recognize it for what it is. A prophecy. One about me and my siblings. But... seven? There's only six of us.

I yank my arm out of her hold and Kalla blinks, then smirks.

"Heard something you didn't want to?"

"I—"

Kalla moves on me. "I speak only the truth. It's a curse settled upon me, just as it is on you. And if there's one thing I know, is you won't survive it. So run along, prinţesa. Run along. And leave Marcus alone. He doesn't deserve to be dragged down with your kind."

I don't want to believe her words, but what reason would she have to lie? Unless... I try to change my stance, to get a better look at her. Noticing the utter pallor of her skin under all the grime.

"How old are you, exactly?"

"Old enough." She retreats into the depths of the cave, but I'm not about to drop it so easily.

"Long ago, my father didn't like muroni. Did you know him?"

She freezes. "No." Though she tries to keep her tone level, she's already given herself away.

"You're lying." I follow after her. "You did know him. Which means your words now could easily be another lie. Clearly, you don't even have the right information. There's six of us, not seven. I think what you really want is to send me down a false path. And possibly exact revenge on someone who's long since been dead. "

She whirls on me, and in the darkness, I can see each feature as it tenses, ravaged by pain. "Your father was a monster. And he got what he deserved."

"What are you talking about?"

"You may not have seen his crimes, but someone else did. And he held Țepeș accountable, as no one else could've." A malicious smirk stretches her dry lips. "Țepeș' death was not of his own doing alone. Did he never mention the bloodlust living inside each of you originals is much darker than any of the rest? That it can consume you, lest you learn to control it? Or did he simply teach you to control it?" A beat goes by, then another, as I stare in mute silence, unable to say anything. "Ah. So it was the control. Unsurprising, given who he was."

I stumble back from the Kalla's words. It cannot be.

That bloodlust inside me, the same one that's now focused on vampir blood instead of human, it's part of my bloodline? Then Nico... and Vlad...

My thoughts go to Liza and Alex. They're the only ones who haven't fought it. They've given in. They control it better than the rest of us, really.

And here I thought they were just psychotic.

"You're lying," I whisper.

She arches an eyebrow. "Why would I?"

I have no real answer to that. My previous thinking, of her wanting revenge, has no bearing given the information she's provided.

"If your maker didn't tell you what demons plagued him, that's on him. And if he didn't tell you more about the bloodlust, and what it can do to those around you, well. Perhaps it's him you should be angry at, not me."

I shake my head. "No. No. I..."

If that were true, then why didn't Father tell us? Why didn't he leave behind a sign, something for us to know about the bloodlust? Or was that what he was trying to teach us, with his strict hunts and controlling behavior? I'd always thought he wanted us to be his weapons. One purpose. One goal.

And on top of that, to leave us in darkness, unaware of someone else being involved in his death? After everything he'd done to prepare us... What if it's that same person coming after me now, and responsible for my sickness?

I shake my head, moving backwards some more. "No!"

"Lie as much as you want to yourself, but eventually the truth will come out." She stares towards the end of the cave. "You should warn him, if nothing else. You're a ticking bomb, and it won't be long before your lust—for blood or otherwise—takes over you. If you care for Marcus, you'll leave, before the craziness of your life drags him into a whirlwind he won't be able to escape."

This is the third time she tries to insinuate herself in our relationship. I don't like that she sees as much as she does, but I'm not about to be told what to do.

"You know nothing about us."

"I don't?" She laughs. "Maybe. But I know Marcus deserves better than you. And if you had half a heart, you'd know it, too."

Unable to listen to more, I run away, cowardly. And with each step away, with each speed I gain, my thoughts run crazy. Impossible. Impossible. *Imposibil.* But it's all possible. It's crazy, but in a darker part of me, I'd wondered, wondered if there was more to this.

And now I know. That according to her there's an even worse monster living inside me. One that will consume me, and those around me. And that Father hid things, important things, from all of us.

What else did he not tell us? What more was there to his death, that none of us know, but we've been suffering in different ways from his selfish decisions?

I get to the edge of a river, and look up. Poenari Fortress. Perched atop a hill, it used to be a massive fortress, with view of the Argeș river. My father's home, a long, long time ago.

A small staircase now leads to what's left of it. I climb up in the ruins, until I'm on the edge of the wall. The last bit of it. One wrong step, and I'd tumble down.

This is where Father's wife died. Where she threw herself off, refusing to be without him. Not knowing that the letter she'd receiving advising of his death was a cruel lie, and Father was still very much alive.

This was where he lost his heart and the last of his humanity long before he became the vampir voivode everyone knew and feared.

Glancing below, I wonder… I could step over. I could be gone. End of story. No monster to rise to the surface, no one to suffer because of me, because of my bloodline. The fall alone will break my body, and without blood to sustain me, I would be done for.

Wouldn't that be better?

Better, than releasing the monster inside?

Better, than living this cursed life?

I can't take being responsible for more deaths. Vampiri or otherwise, I've spent the last centuries teaching myself control. And if all that's about to unravel through no fault of my own, I can't allow it. I can't be the weapon Father intended, not when I've worked so hard to become the exact opposite.

I take a step over the edge. My breath catches in my throat. And in that moment, I'm human again. Completely, utterly human. Completely destroyed. My last shred of control over my emotions is gone, replaced instead by...chaos. I'm mortal in my weakness, in my inability to rely upon my vampir strength. Tears fall down my cheeks, sobs rack my body, until I'm unable to draw in a breath. I bend over, gasping, shouting, crying—a mix of everything.

This loss of control, this pain inside me, I can't—

"Violeta."

No. He can't be here, he can't—and then he is.

Marcus

Violeta's a blur passing by me, almost invisible in her rush to get away from Kalla.

I hesitate for a split second, my gaze going back to the cave, before I take off after her. Whatever's happened, she shouldn't be alone.

But when I follow her scent, I find myself not back at my cabin. Instead, we're miles away, perched atop a mountain. Shivers run down my spine. I know this fortress. I've been here, centuries ago, when I was serving orders.

If I close my eyes, I can still hear it. The clang of metal. The whoosh of the air as a sword slashes through someone's neck.

But when I open them again, my gaze locks on the figure perched atop one of the ruins, several hundred feet above me. Too close to the edge, she sways in the breeze, her gaze unseeing.

Despite the lethargy threatening to consume me, I force my feet up the stairs, until I'm on the same level as Violeta.

"Violeta?"

She doesn't seem to have heard me. Instead, her gaze is completely focused on the ground below. It doesn't take much to figure out what she's thinking. Her entire body's filled with tremors, her teeth are chattering. The wind picks up in intensity, whipping her dark hair around her face, obscuring her features and thoughts from me.

I've seen this before. Hell, I've lived it, many times over. But I'm not about to let her take that jump.

So while Violeta's busy freaking out, I move quickly behind her and wrap my arms around her midsection. She tries to push me off, nearly pulling us both over the edge. Her strength is still in full force, and it takes an extra bunching of my muscles to pull her off, completely.

The entire time, she tries to claw at me, at my hold on her waist, but I ignore it. I keep her back to my chest, pulling her off the ledge. Tightening my hold, until all she feels is me wrapped around her, anchoring her.

When I'd dealt with similar hopelessness—the need to end it all—nothing else helped. I felt lost like a boat at sea, unable to ground myself, unable to think past the anger and panic and everything else in my mind. It's a horrible feeling, not knowing whether you'll ever find yourself again.

Made even worse when you have an eternity ahead to see every single mistake you've ever made. To face every ghost, every demon, should you choose to.

And it makes me wonder for how long she's dealt with this. It cannot be this recent, stuff like this doesn't just happen overnight. Hopelessness builds brick by brick, each heavier than the last when we have all the time in the world to go over our mistakes.

Violeta hasn't talked about her family, or how she was turned, so maybe there's a clue in that. Maybe it's more to do with her disease and inability to escape it. It can't be easy, losing strength. Having everything make no sense.

For the first time ever, I want to find out. I want to involve myself. I want to learn more, as much as I can, about her and what's going on. I don't know what Kalla told her, but whatever it is, I'm willing to help. Violeta's dealing with something *now*. And there's no one around to help her, no one but me.

There was no one around to help me when I needed it. And I've been looking for a way to be useful. Isn't that what my little excursions to the orphans are all about?

I fix broken things. Even if I'm more broken than all of them combined.

Hero complex, sure. But it doesn't mean I can't hold up my end of the bargain.

"Breathe," I whisper in Violeta's ear when she stops struggling against me. "Breathe with me."

"I don't need to breathe."

True. We don't. "But you will anyway."

I draw in a deep breath, knowing she'll feel my chest expanding against her back. If I'm right, it should automatically make her do the same. And I am. It takes two breaths, three, and then Violeta joins in. After the first one, she draws in three more—shuddering, hyperventilating moments.

"Slowly," I whisper. "Slow-ly."

And then I inhale again.

At the same time, I move my feet around hers, trying to force the boots off them, but the tight laces prevent me.

"What are you doing?"

"Shh. Just let me." I drop to my knees behind her, and remove the boots, then her socks, placing each bare foot back on what's left of the fortress floor. Then I rise back behind her, do the same with mine, and wrap my arms around her again. "Feel the ground underneath you."

She shakes her head, but I tighten my hold once more. Refusing to let her go. Refusing to allow her to ignore this.

"What you're feeling is a crash."

"I don't. I'm not. I'm—my family—"

She cuts off, not finishing. Instead, another sob escapes her. I don't know what, about her family, would make her choke up like this, but I don't pay it attention. Not now.

I focus on her breathing. I put my hand on her chest, where her heart used to beat, and press, then release, mimicking compressions. "Breathe with me."

It takes her a moment, then two, but, finally, breaths come out of her again.

"We live forever," I whisper in her ear, keeping my tone low. "Forever. Immortality may be seducing to humans, but it's a curse. Only *we* don't always realize it."

I continue pressing and releasing her chest as I speak, and she leans further into me, not quite relaxing, but allowing me to hold her properly.

"In each of us, there's a shred of humanity left. In some, more than others. And that humanity, every once in a while, it comes back to bite us in the ass."

"I'm old," she whispers. "Too old for that to matter."

"No one's too old. We all remember what it used to be like to *live*. And that panic, of our organs not functioning, of us being inherently dead, that's what this panic is. That's why you can't breathe. It's choking you with past, present and future regrets. Removing your ability to *be*. But you can't let it rule you, Violeta. You have to push past it. To live. To keep living. That is immortality's finest gift."

I don't know how long we stay like that. How long I hold her, breathing with her, feeling the grass under our feet. But it feels peaceful, serene, by the time I stop.

Unwrapping my arms from around her, I turn her to face me, and tilt her chin up. "Well?"

Violeta stares at me. Tears shine in her eyes, but they don't fall. Instead, she rises on her tiptoes and kisses me softly. This, more than any other kiss, rocks me to my core. Drives a knife inside me, because I have to admit I've come to care for this woman, more than I've ever cared for anyone in centuries.

And she's sick. Unless I help her find a cure, I will lose her.

That, I cannot allow. Because the more I hold her, the more I'm around her, the more I realize one unmistakable truth—I cannot lose her. Ever.

Chapter 9

Violeta

It takes us a while to get back to the cabin. Marcus moves slower, still recovering from my previous feeding off him, and I'm constantly checking for other vampiri that may or may not be tracking us. Could Dmitri's goons have found the traces of the other killings already? I have this nagging sense of being watched, but that may just be paranoia compounded by my recent freakout.

And confusion. The way Marcus handled it clearly shows he's had experience, but I've never had a vampir be so... mentally self-aware? Maybe because I live around five others who are constantly avoiding that.

And then there's the fact I'm constantly distracted by his body brushing up against mine. Memories of my feeding off him flood me, bringing to the surface the same bone-melting craving of his flesh against mine... My cheeks are flushed from the memory of how I came all over him. I also want to do it again. I fed of humans before, but never to this extent. And never did I feel the desire I felt with him.

The contrast between the two sensations, and the nagging at the back of my mind warning me that my outburst hadn't been exactly normal, all pile up leading to a mix of emotions I can't unravel all at once.

"You're quiet," Marcus says.

"I'm sorry. For feeding off you and for putting us in a dangerous situation. I didn't really apologize before you brought me to Kalla and, well, I'm sorry. Extremely."

He stops and turns towards me. "Don't be sorry. At least now we know my blood can strengthen you as much as a muroni's. It'll come in handy, I'd wager." He frowns, as if choosing his next words carefully. "What exactly did Kalla tell you?"

"She told me..."

I hesitate. He's treating me with kid gloves, not yet touching upon my outburst or how he helped calm me. But how can I tell him what she said about Father and what's inside me?

Even though he led me to this clue, there is still a part of me that feels extremely vulnerable with him. Even more so now, because of the yearning coursing through my veins. I don't want to have feelings for him, not when I'm known for falling for the wrong person. And the last time that happened, I put my entire family in danger and Liza had to step in.

But I can't deny that there's something between us. Spending these weeks with him in his cabin, watching him work, getting to know his lifestyle, so different from mine... Even before I knew he was a vampir, something about it spoke to me. It's a new lifestyle, something completely different than I have ever known. Maybe that's why it's so appealing to me. More than any luxury I've enjoyed through my new last name.

But what if Kalla was right? What if my bloodlust will put him in even more danger than my presence? Something stops me from being truly honest with him about who I am and until I can figure out why... I need to tread carefully.

With that in mind, I look up at Marcus and say, "She told me enough. But it's not your burden to carry."

"Do you honestly think that I'll let you go through this by yourself?"

He stares at me, frustrated with himself and with me. I know that sensation all too well.

"You can't be making my problems your problems, Marcus."

"Why not?"

"Because I'm not yours!"

His teeth slam together with an audible clack. For a moment, he just stares at me, eyes blazing, jaw clenched. And then he's kissing me again, smashing his lips against mine in something raw, and primal, and desperate. As desperate as I'd felt atop that fortress. It's a kiss that makes my toes curl and my mind erase all thoughts of leaving. A kiss that inflates my ego, that burns through my veins, that makes me want so much more.

In some remote part of me, the rational part of me tries to tell me I need to put a stop to this. But when I try to shove him away, all he does is grip my wrists and pull them around his waist. And then he holds them there, kissing me some more, not letting go until I'm melting against him, lost to the sensations he causes.

Only then does he let me go, enough so that he can look at me and actually speak his mind. "Tell me how you're not mine, again. When you react so beautifully when I kiss you, and when I touch you... There's something here, and it's more than a passing fancy." He moves closer, purposefully brushing his body against mine. "Tell me you don't feel that."

"I do, it's not that. There's something between us, you're right, but, Marcus—"

"You're scared that we don't know each other. I get that. I do. And you have every reason to be." His expression darkens, and he lets me go slowly. "I need to tell you something, as soon as we get back to my place. And then maybe you'll understand why it is that I just can't let you go. And maybe you'll trust me enough to tell me what Kalla said."

A short while later, we finally get back to the cabin. And once we're inside, all I want to do is avoid whatever it is Marcus has to tell me. I can't like this guy more than I already do. He's already gone so out of his way to make me feel at home here, when all I have done is lie to him.

I need to tell him who I really am, reveal my proper identity, so he knows who, exactly, he's fighting for. Anything less would be doing him a disservice.

I could be taking a chance, being so candid with a secret that's so heavy. There's a reason we're in hiding, a reason that only rumors are left of us. And none of it will endear me to Marcus. But I have to try, if I'm to be perfectly honest.

So I take a deep breath and turn to him. "I have something to tell you, too."

He lifts a hand as if to silence me. "Me, first. Before I lose my nerve."

I stare at him. This guy, who's been through so much... Afraid to lose his nerve, in front of little old me? What could be so bad?

It's that vulnerability, present in his eyes, present in the way he's wringing his hands together, present in how he can't quite meet my gaze... It's that vulnerability that makes me stay quiet. And it's that same vulnerability that ends up costing me everything.

"You've guessed I was in the military," Marcus says.

I nod. "I did, da."

"What I didn't tell you, and I haven't told anyone for a long time, is just how bad it was when I was in the military. That's how I knew how to help you with your..." He trails off, trying to find a better way to explain what we both know is a clusterfuck.

"With my breakdown. Call it what it is."

Something about my tone must alert him to the emotions uncoiling in me, as he meets my gaze. His tone changes, softening. "You don't have to be ashamed of it."

How does he see through me so easily? He shouldn't be able to, not in so little time, with so little between us, really. It makes me wonder what else he'd see, if I gave us a proper chance. Thoughts of Nico and how he is with Tassa, how she understands him on such a deep level, whiz through my mind at lightning speed. Could it be the universe has given me what I've craved and I've been blind to it all?

I shy away from those thoughts and clear my throat instead. "I'm not. But that's not what we're talking about. Keep going."

He hesitates, as if warring between his desire to share and the conflicting one of getting answers from me. Finally, he says, "When I was in the military, I wasn't there for myself. I started off as a soldier in a regular human army, but soon, I was turned and drafted into the vampir one. That's where my free choice ended. I was no longer in charge of my future, instead, I was answering to other people. Higher-ranked people than me. Older vampiri than me. An older version of Dmitri's clan—his sire's, until he took over. And...I did things. A lot of things. A lot of bad things."

Something turns in my stomach. It's not uneasiness at what he's telling me. Hell knows I've done bad things in the past and more recently in the present, too. But something about the way he says it... Call it a sixth sense, but I don't think I'm going to like any of this.

"What kind of bad things?" When he hesitates, his expression shuttering, I hurry to explain, "There's no judgement here, Marcus. Not from me."

"You say that now, but I doubt very much that you'll have the same feeling afterwards."

I could say the same thing when you find out about me.

I take a step closer to him. Look him in the eye. Hold his hand, my thumb caressing the back of his. "Tell me."

Marcus stares at our intertwined fingers. "I killed on demand. I didn't realize it back then, but I was playing politics. I was given targets that I thought were actually guilty, and I carried out the orders of their execution. The Ardelean clan used me, and others like me—Guards, we were called—to win their wars against other clans, to expand their territory, and to ensure they always had a fresh supply of human blood. When it suited them, they had us infiltrate human armies to help them turn the tide in certain wars. And as a soldier, I didn't bother investigating any of it, nor contesting orders. It was a different world back then. You took orders, you didn't investigate, you just did."

"How long ago was this, exactly?"

He waits for a moment, a muscle ticks in his jaw, and then he says, "I fought as a human in Mihai Viteazul's army."

"Michael the Brave?" I gape at him. I've been on the side of history, watching it unfold, but Marcus was neck-deep in it. I almost start saying how Father liked Michael because of what he represented—patriotism, after his time—but I bite my tongue. "He unified Wallachia, Transylvania and Moldavia for the first time ever, gaining our kingdom independence for a short-lived time." I whisper, "For all intents and purposes, he's our national hero."

Marcus nods. Shame crossed his features. "I died fighting for him as a human. And I was turned on the battlefield. I kept my purpose as a soldier at the behest of my masters, same as others did. But we were pulled out of Mihai's army when he wasn't useful anymore. We... let him die." He looks away. "It could have been so different. With our forces behind him, the war could've ended differently. We could've stopped being Ottoman vassals so much earlier."

I frown. "This was still early times... End of 16th century, beginning of 17th, right?"

Marcus rubs the back of his neck. "Da, 1600."

"But why... I'm sorry, it's not that I'm trying to bring back bad memories, but I'm having a hard time understanding why the Ardelean clan, a Transylvanian-born vampir clan, would want independence to fall apart."

Marcus meets my gaze again. "Because Mihai damaged the interests of the other major political forces at the time—the Habsburg Monarchy, the Ottoman Empire, and the Polish–Lithuanian Commonwealth. They *hated* what he represented. And while they were mainly human-run powers, Dmitri's father believed in making money. And you can't make money from peace, can you?"

A gasp escapes me. "He preferred war and casualties on any side, because it would make him money?"

"Yeah," Marcus nods. "And it only continued over the centuries. After Mihai Viteazul's time, I—the Guards, too—was inserted into wars on and off. The defeat of the Ottomans at the Battle of Vienna in 1683 marked the beginning of their decline in the region. When the Ottomans started declining, my presence in the wars increased." He lets out a bitter laugh. "There was constant warfare between the same three political forces up until the next century, then... Russia threw its hat in the ring, fighting for the control of the Danubian principalities and Transylvania."

Holy shit. He's younger than me by a century, but...

"Marcus, are you saying your entire existence as a vampir has been spent in the army of some vampir clan?"

"I had no choice in it. They made sure we were glamoured." He hangs his head in shame.

And for a moment, I don't know what to do. I don't know what to say. To live for centuries and centuries simply as a killing machine... Most of our kind would never do such a thing. They'll kill on repeat for their own selfish needs, but not to uphold some ideal. Even us, we went into hiding.

Shame courses through me. It's not Marcus who should feel it, it's us. For staying away. For letting others fight for us. Plainly, judging by his words, many have.

But how didn't I know of this? How didn't any of my siblings?

Another thought hits me, a darker thought. Anger at whoever did this to him. Whoever demanded this much from him. Who would betray such a trust? Because someone obviously did. To put him in wars, over and over again, against his will? And if Marcus says he didn't have a choice in it, that's even worse.

Marcus wouldn't be living here, in the middle of nowhere, if someone hadn't betrayed his trust and the loyalty he's given.

It makes me even more aware of how thankful I am for the upbringing I had. Because my father, he took care of us. He made sure we were safe. He made sure we understood the responsibilities of our new life. He might've had his downfalls and he did abandon us by choosing death, and not revealing everything we needed to know, but at least he was there.

We came out dysfunctional, and not completely right in the head, but we survived.

Can the same be said about Marcus?

"Who...?" I clear my throat. "Whose power were you under?"

He raises his head, and I move backwards at the blazing inferno shining through his eyes. "The same ones we are all under. The royals. The House of Dracul."

It's like the earth shatters underneath me. I feel that same sensation as from the breakdown, only worse. Because that, I was able to understand. I knew it came from Kalla's words, and my own realization of my impending doom. But this...I don't even know how to start comprehending what he just told me.

We didn't employ soldiers, instead we had a small group of dedicated guards. My father didn't use an army, either. He lost his ability to sire new vampiri shortly after turning us.

And when our guards' died, as we were under more and more attacks, it was always just us. Then us and Silva, until his death. And then lately it was just us on the run.

So what the hell..

"What are you talking about?" I frown.

"What do you mean? You do know who the royals are, don't you?"

I open my mouth to say there and then that I'm one of them. To admit the truth. But the words get stuck in my throat.

Marcus must take it as a sign that I don't know what he's talking about, because he starts giving me a history lesson.

"They're the ones who rule us all, the ones whose orders we always carry out. The ones who set up our rules. The rules of the vampir world. The ones we have to follow upon pain of death." He scowls, his words dripping with disdain. "The descendants of the so-called Count Dracula, Vlad Țepeș himself."

Marcus

I stare at Violeta, trying—and failing—to understand the expression on her features. How can she not know who I'm talking about?

I take a deep breath and force myself to let it out. "I'm sorry. I... I still don't really know what your story is, and it's not fair of me to assume."

"Assume what?"

"That you'd know who they are. They're well-known in these parts, but not to younger vampiri. And definitely not for good reasons."

A flicker of pain crosses her features, gone before I can determine whether it's real or not.

"I didn't mean that I don't know who they are," Violeta says. "I do know, of course I do. I just thought that... Never mind. Just keep going with your story."

"I don't have to, unless you actually want to know. I'd meant to explain it as a reason for you to understand more of me, but it doesn't have a happy ending." *And I don't want you to hate me for everything I'm responsible for.*

Her expression softens. "I guessed as much. Just keep talking, Marcus. Please."

I take another deep breath and tell myself that even though I've told the story before, that even though back then it didn't end the way I wanted it to, she is different. I need to give her the benefit of the doubt. Even if it kills me.

"Like I said, I listened to orders. I never contested them. And... It didn't serve me well. On the contrary. I ended up making mistakes, mistakes which might've cost the future of our entire world."

"What do you mean, *cost the future*?"

I should've started with something simpler. I should've started with how I was young. With how I was turned. And yet none of that is as important as the part that I will tell her now. If I can reveal this, be this vulnerable with her, then maybe it'll push Violeta to do the same.

"I mean that I nearly revealed our existence to humans."

Violeta frowns at me. "I'm not following."

"It was a...bloody war. The Ardelean clan was afraid of some new weapons the Ottomans created to fight against supernaturals. We—the Guards—were meant to help with the independence war against the Ottoman empire in the late 19th century. The Ardelean clan thought this was worthy of putting a lot of us in it. So we infiltrated the human army, like we'd done many times before."

I clench my fists, moving my gaze to the knuckles. A brief flash shows them blood red, before I'm back in the present. I've had long enough to cope with my trauma of the wars, but will it ever be truly gone? "There was a lot of blood. Too much. I hadn't felt it in a while, our masters were very clear in what we could and could not do."

Her eyes widen in horror. "Masters?"

"Da, that's what they called themselves. I was... I wasn't born in Romania. Not in the way a lot of us are. This meant that I was automatically lesser in the army. In the human one, and the vampir one, later. They chose where we would go and what we would do. The Guards were a specific squadron meant to carry out missions from the clan leader himself, Dmitri. By then he'd taken over from his father and he hated the Ottomans. He set up generals. We were their pawns. And they were only letting us feed once every week, thus making us more susceptible to their glamour. They were also afraid of humans finding out about us. Ironically, it is what led to our discovery."

She doesn't say anything. Doesn't interrupt. And for that, I'm grateful. It's hard enough getting through the story without questions that'll ultimately shift my focus from the memories to what she might be thinking about them.

"Another soldier and I, we found a human to feed on. He was already wounded. There was blood everywhere and neither of us could resist. As we fed off him, a group of priests came upon us. They knew immediately what we were. They had heard of our kind and they were not surprised that we were actually real. With bloodlust upon us, we couldn't control ourselves, so we killed the priests as well. But it was already too late. More humans had seen us and panic spread in the city. Dawn was coming up and the fact that we were not dying by daylight seemed to infuriate them more. So they attacked us."

"Oh Marcus..."

"No." I hold a hand up to stop it from coming any closer. "I need to get this out. Most of us wanted to leave, some of our glamour and bloodlust had worn off. But our masters didn't want to leave behind traces of our existence. So they verified with the Dracul royals and they were told to dispose of the humans. Which is what we did. The masters didn't get their hands dirty, but we killed each and every single one of them. Every man, woman and child, old or young. I can still remember the smoke clogging my nostrils and making me cough as we burned all the bodies to nothingness and then blamed it on the current tensions in the area."

"How do you know that the royals gave that order?"

The question surprises me. "Because the masters told us. Dmitri himself came and spoke to us."

"Is there no possibility that he was lying? That he was simply saying that to get the humans killed, and no one to contest him? Maybe even to protect himself, since it was his fault that it happened?"

The idea had never entered my mind, and some of my shock must show on my features because Violeta tries to backtrack.

"Sorry, I know it's hard for you to talk about this. It just seems odd that whoever your leaders were at the time would condone such destruction."

A bitter laugh escapes me. "You would think so. But it's not like they had a choice. And the truth is, that's exactly how the royals are."

"Did you meet them?"

My frown deepens at the trembling of her voice. "The royals? No. No one has, at least in these parts."

"How do you know that they're so horrid?"

Something nags at the back of my mind, warning me her defense of these people is not normal. Why would she try to see their side of things, if she doesn't know them? Unless she lied to me.

"Believe what you will." She steps backwards at the harshness of my voice, but it doesn't make me go quiet. I stayed quiet much too long. "But I know what I felt. And for centuries, I was under the influence of these people. Not just through their orders, but through their glamour. They had us doing *everything* they needed us to. Either them, or the people under them. Whether it was on Dmitri's, the masters', or the royals' orders, the end result was the same. All I saw was destruction, pain, ruthlessness. I cannot erase those images from my mind even if I try. If you think there's a shred of good in those people, you're sorely mistaken. The best thing they ever did for us was to disappear from our lives. To stop being royals. To become ghosts. Ghosts that can potentially be chased."

When I look at Violeta again, her eyes are filled with tears. I hadn't meant to make her cry, and the sight tears at me enough to dull the ache in my chest. "I'm sorry."

She shakes her head. "Nu, it's me who is sorry. For all the pain that you've lived, for everything that could have been avoided."

I give in to the need coiling in my gut and pull her into my arms. She tenses for a brief moment then melts against me, and her hot tears soak my shoulder within moments.

Only problem is, I don't know who she's crying them for.

Chapter 10

Marcus

It takes Violeta a couple of moments to calm down. Her tears soak my shirt, and her trembling body only reminds me of the woman on the edge of that fortress. A shudder runs through me. How much pain can she hold, and what is it for, exactly? Does it have to do with the royals?

The more I hold her, the less I care. All I want is to take it away and make sure she doesn't feel it, ever again. If nothing else, the fact I've opened up seems to have made her more comfortable with her vulnerability around me. Will this translate into actual words and truths?

Finally, after a long time of crying, she pulls away and wipes at her face. Her blue eyes are even more brilliant from the tears, and her hair sticks to her face.

“Scuze,” she mutters. “I didn't mean to distract you. Keep going. Tell me the rest of the story.”

“I don't have to. It's not like it has anything specific to do with your disease, or with whatever Kalla said. It doesn't have anything to do with us.”

She stares at me for such a long time that I think she must have lost her train of thought. But then she blinks and shakes her head. “No. It has everything to do with us. Because everything you're saying is part of the world we live in, and I need to understand your view of that world.”

I nod, and gesture for her to sit in the chair. Once she does, I resume my pacing. Now that she's calmer, there's no way I can tell the story without moving. Filled with restless energy, I'm overwhelmed, gesticulating as I talk. Memories I'd long since buried come to the forefront of my mind, filling me with those times.

“After the wars, Dmitri's vampir clans found other reasons to use us. By taking over other clans. striking deals with others. In the last years since I've been on my own, he's brought it down to six large clans in all of Romania. And they have trade deals with others, from the neighboring countries like Hungary and Ukraine. Anyone that falls under the Dracul royals, basically.”

Violeta frowns. “And you think the royals...know...about these changes? Given they've been, um...”

I barely hold back a snarl. “They know. They're just too cowardly to come to the forefront and admit they're behind all this.” When she says nothing else I continue, “Little by little, Dmitri amalgamated some more territory in the area. My sole focus seemed to be consisting of pain, death, and more pain. I started to lose myself in everything—women, drugs, alcohol, you name it. There was nothing I would not try to stop the pain in my mind."

A noise from her draws my attention and I look at her. Violeta does a little shrug. "You remind me of someone, that's all."

"You mean your brother?"

"Da. He also did something similar."

"I'm guessing he's a vampir, too?"

"Da, something like that."

Something strikes me then. "What about your father? The one you said is the reason to you being hunted by these vampiri?"

She looks away, muttering, "Human. He got into the trade—with vampiri—because of us."

The words ring hollow, with none of the truth I've come to expect, but I let it go. There will be plenty of time to ask her more later. Instead, I return to my story.

"Dmitri allied himself with other vampir clans around these areas. What these people did, was cleanse the world to remake it into their own effigy. And all the time, they were taking orders from the royals. And before you say otherwise, for this, we did have letters. Letters signed with the seal of the House of Dracul."

"And were these letters signed by one royal in particular?"

"Da, I'll get to that later."

She seems like she wants to ask something else, but I barrel on before she can.

"I could rehash the story many, many times in many, many ways, but it would amount to the same thing. I am guilty, very guilty, of sins that I cannot erase. Which is why when the latest war was over with—the Second World War—I withdrew. To the mountains, away from all of them."

"But how did they let you leave?"

"Because I had made friends with muroni, and with a lot of people they would not deign to be around, I was a disgrace. It was better for the clan that I was not around to corrupt the young minds they were turning, as they were afraid it would lead to them losing more vampiri down the line. That's why they've left me alone, for the most part. But...there's another reason."

I close my eyes, recalling blonde curls and honey eyes. A plea for saving that I was too late to meet. "One of the vampir clans Dmitri allied himself to, their daughter, Maria, loved me. Once, before things turned very, very bad. I..." I meet her gaze, trailing off. Not because emotions choke me, but because I simply don't know how to communicate what happened without giving Violeta the wrong impression.

She surprises me by asking, "How did she die?"

"She broke one of Dmitri's rules. His clan carried out the sentence before hers—an equally powerful one—even got wind of anything. By the time they had, Dmitri spun the story in his favor, but he knew that if he kept me around I would most likely kill each and every single one of the people involved, including him. Or give them up to the other clan, and lead to their demise anyway."

"Who was the other clan?"

"Does it matter?" My answer must be a bit testy, as she seems taken aback. I let out a heavy breath and cringe. "Scuze, I didn't mean it with that tone. Cazacu—that was her clan. Second powerful one in Romania these days." I shake my head, as if to remove thoughts of those times. "Anyway, Dmitri had no choice but to let me go."

"Just like that?"

I shrug. “Doesn’t mean he left me alone. Like I said, over the decades I’ve had plenty of incidents with his Guards. They seem to have taken my leaving personally, and Dmitri doesn’t try to keep them on a leash. It’s part of why I never got involved with another woman—vampir or otherwise.” I meet her gaze. “And that was the end of it, until you landed on my doorstep.”

“Technically it wasn't on your doorstep. It was in your woods. But that’s debatable.”

I say nothing, waiting instead for the rest of it to sink in. There’s no point telling her that Grigore had threatened the orphans—they’re safe now, and that’s all that matters. Violeta will only feel needlessly guilty.

So I hold off on that piece of information and wait for the conclusions she will draw from what I’ve already shared. That I'm a coward, that I'm running away from the consequences of my actions. That if I’d really wanted to pay for what I had done, I would have turned myself in to human authorities or to the other clan for their own punishment.

But Violeta doesn’t say anything of the like. Instead, she just stares at me, taking it all in as if the mere fact of my revelations has led her to seeing entire new facets of me. Is it enough, though, to trust me?

She surprises me by asking, “Do you miss her?”

It's the last possible question I would have expected.

Do I miss Maria? Once, she was everything to me. But that relationship turned sour, and immortality and long-term relationships doesn’t work out in a fairy tale ending. At least, it didn’t for us. She didn’t understand why I felt guilty over the wars. Not like Violeta seems to understand.

I try to figure out a way to express that, something that doesn't make me sound callous and unfeeling. But there's no easy way, so rather than opt for another cop out, I give it to her straight, not mincing my words.

"We broke apart much before she died. There was no hope of reconciliation, we were simply too different. Immortality has a way of exposing that in light's harshest light." I take a deep breath and let it out on a sigh. "I can't say that I miss her, because that's a chapter of my life that's been closed for a long, long time." Another revelation passes my lips before I can stop it. "I haven't been with anyone for about seventy years. It's part of the reason I have so little restraint around you, to be honest. I've forgotten what it's like. Something that you have easily reminded me of. Which, I guess, brings us full circle to the reason for this conversation in the first place."

Violeta

I don't know how to react. To his last words, and to the truth he's laid out for me to see. This despite not having received the same in return from me.

The truth is my mind is being pulled in so many different directions, I don't know which is the best one to take.

There's the violence. Since my early years and the bloodlust, I've learned to tame that part of myself—until it decided to rise around Marcus. I've prided myself these last centuries on being different than Liza, Alex, Mirabela, but it turns out I'm the biggest hypocrite. Because they, at least, have learned to control that part of themselves for good. By giving in to it, they've learned to turn it on and off like a faucet. I envy that control.

Even now, faced off with Marcus, I try not to think of the taste of his blood, lest I want to feed on him again.

A vampir's true nature cannot be tamed. It cannot be repressed. Doing so only leads to exactly the kind of stuff I've been dealing with. Which begs a different question—perhaps my illness is not an illness at all, but rather a symptom of what it is that I have been repressing. If that's the case, though, that's an epiphany for another time.

Right now, I have a bigger problem. There's Kalla's revelations of what's inside me, but, also, what Marcus has just laid out for me to see. That he was at the beck and call of the royals, or who he thinks are the royals. But I know for a fact that's not the case, because we were never involved in such atrocities. We've been too damn busy hiding.

How many other vampiri have suffered like this? Is this why we are being hunted, as vengeance for putting vampiri through this? Or are we being hunted by the very people who are behind this, and who want to ensure we won't find out and put a stop to it?

I know my siblings noticed the focus of the clans on tracking us down only a few centuries ago. As did I. But we all knew it wasn't normal, that being hunted by our own kin is definitely not the way things were supposed to go.

Or maybe it is. Maybe it's time for a New World order. Maybe our time has come and gone, and now it is up to the rest of the vampir clans to govern themselves.

Even as I think that, I can only imagine the faces of my siblings and how they would react to such news. How they would react to news that someone has been impersonating us, and leading to all of this happening.

And then another, darker thought hits me. What if it *was* one of us who gave those orders for the wars? What if it was our father, or Alex, or Liza? It could've been Vlad during one of his dark moods, or even Mirabela. It could've been me. Maybe for all I know I have a darker alter ego that I'm simply ignoring.

To top it all off, the rest of my thoughts move towards Marcus. Everything that he has suffered. To the exile he has imposed upon himself despite the fact that what happened was not his fault. I know better than most how susceptible vampiri can be after their first hunt. It's why I never turned anyone. To have that power over their mind, when they're in the midst of their bloodlust.

Over the centuries, we've run into some vampiri. Some that use such power for good—such as to ensure their new sired offspring can control their raging needs and not reveal our existence to humans—and others for evil—such as imposing any suggestions in their minds, akin to mind control.

Either way, the responsibility of such power is nothing that I ever wanted to have in my life. And then we lost that ability to sire new vampiri, and, well, it was no longer a question.

Someone obviously failed Marcus and planned to use him as a machine, as a robot, to dispose of humans and to create pain and suffering and death everywhere. But I don't see all the violence. I see the man. I see the soul that is inside, a soul filled with guilt and restlessness and vulnerability, same as mine. A soul that speaks to mine. And I want to nurture it, I want to...

Reality crashes over me. Not only have I lied to him many times by now, but now I have lied to him about the most important part. I did not tell him that I'm one of the royals he despises. And when he finds out... When he finds out, he will hate me.

"Violeta?"

I snap out of my thoughts to realize that Marcus has been watching me. For how long, I don't know. I hadn't planned to cry on him either, and I can only imagine what he thinks about that.

"I'm sorry, for crying. It's not my pain, but it felt like it when you were telling the story. I am so very sorry that you went through all of these things, and that you had no one at your side to help you with it."

Some kind of emotion shines in his face but I cannot name it. Probably because it's such an alien emotion to him that his features are no longer used to it. If I were to take a guess, I would say it's gratitude.

He has nothing to be grateful for, least of all to me when I've been lying to his face. But I can't say any of that.

At my continued silence, Marcus inches closer. He cups my cheeks in his hands and looks into my eyes. "Do you know how much I dreaded telling you that story? Do you know how much I feared that you would look at me differently, that you would think of me differently?"

"Marcus—"

"I meant it as a way to coax you into talking about whatever Kalla upset you with, and your own past. But you know what? I don't need any of that. I just need you, here, now. Nothing else."

I don't have time to say anything. Because his lips are on mine and he's kissing me like his life, my life, and our entire existence depends on it. And it's not a case that I can refuse him, because I want everything just as much as him.

I've *been* craving it, with an intensity that has only lain dormant while we've been talking. But the moment his lips crash on mine, the moment his hands are on me, that fire is roaring back alive.

So I wrap my arms around his neck instead and pull myself closer until there's no space left between us. Until our movements are so frenzied, we're tearing clothes off each other. Until Marcus flips me over and I bend over the couch, my ass nestled against his hardness.

His hand caresses my back ever so slowly, making me moan. I'm so damned sensitive, I feel like I could combust. Then he reaches over my hip, and his questing fingers find my heated core. A low, guttural groan escapes me when he zeroes in with precision, knowing exactly how to make me come.

He'd done it before, after all. This is nothing new. But the way it makes my body hum is like he's the maestro and I'm his instrument to play.

Two fingers slide in my folds, and I spread my legs farther apart, welcoming him inside me. "Marcus..." I need more than his fingers.

His other hand on my hip tightens, and a low hiss escapes him. I turn ever so slightly and get a view of his powerful, corded body over me. His biceps are tense with his restraint, his ab muscles are equally tight, and the way he's staring at me...

His green eyes have melted to a dark mossy color, and his jaw is clenched. Fire. He's staring at me with fire in his eyes, all the while his fingers are pumping inside me, and I can feel that orgasm crashing over me. Wave after wave after wave rocks my body until my legs are shaking, barely able to hold me up.

Marcus leans over me more, and his hardness teases my folds. "Are you ready for more?"

I nod, wordlessly.

A moment later, he thrusts inside me. There's no slow dance, no easing me into it. He owns me with every thrust, his hands on my hips pulling me closer, until he, too, is groaning. A relentless pace, one destined to drive us both over the brink—and one he cannot hold back. The feel of his release inside me brings me to another orgasm, and I crash, boneless, over his couch.

Vaguely, I'm aware of Marcus pulling out, and picking me up to lay me on the bed a few feet away. Moments later, he joins me, cradling me against his chest.

I could say it was rushed, but it was the conclusion to a scene we started long before. When I'd been out of my bath. And to have finally finished that...

"How are you feeling?" I ask him.

Marcus lets out a startled chuckle. "Me? I may not have done this in over half a century, but I'm pretty sure that question is meant for you."

"Believe me, you haven't forgotten anything." I stretch against him. "You.... it was good, Marcus. *Really* good."

"Only good?" His lips brush my forehead. "I'll have to remedy that, then." A pause. "It was earth shattering for me, for the record. Exactly as I knew it would be."

I grin again his chest, and the moment lengthens. But then words tumble past my lips.

"Kalla said some things about my family, that's why I was so...scattered. And about our immortal existence in general. It...it made me think about all the bad I've done, that's why I ended up at the Fortress."

His arm squeezes me closer and he drops another kiss to my forehead.

"Sleep. We'll have plenty of time to talk."

It's been a while since I have slept, at the very least slept the way I just did. Which is probably why it's even more of a shock when I wake up to find Marcus out of bed, and instead by the kitchen table. I don't know what he's doing, but he's hunched over a book.

If I had a heart, it would be jumping out of my chest. Is that my diary that he's looking at? *The* journal, with the crest of the House of Dracul? Should I be worried that he's going to turn to me at any moment now with a look of disgust on his face, and hate me forever more?

I shift in bed and he must've heard it, because he turns to me. Instead of hate, it's hope that shines in his expression.

"I think I found something."

"What do you mean?"

"Those vampiri you killed? The ones that hunted you originally, when I found you. Before I burned their bodies, I searched their pockets. And they had letters, they had a lot of things on them." He must notice my wary expression because he gets up and moves to the bed quickly, then holds my hand in his. "No, no. It's nothing to worry about. I haven't had a chance to look at the stuff but I couldn't sleep earlier and—look. Look at this."

The letter in his hand is plastered in dried blood droplets, but I take it and read it for myself. The handwriting is horrid—I've seen some bad writing in my times, but this is excruciating to decipher. Almost as if on purpose. Unless it's from a human.

As if guessing my thoughts, Marcus says, "It's human. Smells like human."

I nod. "Ok... So, what is it?"

"Read it for yourself."

I do as he asks. And then I read it again. And again. On my fourth read, I have to admit to myself that I cannot believe what my eyes are seeing. This is one of the letters that escaped Liza and Mirabela's notice.

Back when Tassa was kidnapped, they'd found out it was the leader of an order in town who was behind it. Along with a vampir hunter. Those same humans are meant to be protecting us, but clearly their thirst for vengeance is bigger than anything else.

Either way, my sister discovered the humans had been sending letters, to advise the vampiri clans in the area of where we were located. They'd intercepted as many of them as they could, but Mirabela privately admitted to me that she thought more than one had gotten out.

I remember Kalla's words. *Rumors abound... The clans you fear? They* all *know. They're all mobilizing to come after you..*

The witch was right. And this one such letter that escaped us, addressed to the vampir clan in this area—Dmitri's. Advising of where we—my siblings and I—are, and that they could come and kill us once and for all.

Hoping that Marcus doesn't see my hand shaking, I whisper, "This is... about the royals."

"Da, but it's a bit much more than that. Ignore the royals, we don't care about them. They have nothing to do with us. But this man does say something I almost overlooked. He talks about a clan of werewolves that have come to the area."

Dominic's mixed pack of vârcolaci and vrykolakas. Alex has been bitching about them for weeks, not trusting them. It doesn't help matters that our first introduction was over a dead wolf head, which someone had planted to try and start a war between us. Not that I can admit any of this to Marcus, so I have to play stupid.

"What do you mean, wolves? What is all this?"

"It's a new pack of wolves. The type that have not been seen in the area for a long, long time. In fact, probably too long."

"Is it because they always fight with us?"

Guilty as I feel over doing so, it's easy enough to play stupid. I'd been sick, so very sick when Nico and my siblings were having conversations about the wolves, and I only remember bits and pieces.

"No, they don't," Marcus says. "It's odd to say so, but most of the time they are perfectly able to cohabitate with us, sometimes even be friends. I served with a few under Dmitri, a long while ago, before they were killed in a raid." He taps the letter. "This human, however, is saying that he detected spy activity from both camps, meaning the royals and the wolves don't trust each other. So we have to be careful when we go."

"Go? Go where?"

"Violeta, those wolves could have the answer to what it is that you're seeking."

Now I don't have to play stupid. I really am confused. "I don't follow."

"They're not just any wolves. They're *vrykolakas*. Undead creatures who live off hearts of humans, similar to how vampiri live off human blood. And they also live for a long time. The real story behind their existence is very similar to ours. Maybe they, too, are experiencing something similar to what you have. That disease. Or the fact they've only moved here, they might know of someone who has. It's worth a shot to find out, isn't it?"

It is. It's definitely worth a shot, if I want to save my health.

But do I want to lose Marcus in the process?

Chapter 11

Marcus

She's hiding something. I don't know what it is, I can only guess that it's to do with her past. But she is definitely hiding something and I'm not sure how I feel about it. On one hand, it's not like we know each other well enough to be involved on such a scale. On another hand, she has barged into my life like a tornado and to some extent I am entitled to know what it is that she's hiding.

Aren't I?

Following the revelations with the wolves, Violeta paces. And paces some more. And I watch her. And watch her some more—her body movements, her mannerisms, trying to figure out how in the hell did I not realize this woman was a vampir. I still can't shake that off.

Nor can I shake my body's urges, now that I've had her, tasted her fully. It was all I could do, earlier, to hold myself in check. To be mindful of her pleasure and not give in to the animalistic tendencies brimming in me. I've never felt something so intense–it's probably why I couldn't sleep after. Images of her mouth on me are enough to drive me to distraction, like she's become my sun and I'm but a poor orbiting planet around her brilliance.

And I don't like the idea she'd be snuffed out by this disease in her.

"What is it that's holding you back?" I finally ask.

She turns on me, frowning. "It's not so much holding me back, as it is that wolves are unpredictable. Especially these kind. And if there's been spy activity, surely they'll be wary of strangers? Especially vampiri?"

"You can keep worrying about it, or we can just go. And then you'll know once and for all if your worries have a foundation in truth or if they're just pure imagination."

"How would we even find them?"

I shrug. "I know these woods better than most. Plus, the letter has a human scent. Once we track it, we can find out from the human where the wolves are, and go from there. I know it's a long shot. They may have no information whatsoever. But... maybe they do."

Violeta stares at me for a second longer. I wish I knew what she was thinking, but her gaze is impenetrable. It's moments like these that make me question how much, if anything, I know of her. Who is this woman I've let into my bed? And then, it's those same moments that make me realize I don't care. She could be an assassin, and I would still feel the way I do about her. I would still need her. I would still crave her.

I turn away, not wanting those emotions to show on my face. Out of the corner of my eye, I see Violeta finally nod. I'm on my feet the next moment, grabbing a knife, and then I'm out the door. She follows close behind, her bag over her shoulder.

Between my tracking skills and knowledge of the woods, it takes me little time to find the spot. The human was surprisingly careless, leaving his scent and footprints all over the place. But once we get to him, his abode is not what I expect in the least.

I start scenting other things from the letter. Fear. Paranoia. It's enough to make me pause in my tracks. Blindly, I reach for Violeta, tugging her back in the shadow of the trees.

"What is it?" she hisses.

"You don't smell that?"

She shakes her head. Of course she doesn't—my blood must be wearing off already, meaning her vampir strength will also wane by the day's end. All the more reason to be careful.

I take my time inspecting every tree foliage, trunk and bush in the area. Something feels off, too still. Unsheathing my knife, I crouch lower to the ground, my eyes scanning every shadow of every tree.

"Stay here," I tell Violeta, then move into the clearing, heading straight for the cabin door. The scent of fear and paranoia only intensifies the closer I get to the door.

And just as I'm about to knock, there's a whoosh of air behind me. And the bite of an arrow tip against my neck. "Don't fucking move."

A moment later, Violeta's scent envelops me. "How about *you* don't move, asshole?"

I close my eyes. She should have stayed hidden, not barged into this. Who knows how many are here?

I turn, slowly, until I face the man who'd snuck up behind me. And the contradiction of his features is enough to make me wonder what the hell we've stumbled into.

He looks human...for the most part. But there's a reddish tinge to his eyes, one I've seen in bloodlust-crazy vampiri. He *smells* human, though. A flicker of hope rises within me. Could he be suffering from the same thing Violeta is?

Before I can investigate, another shape blurs behind Violeta. When she stops moving, I see a woman wearing a hood that's seen better days. She levels a stake at Violeta's neck, grabbing her without a second's hesitation.

"Let my partner go, and I'll consider making your death painless."

Judging by the red eyes under the hood and the regular human smell around her, she's in the same state as her companion.

I hold my hands up. "There's no need to hurt us. We've come in peace, to ask some questions of the man who lives here."

A smile curls the lips of the woman. "Two clueless vampiri, stumbling in our trap. What a day this is turning out to be."

The man steps back until he's by her side, the tip of his arrow still pointed towards me. "Go on then," he says. "Knock on the door and get the bastard to come out. We haven't been able to enter the house."

I frown, glancing between them. "What do you mean, *haven't been able to*?"

"Wards," Violeta says. "New vampiri can't enter a human house without being invited in, only older ones can. Except these two aren't vampiri, they're humans." She turns her head to the side. "I'd wager even...hunters. Aren't you?"

"So what if we are? It's about time we used your kin's strength against you. Hunting you is getting harder and harder otherwise."

Violeta's blue gaze meets mine. I give a slight nod, enough to let her know we're on the same page. Now that we know what we're dealing with, we can eliminate them.

Hunters. This is what Dmitri's people kept pestering me about, and all along two of them have been staking out a human's hiding spot. The same human who knows the location of wolves and the royals? Keeps getting weirder and weirder.

"So, what, you drank vampir blood?" I ask. "That alone wouldn't give you this strength."

The woman snorts. "Not just vampir. Muroni, too. They said it was best to mix them for longer-lasting effects."

They?

"Shut up," the man hisses. "And stake her already. This is taking too long." His twitchiness reminds me of humans I've seen hooked on drugs.

He adjusts his grip on the bow, then releases the arrow. I feel it hit, embedding itself in my flesh, but I don't let the pain register. I've had too much experience blocking it, it's practically an art now.

I take a half-second to move. One moment I'm standing by the door, the next I crouch low and swing my knife at his thighs, slashing both. His grip releases his weapon and I move him into a chokehold, using his body to block mine in case the woman gets any ideas.

"Let's try this again. Let *my* partner go, and then I'll consider allowing you to live."

The woman opens her mouth to say something, but Violeta shoves her head back, head-butting her. The crack of bone fills the air, followed by the scent of blood.

Violeta whirls on her, then, and with a quick snap of her hand she's got the girl's neck snapped. I follow suit and dispose of the one I'd been holding, then yank the arrow out of my shoulder.

"Goddamned mess," I mutter. "Next time I tell you to wait, *wait*."

Violeta rolls her eyes. "You know, just because I allow you control in bed doesn't mean I'm relinquishing it everywhere."

I scowl at her. "Your life is at stake here."

"And I handled myself, didn't I?"

She pushes past me and with one shove of her shoulder, the door handle snaps off and the wooden panel sways inside.

The dilapidated cabin is a sad excuse for a shelter. I push the door open and hear scurrying to the side—rats? When I turn, it's to find someone curled up, wrapped in covers.

"We mean you no harm," I say.

He shudders in his blanket then looks up. He's holding something in his hands but I can't tell what it is, with the light and the way he's huddled up. My soldier instincts warn me it could be dangerous—could be a weapon.

But I know in order to get through to him, to get the information we need, it would be best to try for honesty rather than mistrust.

"The two vampir hunters outside are dead. They seemed eager to come in here."

His wide gaze flies to the barricaded windows. "They've been waiting, prowling. Unnatural, what they did to themselves. Not supposed to be like this... Not supposed to be..."

He trails off in incomprehensible mutters. I chance a step closer, pulling out of my pocket the crumpled letter.

"We found this," I say and hold it up. "It has your scent all over it."

A silence, then, "So?"

"So..." I move closer, and Violeta enters behind me.

His eyes shift to her, widen, and he trembles. Is it because he knows her? Or is it because he can tell who and what we are? Perhaps some instinctual wariness has finally seeped into his addled human brain.

Another step towards him. This time, I smell alcohol wafting off him in waves.

"It's a free country," he mutters. "I can write letters."

"Sure." I widen my stance, and his trembling increases. When I want to, I can be intimidating. Good. "The problem is *what* is in that letter. Some would say going against the royals is akin to signing a death warrant. Yet you did it anyway." I shrug carelessly. "I'm only here for one thing, and one thing only. The wolves you mention. Where are they?"

He glances behind me, then back at me. "What's it to you?"

I clench my jaw. "No business of yours. Tell me, and we'll walk away and leave you to your pathetic existence."

"Okay. Okay, fine. The wolves are nearby, they're in a campsite not too far off. I can take you there. I've staked them many times but first—"

He moves, and for a moment I think he's about to stand. But then he tosses off the blanket and out comes a crossbow. He shoots once, and the arrow barely misses me. Then he reloads, turns the nozzle to Violeta and shoots again, this time nicking her in the shoulder.

Her soft gasp of pain is lava to my veins. I advance on the man, ducking his poorly aimed arrow, and punch him in the gut. I'm fairly sure I feel bones breaking. When he crumbles to the ground, I bend over him and pick him up by his throat. His eyes bulge out of their sockets as he tries—and fails—to rasp a few words.

I freeze in my intent. To take a life, when I've sworn not to take one again. The vampiri hunters outside were scum, completely tainted. But this? A human life, of all things. My rage for Violeta, for her being in danger, has overwhelmed everything else.

I prided myself on having everything under control. Since I left my vampir clan, I even managed it. I'd built myself a routine, a life. Isolated, but plain and simple. And then *she* stumbled into it, and tore it all apart with her sweet smiles and alluring body and complex personality.

And now... Gone is my every principle, consumed instead by my feelings for her.

Feelings that are getting stronger and stronger, and harder to ignore every day.

Feelings that scare me.

Feelings that overwhelm my impulse to not take a life... Almost on autopilot, my gaze meets the human's. My entire energy zeroes in on him.

Violeta

I stare at this man, this vampir, and the way he holds the human. He took an arrow for me, and the man's eyes are wide, but Marcus doesn't care. He's on him in a beat, his fingers around his throat, lifting him effortlessly off the ground.

This is the soldier. This is what he warned me about.

When he told me he's not all good, that he did monstrous things, *this* is what he meant.

I've seen countless acts of violence from my siblings. Liza and Alex, especially, seem to have a taste for the killing of others, for inflicting suffering in new and unusual ways. It's why I don't hunt with them anymore. It's not that they're psychopathic monsters, although to some extent they are. I can't excuse their behavior. But they have their own issues to sort through, and violence is how they do it.

But Marcus...

I'm starkly reminded of what he revealed to me, about working for the royals. About being out of control, and under someone else's control. Being a good soldier, taking orders, carrying them out. About losing little pieces of his soul.

I don't believe his claims that my family ordered the deaths of hundreds of thousands. There must be something under all that, something Marcus himself is unaware of.

But until I find out the truth, can I let him carry out this violence, even if he thinks it's for my own good? If he's killing someone to retaliate for me being hurt, is that even appropriate or will it only hurt him more? Will it only be another notch he's added to his belt, another killing for the royals he hates?

"Marcus..."

He doesn't move, frozen in some sort of a trance. It doesn't take a genius to realize why, and for the first time I wonder when's the last time he killed cold-blooded, and not in self-defense like we did outside with those hunters. I know I won't have him do so for me.

"Let him go."

He does nothing, instead clenching his fingers around the man's throat.

"Marcus, *let him go.*"

Still nothing. And the man is turning blue in the face. Shit.

I don't want to, and I don't even know if it'll work, but I have to try. Only one thing will make him listen at this point, and that his masters, the royals, ordering him to—and that's a direct order from a royal, much as it pains me to do it.

Behind his back, I pull out a small dagger and cut my palm, as deep as I can. Blood gushes to the surface. And as it gushes, Marcus' head tilts to the side, his nose up in the air.

I move around the human, instead capturing his gaze with mine. The blood will enthrall him, but it's my voice, once he feels my essence, that will compel him. I shake off the gut-clenching sensation that this is wrong, that I shouldn't be exerting my will on him, and instead speak as clearly as I can.

"Marcus, I order you to let him go. Do not try to kill him. Do not kill for a royal or any master. Never again will you lose your freedom to someone else's whims, unless it is done of your own free will."

Marcus is frozen for a moment longer. Then he gasps, his eyes go glazed, and he lets go of the human. He collapses to the ground in an unconscious heap, while Marcus falls to his knees, gasping loudly.

I then turn on the human, knowing full well I can't let him live. He's too busy gasping, trying to regain his breath, to see me coming.

"It was a stupid move," I whisper.

He looks up then, his eyes wide. I'm already descending on him, using the dagger to cut his throat. Blood gushes out, and I don't feel the slightest incline to drink it. But Marcus'... I inhale his scent deeply, then turn to my own wound, licking it closed.

I wipe the knife on my dark jeans and sheathe it again, then walk over to Marcus and kneel in front of him.

At first, I'm afraid of touching him. His eyes are still glazed, and to anyone else he'd seem catatonic. I know our blood, when used with the power of glamour, turns vampiri into good little soldiers, unable to fight it off. It's a power I've only used a handful of times in my life. One I know some of my siblings will not even touch—and others will, when it suits their purposes.

We're all aware of the choice we take away from those we use it on, though. Of the moral dilemma. In this case, I'd done it to protect Marcus, but also to protect myself. Does that make it a right choice, an evil one, or just a selfish one?

Staring into his glazed expression, I clench my fists to hide their trembling. I hate it. I never wanted it for him. And I will never use it on him again, but it was the only way I could think of to stop the truth from coming out. From losing him. And even if it means I'll lose him sometime later once he finds out... it's a choice I made. Not gladly, not under coercion, but my choice.

After hundreds of years alive, I know how to be accountable, especially for the bad things I've done.

"Please forgive me," I whisper, and reach out.

The moment I touch him, he jerks, stumbles backwards, looking around.

"Are you all right?" I ask.

His eyes land on me, as if he's coming out of a nightmare. "What just happened?"

He shouldn't remember any of it. I really hope he doesn't,

because it'll be hard to explain how in hell I was able to glamour him, when it's only possible for a vampir older than him to do so. And Marcus thinks I'm younger. Not only that, but it would also bring about questions of how old I am, and it would be a dead giveaway for my true identity.

Instead, I say, "I killed him. He's gone. And we have the information we need."

Marcus glances between me and the dead human. For a moment, I don't move, tenser than ever. Will he remember? Can he fight it off? Will my disease have worn off even this ability, in the end? And if he does, if he realizes what I did, what can I say to justify it?

Nothing. There's absolutely nothing I can say.

But I shouldn't have worried, because after a quick glance around, Marcus only nods. The glazed look fades away, replaced by his usual green hue. "Then let's not waste any time."

Chapter 12

Marcus

I burn the human's body outside, though there's no real need, given Violeta didn't leave any vampir bite marks on him. The slash of the knife could've easily been attributed to a robbery gone wrong, and that's if this was ever discovered.... Doubtful, in these parts of the woods.

Once the fire has incinerated most of his remains—and the vampir hunters'—I head back inside. Violeta's thrown a blanket over the bloody area, and moved to the opposite corner.

I try to hide my frown, but something doesn't add up. I want to ignore that nagging feeling telling me more is going on, but my soldier instincts tell me otherwise. So even as I move about the small cabin, I'm going over it in my mind.

I'd had the man's neck in my hands, then he was gone, and I was on my knees. And she killed him. And now she's moving around almost robotically, her shoulders hunched as if she did something wrong.

Which is absurd, because all she did was save us. Right?

"The wolves..." I trail off.

She starts, glances at me, and looks back at the ground. "I, um...I'm just a tad tired. Do you think we can use his house and sleep, then take off in the morning?"

I arch an eyebrow, looking pointedly at our surroundings. "Here?"

She nods. "I don't feel like I've got the strength to head back to your cabin."

"I could carry you?"

All I get is a pleading look and a shake of her head.

I frown. "I really don't want to waste any time. Not when it's so precious to you."

If anything, my words seem to only affect her more, and she glances away. "I get it. But I'm fine with it. Please?"

It's only a sign of my deep infatuation that I give in so easily, and start cleaning the area and preparing a spot for us to sleep far away from the bloodbath.

"What's your family like?" I ask as I brush my fingers through her hair gently.

I managed to find us some cleaner blankets in the man's home and set them on the floor, then offered Violeta my chest to rest on. She's been curled up against me for the better part of an hour, but I can tell she's not asleep.

What's she thinking of? That's the million-dollar question.

I've had no build-up to my inquiry, but there's a larger part of me that demands to know. I've avoided it as much as I could, giving and giving in the hopes it would have her open up, but all it led to is more silence. And I *need* to know where she's from, everything about her, and those around her. It's an urge in my being, as strong as my need to hold her close.

Violeta tenses in my arms, then seems to relax. Whether it's genuine or in an effort not to get my guard up, I don't know. I can't see her expression, snuggled as she is against my side.

"They're, umm, different," she finally says.

The words are loaded with meaning. I can't tell which of it is good and which bad, so I continue my ministrations, moving my fingers across her scalp as I massage it.

In the silence, she speaks. "My brother, he and I are close. More so than with the others."

"Others?" A chuckle escapes me. "How many siblings do you have?"

"Five. We're six in total, including me," she says quietly. Then, a bit quicker, she adds, "Adopted."

Shame runs through me, hot and uncomfortable. Here I was thinking she's hiding something, when all it was is the same as me—an ugly past, one unworthy to pass the lips of the people we've become.

I pull her closer in a silent, comfortable hug. It's the only way I know to communicate I get what she means, and she doesn't have to dread talking about it. Not with me.

After another beat, Violeta sighs against my chest. "It was hard, growing...up. We're all very different and some of us, well, immortality only enhanced some really bad traits and took away some good ones."

"So they're all vampiri?"

There's a slight pause, and I want nothing more than to look in her eyes and understand these hesitations. Instead, I force myself to respect her space, and give her the time to answer.

"Da."

"That's hard." I take a deep breath. "The hardest thing I've ever gone through is seeing those I loved die, and being unable to save them. To sit by and watch the people you grew up with become the worst versions of themselves... I can't even imagine." I pause. "Do you see them often?"

"Occasionally," she mutters. "We used to hunt together, but not so much anymore."

"Because of them changing or...?"

Her voice is darker when she answers. "Precisely because of that."

I squeeze her closer. "I'm sorry, Vi. It's one thing to see humans come to the end of their lifetime, but your case is much worse, in many ways."

"I suppose." She pauses. "Why didn't you save the humans? The ones you watched get old and die, I mean. You could've."

"Because saving them would've meant also turning them into monsters."

She looks up at me. "Is that what you think we are, then?"

Her words are heavy, laced with meaning yet again. I take my time answering, rolling over the words in my mind, trying to determine whether they're what I truly believe or not.

"I don't know," I whisper. "We're not natural, that's for sure."

"Does that make us monsters?'

"Nu. Different doesn't mean monstruous. But... our actions do. And I know I've done plenty of bad things to earn the moniker."

She breaks our gaze and buries her head in my chest, growing silent once more. I think that's the end of it, but then she speaks. And it's the words I've been waiting for, but not quite the content I'd expected.

"I did, too. When I was first turned, I couldn't control my bloodlust. It was...bad. My brother, Nico, helped me—he'd been turned before me so he had a few years of experience—as did my sire. But it was hard." Her palm on my chest clenches into a fist, as if she's angry at herself. "I'd always been a sickly child as a human. Being unable to hang out with others, or play, it made me a shy person by nature. Then when I was turned..."

She trails off, drawing in a shuddering breath. It's funny, the things we do on autopilot even though we don't need to.

I squeeze her against my chest. "You found it alluring."

She tosses her head back to meet my gaze again. The blue in hers is darker, conflicted. "Da. Very. I took full advantage of everything I was able to do, sometimes not realizing the bloodlust was upon me until it was too late. If it hadn't been for my brother, I would've hurt way more people than I did. And still I didn't really listen. Not until the worst happened."

"You killed an innocent?"

She closes her eyes, then opens them again. This time they're filled with unshed tears. "A child. I didn't mean to, at least I don't think I did. I can't even remember doing it. I just remember waking up to her body, that cherubic face, the blond curls, the pale skin and blue lips…" She shudders. 'I've never forgiven myself for it." Her tears flow freely, bathing her cheeks.

"Ah, precious…" I risk a thumb to wipe away her tears. "We've all done horrible things. You shouldn't be blaming yourself forever over something that happened so long ago. You've grown, since. I see you for the good person you are now."

"I'm not, though."

"Shush." I bend forward, kissing her softly, before resuming my position.

This is what I've been waiting for. This vulnerability, this openness, this sense of communication. To finally understand what makes her tick, to have her opening herself up like this to me is even more euphoric than the sex we'd had.

Violeta stares at me, then bites her lip. "In many ways, I guess I had the opposite of your upbringing. I had too much freedom, when you had none."

"True." It's also a good insight into why she had the breakdown she did. Knowing her now, the person she is, those victims must've weighed heavily on her mind. Centuries of not dealing with that guilt would compound into her desire to put an end to it. "Is that why you were atop Poenari, after you saw Kalla?"

Violeta nods and breaks eye contact, burying herself once more in my chest. "Da… She said, or rather, warned me against the blood-lust. The same that's been in me, only she said it's getting worse. She didn't say why, specifically, but it could be this disease. I… I'm scared, Marcus. I don't want to be the person I was back then. I don't want to wake up next to another dead child."

"I won't allow it to happen, I swear it."

Whether it's the firmness in my tone, or my words hit their mark, she's quiet again for a bit.

"Can they help, do you think?" I ask her. "Once we find the wolves, find out what they know, will they be able to help with your disease?"

"Maybe." The one word is barely above a whisper.

"I don't want to lose you, Violeta. Not when it's this early in our relationship."

She says nothing, and I realize that whatever it is I've said, she's shut down on me. I'm familiar with the mechanism—used it all the time, really—so I don't try to push for more. I'm more than happy with what she's already given. Instead, I allow my head to fall back and stare at the ceiling.

I wouldn't have expected to fall asleep, away from the safety of my home. It's been such a long time since I tried, that nothing else would do except the four walls I know inside and out.

But with Violeta in my arms, with the night outside as quiet as ever, it ends up becoming easier than I thought.

I don't know what time it is when I wake up, aware of my raging hard-on. And what's causing it—Violeta, her hand on my flesh, stroking me and teasing me to oblivion and back.

My rational mind, the one warning of unfinished conversations and too many feelings abounding, tells me to take it slow, to ease out of it, to breathe. But my primal side, the darker, rawer side of me is already on the brink. All it'll take is one perfect touch of her hand and I'll shatter.

"Vi—" Her strangled name dies on my lips.

With a grin I can sense more than see in the darkness, she bends her head towards me, kissing my neck, my chest—when did she take my clothes off?—and lower still. I dig my hand in her scalp and tug upwards before she can distract me with her lips on my hard-on again.

"We have to leave in a few hours." I don't recognize my own voice, halfway between a whisper and a growl.

She grins, licking her lips. "Or, we don't have to. It's snowing outside, and quite heavily. What's a few more hours?"

When she straddles me and rubs herself sinfully against me, I forget all reason. She's taken off her sweatpants, so the only barrier is the thin material of her underwear. And even that's soaked, a testimony that her need is as bad as mine is.

The rational part, the one demanding slow, is pushed to the back, and I let passion rule us both. In one smooth move I push up her shirt, bury my face in her breasts, and pull her hips over mine.

Her moan, my groan, fill the empty space. Even through her clothing, I can feel how warm and ready she is for me. She lifts herself over me and her hands move to the elastic of her underwear. She shimmies out of them, lets me slip them off one leg, then the other, and resumes straddling me.

This time, there's no barrier between us. Nothing to keep us apart. Just her skin on mine, her heat beckoning me inside her, and her scent filling my senses.

I let out a growl as she takes me in her hand, and slowly, inch by painful inch, allows me inside her. When I'm all the way in, I drop my head to her chest. One hand moves to her breast, pinching and tugging on her nipple. The other's already shifting from her hip, to between her legs, seeking that small bundle of pleasure that'll drive her crazy.

This isn't smart. None of it is. The emotions in my chest, the desire in my loins—I don't just need her. I *crave* her, like an addict craves his fix.

"Marcus..." Her hand is on my cheek, forcing my gaze upward, colliding with hers.

My thumb increases the friction on her clit, my fingers pinch her nipple harder, and her lips part open on a long moan.

"I—I can't..."

I grip her hips and move her up and down me furiously, thrusting into her as she tightens around me, milking me for everything I've got. I close my eyes in sheer bliss at the feel of her over me.

"Fuck." It's a hiss, a whisper that breaks the darkness.

I pull my mouth away from her breasts and look into her eyes. My hand is on her nape, pulling her down for a fiery kiss as I thrust deeper inside her.

I'd give her everything and more, for this particular taste of heaven.

When I wake up next, Violeta's asleep in my arms. I haven't slept this long for ages, let alone with a beautiful vampir like her in my arms.

One who could die at any moment, if she doesn't follow the new clues we've found.

I force the thought away, refusing to let it ruin the blissful sensation. But like a nagging mosquito, it's back over and over, not letting go until it's fully front and center of my mind. Doubts assail me. Did Violeta initiate the sex in order to distract me and delay our finding the wolves?

Why would she even do that? They're her best chance at finding answers, for good.

Unless... could it be there's something else she's hiding?

My mind wanders back to the previous day, to the dead human, to that odd blackout moment I'd had. What had happened, exactly?

Violeta stirs in my arms, muttering something. I don't catch all of it – it's some old dialect of Romanian she's speaking. But it only serves to add to the questions in my head. Just how old is she, exactly? And who turned her?

So many questions, so few answers.

They all mix in my mind with the battles I've been in, the things I've seen, the things I've *done.* The unexpected attack from the hunters, followed by the human's dead body are reminders of the bloodshed I've caused—and of everything I can never forget.

With a sigh, I wrap my arms around Violeta and nuzzle her hair. "I've got you. And I'll keep you safe, I swear it." *On my life.*

Violeta

The next morning, I wake up stretching. Marcus stirs at the same time as me, and I debate distracting him with sex again once more. But I don't want to taint the memory of the previous night with games. He doesn't deserve it, not when all he's doing is trying to help me.

I'm pretty sure the pack of vârcolaci that letter referenced is the same one who'd met me back at the castle. Meaning they know my scent and they definitely know my face. Ergo, my days with him thinking I'm some innocent, reformed vampir, are basically at their end. The moment we land in Dominic's territory, the truth will come out.

But whether or not this trip will reveal my true identity, it's time to bite that particular bullet.

We get ready in silence and I reach for my bag at the same time he does. I try to ignore my trepidation when his hand wraps around the worn leather strap...

Then he hands it to me, and I etch out a smile. "Thanks."

Marcus nods and heads to the door. I'd expected the same openness from the previous nights, but today he seems lost in thought. Just as I'm about to ask him what's wrong, he opens the door... and freezes.

I rush to his side, only to be confronted with the same view. A semi-circle of wolves of all shapes and sizes is blocking our exit path. And they're not just any wolves.

My eyes land on the black fur and blue eyes of the leader.

Marcus moves in front of me, stupidly protecting me yet again. "We mean you no harm."

I tap his shoulder, lowering my voice to a whisper. "It's the wolves we're seeking."

"How do you know?"

I can't really say I know the leader, can I? If I do, Marcus will ask more questions. Too many. And then the truth will come out earlier. I may be all right with it if it happens, but I don't want to push it. It's selfish, but I'll take as many moments as I can of having him look at me this way. Like he cares. Like I'm valued. Like I'm...his.

No lie comes to my lips, though. He turns to stare at me, and the leader takes that moment to shift back to human.

Fully naked, his arctic gaze lands on me. "What are you doing on my territory, vampir?" He sniffs the air, and adds, "And killing, no less?"

Shit.

I move past Marcus without answering him, and instead walk a few steps closer to the wolf. Marcus makes a noise behind me, but my attention is focused on the wolf. I ignore his ripped body—though, seriously, it's a work of art—and focus on his harsh features.

"The killing was self-defense," I mutter. "And, as for why I'm here… I'm looking for you."

He stares at me a beat, then at Marcus, and nods. "Fine. Follow us to a place we can speak in peace." In a beat, he's back to his wolf form, and walks among his wolves.

Though Dominic's fur and appearance is fully wolf, his followers seem…worse for wear. Their fur is equally as dark as his, but more matted. They're larger than regular wolves—larger even than some of those in his pack—and their backs are hunched over. Yellow eyes stare at the world around them with wariness, but when they land on Dominic, they're filled with respect. An interesting paradox.

Half of Dominic's team follows him, the rest closes in on me and Marcus. It's evident his words weren't an invitation, but an order, so I sigh and follow him, knee-deep in the snow. After a moment, I catch Marcus' echoing footsteps behind me.

This should be interesting.

Chapter 13

Violeta

As it turns out, the wolf camp is a bit of a trek away. Marcus didn't comment on their appearance, and I can't tell if he's ruminating some deep, dark thought concerning my revelations last night, or if he's just happy that the wolves found us before we had to go find them.

So far, Dominic hasn't said anything else. He only shifted back to wolf form, then effortlessly pranced through the trees as we'd followed, surrounded by his pack.

After the initial slow beginning, the wolves take off on a fast run, and so do Marcus and me. At least, until my stupid disease awakens with a vengeance. It'd been quiet though I've felt my energy dwindling since using the glamour. Still, Marcus' blood kept me going longer than the muroni concoction.

But now one moment I'm whizzing through the trees, faster than a hawk on its prey. The next, it's like I run out of steam. Everything slows down around me, gets blurry. In the moment it takes me to realize my surroundings, I'm stumbling. My hand rasps against a tree's trunk, but can't get a grip. It's like my muscles have stopped working.

And then I'm stumbling, tumbling, rolling downhill. Snow seeps in my clothes, mud coats my legs and, somehow, by some idiotic miracle, I don't smack my head on a rock. I come to a stop when my back hits a fallen tree.

A groan escapes me. I try to get up but, same as before, my muscles simply won't cooperate.

Worse, I can't even blink to keep my eyes open. It's as if someone hit the off switch, and my leftover energy has evaporated. My hand slips off the snow when I try, and I just give up, lying against the tree, trying to regain my breath and a semblance of where I've fallen to.

Snow crunches in the distance. I blink furiously and finally my eyes settle on Marcus heading my way. And he's not alone—a pair of vrykolakas have followed him.

His expression, hidden from the wolves behind him, is as neutral as can be. But the shine in his eyes tells me there's more, that he's truly concerned about my state of being. I try not to see hope in it. Hope that we have a chance to actually end up together, given...everything he still doesn't know about me.

Last night, he'd asked me about my family. And I'd been able to talk about them, carefully choosing my words so I didn't give anything away that could hint at my true lineage. But I'd also been able to tell him other things, things that I didn't have to lie about. And it had felt so good... But also bittersweet. After the kindness he'd exuded, it had taken all my willpower not to reveal everything and beg his forgiveness.

And now, these wolves... I'm worried what they'll say. They know exactly who I am, and whatever it is they want with us, it won't turn in my favor.

So when Marcus bends over and holds out his hand, I relish the touch of his fingers against mine. His strength as he helps me up, dusting my ass of the snow. The concern in his voice as he moves that much closer to me, his lips by my ear.

"Are you all right?"

No. I'm anything but. And soon enough, you're going to hate me, and I can't do anything to stop it.

At least he doesn't seem stony-faced anymore. Biting back my words, I nod instead, and we head back up the path, me leaning on Marcus most of the way.

Dominic tilts his wolf head at us as if asking what's wrong.

"I'll explain later," I say. "Let's just get on with it."

Since I'm moving unbearably slowly, Marcus picks me up in his arms and continues following the wolves at vampir speed. About an hour later, we finally arrive at an encampment. Trees were cut to make way for a semi-regular circle of houses, all in various stages of construction, and spread apart. On the edge, where the forest continues, more wolves lie down in the snow. They seem to be separated in clusters—I count at least another twenty. That, plus the ones who'd come for us, makes for a nice thirty.

Alex was right, then. There's a lot of them, and they really are settling down.

I glance up at a cliff in the distance. A shiver runs through me. I've hunted close by here before. All my siblings have, meaning we're way too close to my family. If Alex or Liza come hunting around here...

Stop it. They won't. They've been told to stay away from the wolves.

As if they ever listen... Especially Alex.

He's had it in for these wolves since they first arrived here, even thought they were responsible for some stuff earlier on. Of course, it turned out that was humans trying to make it so, but that didn't get him to cool off at all.

I'm worried. More than worried to be running into anyone I know. There are so many things to consider, all of them worse than the last. Assuming the wolves meant this to be an informal, casual conversation, and not a kidnapping, they'll be in danger because of me. And with vampir hunters in the area, Dmitri's clan aware of me, and Kalla's hint of rumors that more vampiri are coming... I'm starting to wonder if I should warn the wolves to get out of here while they still can.

Though I'm in fresh air, I can feel the walls closing in on me. Soon I'll be forced to deal with my choices... Too soon.

We're led to a small house, built in the old style. A wooden frame—timber, by the smell of it—with earth and straw infill, while another house has mud bricks. Inside, the furnishings are minimal. A carpet, table and chair, and a bed in a corner with a straw mattress.

A redhead gets up from the table. I remember her all too well. A few weeks ago, when the wolves showed up at our castle, she was there. She was the only one not in wolf form, because she's fully human.

I remember my surprise at that. Vârcolaci are, by nature, volatile. But her and Dominic, in as far as I could tell in the short time, were equal partners in this. I still remember the magic coursing through her, shining in her gaze when Alex tried to hurt her mate.

But there's no glint of lightning in her eyes this time. Instead, she nods at a younger version of Dominic. He's sitting at the table in front of her, tapping his knuckles nervously on the worn wood. Twenty years or so younger, he looks exactly like his father except for the hair, it's a lighter blond hue. And he definitely smells human and wolf, but also...something else.

"You can go, Luca," Lucrezia says. "We'll talk more later."

I try not to stare too much, but his scent is interesting. A mix of wolf with spices, like something exotic. My gaze lingers on the redhead again. I'd thought she was a witch, but now I'm starting to wonder if there's more to her.

Luca—their son, I presume—shoots us an annoyed glare and leaves. Clearly, we've interrupted something.

Dominic then turns back to human form and heads for some clothes. A few moments later he faces us again, this time dressed in jeans and a simple shirt. "Take a seat."

"Is that an order?" Marcus asks.

Dominic rolls his eyes. "No orders around here, vampir. Cool your jets." He sits down first as if to gesture how normal it is to do so. The redhead shakes her head, a playful smile on her lips.

"You never were a people person, Dom." To us, she says, "My name is Lucrezia, but you can call me Luz. This is my mate, Dominic."

"I'm Violeta," I mutter, "and this is Marcus."

Lucrezia nods, focusing her gaze on him. "For the record, we don't intend to harm you, and you can leave here at any point."

"After you answer some questions," Dominic corrects.

I sit first, but freeze against my seat when he speaks again.

"I know you." His eyes narrow, taking in my expression. "Weren't you—"

"In the woods, running the other day," Lucrezia intervenes.

My surprised gaze rises to hers. There's something in there, something warning me to go along with it. How could she know that I want this kept quiet from Marcus?

"I...Da." I trail off unsure what else to say. Or, not say.

"You saw her?" Marcus intervenes, placing a hand on my shoulder. I feel his presence behind me like a rock, and the tension radiating off him. "When the vampiri were chasing her, *you saw her*, and you didn't help her?"

Dominic glances between me and Marcus, as if weighing his words. I worry he won't follow Lucrezia's lead, but then he does, in a roundabout sort of way.

"We don't get involved in vampir affairs."

Marcus' hold on me tightens. "And yet, you just did. You practically ordered us here, without much of a choice."

"Because you killed on our territory."

"Violeta already said it was self-defense."

Dominic arches an eyebrow. "And you're telling me as her mate, you couldn't defend her?"

Marcus' hand drops from my shoulder, at the same time as I lean forward. I must've heard wrong. "What did you just say?"

When I glance at Marcus, he's frozen, his expression completely stunned. I turn back to the wolf. "What do you mean, *mates*?"

Lucrezia steps forward. "You must both be hungry. Why don't I get you something to eat?"

"We drink blood," Marcus says after a beat. "And I'm more interested in hearing this."

Dominic sighs and leans back in his chair, crossing his arms over his chest. His expression is halfway between sardonic and annoyed. "Do vampiri not have mates?"

"No," I whisper.

Not normally. Except, Father did. Only he called her his consort. And Nico and Tassa... I'm pretty sure she's his consort, given how she has affected his life in such a short time. Could Marcus be that for me, too?

The irony of the situation isn't lost on me. I'd left the castle, left my siblings and everything I knew was safe, only to be tossed head-first into the big, bad world out there. And it so happens that it's filled with more minefields than I would've thought.

"Not that I know of," Marcus says. "What makes you think we, specifically, are mated?"

Lucrezia sighs, nudging Dominic as if to warn it's his fault for starting this conversation. "Your energies are aligned."

"How would you know this? You've only seen us for a moment."

Unable to speak, stunned into silence, I can only listen. And remain thankful for Marcus' presence here, for his ability to take this in his stride. Because I sure as hell am not.

Lucrezia shares a glance with Dominic, and it dawns on me. "You've been watching us, haven't you?"

Dominic nods. "Of course. You kept killing on our territory."

My territory, I want to correct him, and barely hold back. The glitter of amusement in his eyes is akin to a dare. He did that on purpose, trying to make me slip up.

I clear my throat, fighting hard to keep a neutral mask. "So you're not just talking about the human, then."

"No. I mean the two, or was it three, rounds of vampiri you killed, darling. Not to mention the two hunters. Care to explain that?"

That glint is still in his eyes. Bastard's doing it on purpose, putting me in a situation where I either answer like a vampir who's worth nothing or get annoyed like the royal I am.

"I... The vampiri were hunting me. I had to defend myself."

Dominic nods. "I can understand that. Even if I don't understand your mate not defending you."

"He's not my—"

"I'm not," Marcus says at the same time. The certainty rolling off his tongue stings, I won't lie.

Dominic chuckles. "Could've fooled me."

I focus on Lucrezia instead, since Dominic seems to be enjoying our confusion all too much. "I don't understand. What exactly do you mean by our energies align?" What I really want to ask is, *What the fuck are you*, but I hold off on that. Manners first, after all.

Lucrezia gives me a tight smile. "I'm what you call a Solomonar. Ages ago, or so I'm told, they were witches and warlocks trained in use of magic by zmei. They would ride them into battles, like soldiers."

I gasp. "Zmei? But they're... You mean the dragon shifters of the Carpathians? They were extinct!"

"Not quite, no," Lucrezia says. "Two brothers survived, and we happen to know both of them. They're the ones who suggested moving around this area, actually."

"Luz..." The single word is both a growl and a warning from Dominic.

Not that it deters Lucrezia. She sits on his lap, and continues, "See, we were living on the other side of the Carpathians originally, after moving from the United States. Dominic was born here, and when it was time to return with our pack, we chose the area that was most familiar. But the land was no good, and the wolves were getting restless. We didn't really know where to turn. At least, until Tytus—one of the zmei brothers—mentioned this area here."

"How convenient," Marcus mutters behind me.

"I said much the same." Dominic smirks. "But between my mate and my pack, I was outnumbered."

"So, this whole energy aligning thing…" I trail off meaningfully, hoping she'll give me the answer I seek.

Lucrezia shrugs. "My powers developed oddly over time. I still channel zmeu magic, and thanks to a few experiences, I'm able to see past the, hmm, corporeal form. Everyone emits energy. You two happen to match." She points to Marcus. "Your light shines through her darkness."

He scoffs. "You must mean the opposite."

Her confused gaze lands on me. I can't admit the rest of what Kalla said, this would be the worst possible time for that. So I keep my mouth shut, resulting in an awkward silence.

Dominic breaks it by tapping the table a few times, then that arctic gaze lands on me again. "Mate subject aside, what happened, earlier? You weakened. Vampiri don't weaken."

I tilt my chin up. "Well, I do. I don't know if it's a curse or whatnot, but I've been sick for a while. Two years and some. It's why we were searching for you. We found a letter speaking of your return to these lands, and Marcus said because of your wolves being…special…that maybe there might be a clue here to fixing me."

"If by special you mean undead, that is true. It's something I'm trying to fix."

"How would you fix something like that?' Marcus asks.

Dominic sighs. "By making sure they don't do what landed them in the undead category in the first place."

I inhale sharply. "That's possible, then? There's redemption?"

Dominic nods. "Of a sort. I'm still understanding it, even after a quarter of a century caring for them, but it's not *im*possible."

I'm silent for a longer moment at his words.

Lucrezia adds, "What, exactly, are your symptoms?"

It's my turn to share a glance with Marcus. He nods, silently indicating I should explain everything.

By the time I'm done, both of our hosts seem shocked. Then they share a look and Lucrezia stares at me, but her expression is different. "Why don't you two get some rest, and we'll ask around. You can use this house for the time being."

"Isn't this yours?" I ask.

She shakes her head. "No, it's more of a guest spot. We'll be just across."

They're gone sooner than I thought was possible, leaving me and Marcus behind. And, somehow, my head is even more filled with questions than before.

I turn to him, not knowing exactly what to expect.

Marcus

Mate.

They said *mate.* Is that the impression we give? Aside from the energies fusing and all that crap. Dominic didn't seem to think in those terms, so something else must've given him the impression.

I try to think what could've done so. After all, yes, I was very glued to Violeta as we made our way here, but I'm a useless defender according to him.

"Are you all right?"

I face her hesitant expression. Unsure what to say, unsure if I am, as she says, all right. Am I?

Mate. The word itself sounds so...final. Could I actually be what she needs, when I'm missing so many pieces of my own soul? So many of them gone to the horrid acts I've committed over the centuries.. Is there anything left of me to give other than my body?

I clear my throat. "The better question is, are you?"

She takes a step closer to me, as if encouraged by my words. "Da. I didn't know if... What Dominic said, I mean..."

I take a deep breath and let it out in a shudder. "If it slapped me across the face? Yeah, it did. I just didn't expect it, is all."

"Neither did I."

"Especially when our world doesn't have mates." I let out a short chuckle, but Violeta looks away. I touch her shoulder. "Does it?"

She meets my gaze and gulps. "I.... I think our term for them is consort. A vampir consort. But... they are rare."

I frown. "How rare?"

"Rare enough that finding one is... Well. I, that's to say, my father, he said consorts are nearly impossible to find because the darkness in us usually doesn't like to be shoved away by light. We're more likely to self-destruct any relationship than, well, learn to work on it."

I think back to Maria and how easily it all fell apart. Maybe there's some truth to it, after all.

"Have you ever been in love?" The words are not what I expected to come out of my mouth, at all. But there they are, a tangible force between us.

Violeta's crestfallen expression tells me immediately it was the wrong question to ask.

"I'm sorry, I have no right to ask. It's this wolf's idiotic comments, I—"

"I was." She lets out a shuddering breath. "I mean, I think I was. In retrospect..." She frowns at me, biting her lip.

"What is it?"

"I guess, what I'm trying to say is... What I thought I felt for him doesn't compare to the intensity of my feelings for you. And—I get it. I know you lost someone, you don't have to make declarations you don't mean and I don't expect you to, but you asked and I—"

Her tone, the shaking of her voice, the way she's looking me, is more than I can take. The tangible energy between us shimmers and pulls, and then my hands are on her shoulders, and my mouth is crushing hers, stifling the rest of an apology I have no intention of hearing.

She *feels* for me. This gorgeous woman, this force of nature, feels for *me*. A hermit, a fucking nobody in this world.

When I pull away, it's only to cup her cheeks in my hands, caressing every line on her features. "Your words humble me. And elate me. What I feel for you, Vi, it's not... I can't put it into words. I can only show you. If you'll let me."

She nods, and the movement brings her lips to brush up against my fingers. With a groan, I capture them once more, this time in a more fervent kiss than the last. Fire rolls through me and into her, until we're both panting, shedding clothes, uncaring that we're in a village of strange wolves and that the explanation to her cure must be around here somewhere.

For once, there is no vampir world.

No werewolves.

No disease.

Only us, and the feel of her skin against mine, and me inside her, and the way she clamps her legs around my waist and pulls me in deeper, arching under me, begging for more.

I can't hold back. I sink my teeth in her neck, intending only to mark her, but instead her blood flows into my mouth, and then she's sinking her fangs into my neck, and I don't know where she ends and I begin anymore.

The eroticism of the connection only drives me deeper inside her, reducing me to a mindless beast until I stifle my roar against the same skin. With a lick of my tongue, I close the wound on her neck, then pull back. Try to lift myself on my elbows.

Violeta looks at me, all flushed, more human in that moment than any vampir I've ever bedded. She smiles at me with glazed eyes. "You're like a sweet wine, my darling. Getting better with every sip."

I chuckle and roll off her, pulling her atop me and covering us with a blanket. "Want to bet the entire wolf village heard us?"

Her soft laughter is stifled against my chest. "Well, they do have great hearing... So it's their own fault. And all that talk about consorts. What silliness."

Within minutes, she's asleep in my arms, but I lie awake much, much longer. What she easily dismissed as silliness, I can't help wondering if there's more to it, if there's an actual truth to such things.

I push away a lock of her hair and kiss her forehead. I guess I'll soon find out.

Chapter 14

Violeta

It can't be more than a few hours when soft rapping by the outside of the house wakes me. I move out of Marcus' arms, surprised the noise hasn't woken him. Then I get dressed and poke my head outside.

Dominic's leaning against the wall of the house, Lucrezia by his side. Something about their expression makes my heart drop in my stomach.

At least until Dominic sniffs the air and snorts. "Not mates, my ass." He turns to Lucrezia. "You owe me ten bucks, draga mea."

She shoves him out of the way with a mock glare and heads towards me. "Don't mind Dom, he has no filter."

He grins behind her back, but the grin falters when it lands on me. "No filter, perhaps. But *you*, vampir, you have no honor. Why are you lying to the other one about your true identity?"

My eyes widen and I glance everywhere but behind me, hoping Marcus still isn't awake. "Can we please talk about this somewhere else?"

Lucrezia nods and grabs my hand, tugging me to a house farther down the path, nestled right in the woods. When we enter, the coziness surprises me. A bit larger than the one we'd spent the night in, it's light and airy, with everything in shades of dark gold and browns—the carpet, the furniture. A small kitchenette is set up in a corner, and past it, a hallway leads to another room. The walls are filled with decorative handsewn curtains and tapestries.

"Where's Luca?" At their surprised glances, I add, "He's your son, right? I noticed him earlier when we arrived."

Lucrezia laughs. "He's too old to be living with us."

Dominic snorts. "Are you kidding me? The minute he turned eighteen I kicked him out." He adds in a mutter, "Not far enough."

"He's only grumbling because they're so alike," Lucrezia says. "But he won't be bothering us here, no one will. Have a seat, please. Would you like a drink?"

I'm about to decline, but she opens a decanter and the smell makes my mouth water. In an almost trance, I watch as she pours me a glass. Judging by the thickness and the rich burgundy color, that's no wine. It's blood.

The moment it's poured, I've snatched the glass and downed it in one shot. Not once do I bother to breathe, or think that it might be poisoned, or a trap. I just drink and drink until there's not a drop left. If it didn't make me a total savage, I would snake out my tongue and lick the inside of the glass, but that's too much, even more for me.

As if guessing my thoughts, Lucrezia pushes the rest of the pitcher towards me. "Have some more, please."

I hesitate. Now that the glass is empty, my better sense kicks in. "What is that, exactly?"

"I should've thought it's obvious," Dominic says. "Blood."

"Da, but..." I bite my lip, hesitating in how much I can say. Then I give up. I'm tired of keeping these secrets, of having no one to share them with, of always being on my toes and watching what I say. "What kind of blood? I haven't been able to drink human blood in...a long time. Didn't feel the need for it. I vacillated between red wine, and human food, until my brother's girlfriend found a potential cure with muroni blood. But it only staved off the symptoms. The last time *any* blood rejuvenated me like this, it was Marcus'."

They share a glance, and Lucrezia pushes the pitcher towards me again. "Then have more. Please. We'll explain what we know, but it's best you keep your strength up."

"And your mind open," Dominic adds.

This time, I don't hesitate. I pour more of the drink, and have another glass. And a third. By the time I'm halfway through the fourth, I start getting that sense of slushiness inside me, and I pause, licking my lips.

"Okay. Consider me enraptured. What, exactly, did you want to tell me about my condition?"

Dominic takes a seat next to his mate, and leans forward. He watches me closely for a moment. I don't know what he's looking for, but he seems satisfied enough as he nods.

"Bine. All right. So, what exactly do you know of your ancestry?"

"Not this again," I mutter, before raising my voice to a normal pitch. "I've had this lesson before from a muroni."

Luz frowns. "A what?"

"Vampir of the caves," Dominic explains. "They live around these regions, though to be honest I thought they were gone. No matter. Humor us, te rog."

I find it odd he's polite enough to say *please,* but I repeat what Kalla had told me, and how that particular meeting had gone. When I'm done, Dominic's leaning back against the chair, his legs spread in the most comfortable position ever. Meanwhile I'm tense and annoyed, and the rest of that pitcher looks too damn good to ignore.

At a loss, I try to pace myself and wait for their reaction. Turns out, I don't have to wait long.

"The muroni didn't have the story wrong," Dominic says. "But she also didn't have the full thing. Before I get into that, let me tell you how my pack came to be. Twenty years ago, they were a mess in need of dire guidance. They landed in the town I was living in—with a different pack—and started causing havoc." His gaze goes to Lucrezia. "If it hadn't been for my mate, I never would've figured out the link."

"Which is what, exactly?"

He clears his throat. "Vlad Țepeș was Prince of Wallachia, as you know. What this land was called before...in the past, I mean. You and your siblings may have been his chosen vampir offspring, but his actual line was carried on by his human children. Cue a few centuries down, and my great-great-great-grandfather emerged from that lineage."

I gape at him. "You're...related to Father?"

Dominic makes a face. "Yeah. Believe me, it was a shock when I found out, too. Born out of wedlock, my dad was a bastard to one of

Vlad's offspring and a piece of work, but still technically had heregie—heredity, blue blood."

"I know what heregie means. It's what makes *us* royals in these lands."

Dominic rolls his eyes and he's about to continue when I interrupt.

"Hold on. Father—Vlad—carried the vampir gene. None of us have been able to shift in centuries, except for the muroni. So he can't have been... I mean the vârcolac... That's passed on through family."

Dominic arches an eyebrow. "Vlad was a carrier of both genes, originally. He *was* able to shapeshift, and he passed that onto you. But when he lost that ability, so did you, because he was your sire and you were his immediate offspring. Muroni were able to keep their abilities because of how they became muroni. Bottom line is, the vampiri and werewolves in these parts, they can all trace their lineage to him."

I frown, recalling something my siblings had argued over. "But your vrykolakas, they're not regular vârcolaci. Wolves. They're...something else entirely."

Dominic inclines his head. "Da, because there's more to the story. My old relative, after a few crimes and such, was excommunicated from his community by a Romanian priest. Some said at the time it was a political move, destined to kill the last of the line of Vlad the Impaler. In the legends, they always say that if a poor soul dies excommunicated, then he returns to life as a vârcolac. Of course, they forget to explain you need to have the gene carried through the family."

"And your great-great-whatever had that gene, through Father."

"Indeed. So after he died, rather than move on, his soul was tortured and wouldn't let go of the body. He was resurrected as the undead and haunted his entire community. This led to the priest himself being excommunicated, and the town by comparison. The then-king dispatched a group of soldiers to kill everyone and cleanse the area, but it was already too late. They had died at the hands of my relative and returned as undead vârcolaci. This was the first full tribe of them in that area, and they roamed the land recruiting many more with them."

"Vrykolakas," I whisper.

Dominic gives me a mocking thumbs up. "You're on point."

I chew on my bottom lip. "But then, are you a vrykolakas?"

Dominic shakes his head. "I'm not. Because my great-great-grandfather, he was cured of his vrykolakas tendencies. Instead of living off blood and hearts of humans, he was taken back into the fold of the Church and re-blessed. This drove the Darkness out of him, he became a missionary for peace. His life's work was to cure vrykolakas of their evil and turn them onto the right path." He shrugs. "I sort of picked up where he left off."

"So your pack, they're mixed?"

"Da. Which is why, I'm guessing, your siblings were spooked."

"Yeah," I mutter. "That would do it." I take the refilled glass from Lucrezia and frown between them. "As interesting as this information is, I still don't get the link to me."

"You've already made the connection that your maker is ours as well. Well, my wolves'. But the truth lies in his life as a human, not as a vampir."

I slam my palm on the table, filled with an anger I cannot explain. "Then *tell me* already! I'm sick and tired of riddles and half-truths."

Dom growls and leans forward. "Calm yourself, or this conversation ends here and now." He grabs the glass out of my hand and nods at Lucrezia to take it all away.

Shame courses through me at my outburst. They might be unconventional, these two, but they've hidden my lie when they could've just been honest with Marcus. And right now, they're trying to help. They don't deserve this.

When Dominic sees I'm quiet, he adds, "Bine. I'll start off with a common myth, something that not many know outside of this part of the world. See, our world, our destinies, are not in our hands contrary to what most human self-help books will have you think. On the contrary, there is a much wider universe beyond our comprehension, one comprised of gods and goddesses who have always watched over us."

"Gods and..." I glance at Luz. "Tell me you don't believe any of this."

"I wouldn't have, except recently I've been faced with the truth of it. We've run into Hades himself, Violeta. And it's all real, but not quite the way we've learned."

"Meaning?"

"There isn't one pantheon of gods, there's more than one. All of them, in fact, have split the Earth into areas they govern. The Celtic pantheon has the northern lands, the Greeks have the Mediterranean, and on it goes."

I tap my fingers against the table. "Still waiting for the punch line."

"The point is," Dominic says, "we're not masters of our fate. We can ignore said directive, but at the end of the day we have to fight against others. Anyway. Vlad, too, was not truly master of his destiny."

I stand straighter at that. "Go on."

Dom leans back in his chair, obviously deeming me less of a threat now that I'm no longer volatile. "You know Vlad himself fought the Ottomans nonstop. A big reason behind that was because his father actually made pacts with the sultan of the Ottoman Empire, and Vlad suffered due to that. Many say he suffered a great deal under the sultan when he lived with him for years as a child."

I cringe. "You sure seem to know a lot about him."

He shares a secret look with Luz, and an odd smile tugs at the corner of his lips. "I've made it my mission to know, after finding out—Well, I'll get to that in a moment. Anyway, back to the Ottomans. Vlad fought them using surprise attacks and psychological warfare. Some of the best in the land, especially given the times. But he was excommunicated by the Church for refusing to bow down before them."

It's an odd picture, with the father I grew under. I know many thought him cruel, but I saw in him only hurt and pain. I mean, he did teach us those same tricks—of surprise attacks and psychological warfare—but it was for our survival. Not to go out and commit unwarranted genocides.

"If you're about to say he was a horrible human being, I'm getting ready to refute it. Just so you know."

Dom laughs darkly. "I wouldn't claim to start such an argument with one who's lived with him. No, that is not the point of my story. Rather, back to the excommunication. You know then that he married a catholic princess, and it is the reason he was eventually cast out by the Orthodox Church. But there is a deeper, darker story within this. And it has to do with his first wife."

I rub at my chest. Despite the centuries, I remember Father's pain when he spoke about her, on the rare occasions he did so. The look in his eyes...

"She killed herself," I whisper. "He told me the Turks had seen on one of their many delegations how much he loved her. Their best ammunition against him was to hurt her. And when they couldn't get to her directly, they sent a letter advising of his death. She...cast herself to the river below Poenari Fortress, and was lost to him."

Lucrezia closes her eyes at my words, as if feeling my pain. When they open again, the brilliant green is filled with tears. "Yes. Vlad continued to live in much, much pain, for years upon years. His second marriage gave him no joy, he closed off to his new wife and the possibility of a new future together. But, most of all, the guilt that he wasn't around to protect his first wife ate at him."

All of this rings too close to home. "How do you know all this?"

"Because I found Vlad's tomb. It's why I returned here, I wanted to know more about him."

A gasp escapes me. "We hid it! We made sure that no one else would find it! If you so much as opened it—"

Dominic lifts his hand in a placating gesture. "Relax. I did not desecrate him, but I needed to know. Luz was able to pull from within this notebook. His thoughts, buried with him."

My gaze is glued to the tiny booklet he sets on the table. The worn spine, the crest of Dracul on it. How many times did I walk in on Father scribbling in it, only to see him hide it thereafter?

"That...wasn't with him, when we buried him," I whisper.

"Because it was left with someone else. Once you buried him, they went in and returned this to its rightful owner."

I frown. "Who was it?"

Dominic shares a look with Lucrezia, and she clears her throat.

"I'm not sure of his name, only that he's dead and he was Dacian. Warlocks who use blood magic, and serve a dark god of death—Zalmoxis."

A shudder runs through me and my gaze returns to the book. "What would Father have had to do with them?"

"I'm glad you asked," Dominic says. "Because within this notebook lies the other part of the story. There is a reason not much is known of Vlad's first wife, and that historians haven't been able to trace a lineage for her. Because they were looking for *human* ancestry."

I'm so focused on the notebook, it takes a moment for the words to register. When they do, I snap my gaze to Dominic's. "Are you saying she wasn't...human?"

"Da. More than that, she was not even part human, like you were at a time, like I am now. His wife was Zalmoxis' daughter, and his prized possession."

"Zalmoxis... The same god of death the Dacians worshipped?"

Lucrezia nods.

I try to think back to everything Dominic had previously said. "And according to you, deities are very real so... You're saying Zalmoxis is in charge of the Romanian area?"

"And more of Eastern Europe, yes. His daughter fell for Vlad when he started killing the Ottomans, drawn in by his ruthlessness and who knows what else. Zalmoxis thought him a hero, perfect to defend his daughter. He took a chance on a human, and it paid off... Each of Vlad's victims went to feed his power. The more criminal, the better."

"And my father knew all this?"

Dom nods. "Yes. Zalmoxis gave him everything—strength, supporters, luck to escape the multiple assassination attempts. A shape shifting ability, and even, by some accounts, magic. All he had to do was use those skills to protect his wife. But when his wife died, when he wasn't able to protect her... Zalmoxis never forgave him. He watched from the shadows as Vlad married again, and the moment he became excommunicated, Zalmoxis knew Vlad would come to him and ask for help. So he took Vlad's pain, and made him a vampir, the first of his kind in these parts. A royal, by all accounts. Zalmoxis did it all so he could have Vlad hunt the rest of the Ottomans and make sure anyone responsible for his daughter's death was.... obliterated. But what Vlad didn't know was the curse built within this gift... A curse that wouldn't make its way out of the shadows until much, much later."

"I don't..."

Lucrezia steps in. "Zalmoxis allowed Vlad to create his army. To create his sons and daughters, like you and your siblings. But then that all stopped. Vlad himself, his mind started going, correct? We saw it in the notebook."

"I... Da. He wasn't himself. He kept saying he wanted to end his existence while he still had the strength of mind to do so."

"That wasn't him talking. It was Zalmoxis, whispering in his ear, demanding what was left of him. Telling him everything that you six would suffer. And when he had him, when Vlad was finally dead, it wasn't enough."

The cruelty of such a being rips me apart, just thinking of it. Everything Father had suffered in those times, everything he couldn't tell us... I should have taken that damned notebook and read it cover to cover. Maybe then I could've stopped his demise.

"What more was there to give?" I finally whisper to Dominic.

"Everything Vlad had built." He taps the notebook. "That bit isn't in there, but it's what I've been able to put together thanks to help from our zmei friends."

Lucrezia steps in at my confused gaze. "The zmei, they used to protect gods. They've lived for millennia, so they know more about these beings than we could ever hope to discover. Their help has been instrumental."

"Remind me to send them a postcard," I mutter. "If Zalmoxis wanted Father's legacy gone, then how come we're still alive?"

Dominic tilts his head, all amusement gone out of his expression. "Are you, though? You're in hiding, and you've just admitted to suffering from some mysterious disease that saps away your strength. A strength you only get back when you're given blood *filled with darkness.*" He gestures to the decanter. "That's from my wolves, the vrykolakas ones. The same ones that come from Țepeș' lineage."

So many puzzle pieces, all clashing in my mind, demanding to be fitted so they form a full picture. But all I can think of is Father's suffering, and the mentioning of mates—consorts. It's no silliness, after all.

Dominic is relentless, though, and he continues. "Let me paint you a picture. How do you make someone suffer? I don't just mean basic torture. But real suffering that is felt in their gut, enough to drive them to the brink of insanity?" When I say nothing, he continues, "You lift them to the top. Make them king of everything. Give them everything they've ever wished. Then you take away what gives them purpose, little by little." Another pause, and he says, " Zalmoxis incited vampiri to go against the royals—yourselves—and killed off your armies. Until you were alone. And then...he went after you. That's why Vlad's offspring can't create vampiri of their own."

I shake my head. "Why not just pop down here and kill us, have it done and over with?"

Dominic sighs. "This bit, we got from our zmei friends as well. See, Zalmoxis isn't a free god. Not really. He's been imprisoned in Tartarus for the last few thousand years. That's why his daughter was on this realm in the first place, he was hiding her from the other gods' wrath. And then she fell for Țepeș... And he lost her for good. And thus, he wants Vlad to feel the exact same loss in each and every single one of you. To watch you die horrible, atrocious, mortal deaths..."

"Unless you find your mates."

A gasp escapes me. "What!? But that's impossible! Vampiri don't have mates, that would imply there's something of us worth saving!"

"A true mate coaxes light out of the Darkness, and souls out of hiding," Dominic says. "With a mate for each of you, you all could continue the line and take your rightful place. The specifics, those elude me, but I trust that's enough of a history lesson to get you started."

"But what of my disease? You said this was all tied with it."

Dominic nods. "The disease is a curse. Zalmoxis' play. The curse takes effect if a vampir has lived too long without its mate."

"But we've all lived centuries without them!"

"Mm, are you sure about that?"

I lean forward, holding back a scowl. "Are *you* sure about all this bullshit you're spewing?"

He grins. "One thousand percent. Say what you will, but one of you has met their mate. It's what triggered the curse."

Lucrezia speaks more softly. "Is it possible one of you did and didn't tell the others?"

I frown, thinking back to my siblings. "Only Nico comes to mind, but he only met Tassa a few months ago. I've had this blasted disease for two years!"

"Would they say for sure if they had, though?" Lucrezia asks.

"Nu—I—My siblings are—you've *met* them!"

Dominic shrugs, unimpressed. "Then you'd best go back and ask them. Tell them everything we told you, and warn them. Unless the one who met their mate comes clean, you won't know the full facts."

"But why did the curse hit me first?"

"I asked Tytus about that," Lucrezia says. "He's one of the zmei brothers who lives in the Carpathian region, and my mentor. He said curses, as a rule, attack the weakest link. In a vampir case, it would be the one who's weakest, drank less blood..."

If I could pale, I would. Because that describes me to a T.

"And it will attack the female first, before killing every male after," Dominic adds. "As per Zalmoxis' decree. Until none of the House of Dracul are left."

"But... is there no way to talk to Zalmoxis?"

"No."

"And if we get the mates...our consorts... Then what?"

"That bit is yours to solve. I can't be giving all the answers, can I?" Another half-shrug. "Truth be told, we don't know. That requires getting into a god's mind, and none of us have that power."

I shake my head. "This is insane."

"But it's the truth." Dominic points to the notebook. "I'm not just pulling it out of my ass."

"I'm going to have the hardest time making my siblings believe me."

Dom pushes the notebook towards me. "Then take this with you. Use it as proof."

"Or, you could come and tell them."

He laughs. "I'll leave that task to you. I've got plenty here to keep me busy."

I'm left in a daze after everything he reveals. And as I stare at the notebook, flip through the pages, recognize my father's writing, I feel the oddest sensation running through me. I don't realize what it is until tears fall freely down my cheeks.

I miss him.

I miss Vlad Țepeș—Father, the ruthless warrior, the controlling sire—and wish to hell and back he was here to tell me what to do with this information. Because try as I might, I've got no damn clue.

Chapter 15

Violeta

In a daze, I eventually leave Dominic's house and make my way to the guest area—the house we were sleeping in. I nearly collide with Marcus, who's rushing out.

"There you are." He grasps my shoulders, squeezing them. "I thought something happened." He takes a closer look at my expression and must notice something because he frowns. "What's wrong?"

I shake my head, biting the inside of my cheek to keep from crying, or screaming, or both.

I don't know what to do with the information I've been given. Yes,

I need to go home and explain it all to my siblings, but beyond that. Consorts? *Vampiri*, with consorts? None of it makes any sense.

And Zalmoxis... I used to think we were the apex predator, even among the supernatural world. Now, I find out there's so much more out there. Things we have no control over, but that control us. A god's fancy is the cause for all this... How are we even supposed to fight a god?

Because I know my siblings, and they won't take this lying down. We've been independent for so long, the last thing they'll want is commitment, especially to something as forever-sounding as mates.

And worst of all, I can't tell any of it to Marcus. Because doing so would mean admitting everything else I've lied about. Including my lineage.

"I...nothing."

He frowns, his grip tightening on my shoulders enough to stop me from moving. "It's obviously something. Is it the wolves? Did they say something?"

"In a way, yeah. It's about my disease, but I don't... I don't want to talk about it. Not just yet, anyway. Will you allow me that? Please?"

He opens his mouth as if to dispute it. I can see the conflict on his expression, and the confusion. A few nights ago, I'd opened up to him easily. But no matter how much I may want to now, as well, it simply won't happen.

When I say nothing, Marcus nods. "Whatever you need."

In silence, he ushers me back inside the house and closes the door behind me. I take off my shoes and curl back under the bedsheets, slipping the notebook Dominic had given me into my bag. I feel the bed dip as Marcus joins me, wrapping his arms around me and pulling me to his chest.

But the only thing I can do is cry, and wonder how the hell I can avoid losing him, if I tell him the truth.

I wake up to noises outside the guest house again. Only this time, Marcus isn't in bed with me. It takes me a groggy moment to gather my bearings. It's not weakness, not in the sense of the disease—curse, it's a fucking curse cast by a divinity not a disease!—has caused in the past. More of a slushiness like I'm filled with too much of a good thing.

After a beat, my brain kicks in and I focus on the voices outside, recognizing Marcus' immediately.

"You must've told her *something* because she came back crushed."

"What I discussed with her is between her and me only, unless she chooses to share it with you."

Dominic. Shit. Marcus must've sought him out after I crashed. A beat of relief rushes through me that Dominic's willing to keep my secret still, though he evidently doesn't agree with it.

"So butt out." Dominic's words are final, and I cringe, already getting out of bed.

There's a scuffle, and I take that as my cue to rush out of the house and come between them—in the nick of time. Last thing I need on my hands is an interspecies incident.

I press my hand to Marcus' chest, meeting his eyes. "Please. You shouldn't be fighting him."

His expression is harsh, jaw clenched and eyes glaring at Dominic, fists ready to strike. It reminds me of that human in the woods, who he'd been willing to kill so easily for me. What have I done to him, other than complicate his life these last weeks?

Maybe Dominic is right. Maybe I should tell him once and for all and get it over with. He'll hate me, but at least he'll be safe away from me.

Marcus softens almost instantly when he turns to me, though his body is just as rigid. "I'm sorry. It's not that I'm trying to intrude on something you don't want to share, but I'm worried."

"I get it." I take a deep breath. "How about we pack up and go back to your place?"

"You don't have to," Dominic says behind me, causing Marcus to scowl at him. "You're welcome to stay here as long as you wish. You must have many more questions."

I face him with a weak smile. "Thanks, but we both know it's time I leave and deal with everything you've told me. And while your hospitality is great, truth be told I've got a clan of vampiri tracking me. Last thing I want is to bring those problems at your doorstep while you're settling in."

He opens his mouth as if to add something, but only nods. "Offer still stands. Wouldn't be the first time we fought off a couple vamps."

"Mulţumesc. I truly can't thank you enough for everything you revealed."

With one last glare to Marcus, Dominic turns and leaves.

My words have only caused Marcus to be more curious, more intrigued. His eyes follow me as I let go of him and step back, already withdrawing in my own mind, trying to find a way to tell him something, *any* part of all this, to ease his worries.

"Are you sure, Violeta? If we need to stay longer, if you need more information for the cure—"

I bite back the bitter laugh threatening to escape me. I have more than enough information, I just don't know what to do with it.

"I'm sure. Let's go."

We pack our meagre belongings and leave after I say goodbye to Lucrezia. It's only as we leave that it hits me I didn't ask about the strike of lightning from the first time I'd seen her... but that's a question for another day.

I focus on rushing through the trees, the bag on my shoulder heavier than before. At least my forces are replenished. Now that I know why, I'm unsure how to process it. I need my siblings—but Nico, the one I'd go to, is away on vacation. I already interrupted him once, can I really do it again? And how would I even go about explaining everything I've just learned, when I'm having a hard time believing it myself?

Marcus notices my newfound strength and comes up to my side. "Feeling better?"

"Da."

He frowns at my curt reply and drops back. Tears sting my eyes again. If he's my consort, I'm doing a shit job of being a good consort to him, that's for sure.

I don't get a chance to redeem myself. Because as we go by a ravine, I catch movement out of the corner of my eye.

"Marcus, watch out!"

I come to a full stop, digging my heels in the earth for grounding, and face the squad of vampiri in a crouch, hissing. I take out the first one before he can attack, and Marcus is right there, protecting my back.

Somehow, he grabs hold of one of the vampiri's knives, and then he's dancing. All I see in my periphery is him slashing, ducking, evading vampiri. Cracks of bones and agonized screams fill the air.

I tear off one attacker's throat then blindly look around, searching for Marcus, and find him fighting three others. Even when they seem to make contact, he has no reaction, almost as if he feels no pain. He's a complete, utter machine, in his element like I've never seen him.

And he takes my breath away.

A whoosh of air behind me warns of an incoming hit, and I duck someone's sword. *Since when the hell do they bring swords to a hand-to-hand fight?* I grip the vampir's wrist and twist it, breaking it.

She gasps, but I'm already tossing her over my head, and facing the next one. For long moments, I get lost in the fight, trusting Marcus to be able to protect himself.

But then I don't pay attention for one stupid moment, and it's one moment too many.

A vampir grabs Marcus and levels a stake at his heart. I freeze.

"There, that's better, Majesty. Let's have a nice and quiet chat, shall we?"

I don't hear the rest of his words. I only focus on the one meant to doom me—Majesty. When I meet Marcus' gaze, I see the emotions playing out. Confusion, stupefaction, then anger. He already had all the pieces, it's no wonder he connected the dots so fast. I sense it with more than my eyes. It's in my boiling blood, in the ache in my heart, and the air I'm drawing in that suddenly feels stifling.

Then Marcus moves, a flurry of quick, precise actions that decapitates the vampir who'd held him, before launching himself on the rest. During our last attack, he'd been weakened by me feeding on him, and I didn't get to see his full rage. Now, it's all there—the ruthless soldier, taking out his emotions on someone else.

"Marcus!"

He doesn't react to my callout, and vampiri are already heading for me. I settle back in a crouch, then attack before they get a chance to. I pull one to me, crack his neck, then rip the entire head off his body. Next, I move to the two on the side, grab their stakes and drive them into their hearts—they collapse.

Their blood surrounds me, enough to call out to me. The damn bloodlust sings in me, stronger than a siren's song.

I slam a vampir against a tree, and this time sink my fangs into his neck, drawing in just enough to keep me going.

When I release him, my eyes land on Marcus again.

Like a god on a rampage, he clears every vampir down to the last one, in a perfect dance of death I can only watch, mesmerized and immobilized. And then he turns to me. Blood soaks his shirt and is spattered on his cheeks. His green eyes are blazing.

Without a word, he walks to where I'd dropped my bag and opens it. Rifles through it... And then picks up the notebook with the House of Dracul crest.

A muscle ticks in his jaw.

Slowly, unbearingly so, he drops it back in the bag, and tosses the whole thing at my feet.

His scorching gaze finally meets mine. And in it, all I read is condemnation.

Marcus

Majesty. She's a fucking royal. That's why she's been so secretive, that's why she's been hiding from me. And playing me like a fucking fiddle.

My stomach roils when I think of all that we did, of the many ways I worshipped her, of how I've been *caring* for her. Enough so that I started entertaining the stupid notion of consorts. What it would feel like, be like, to have her by my side forever. To continue to care for her. To love her.

I idiotically believed in the fairytale the wolf was selling. It's why I was so worried for her, why I couldn't wrap my head around her sudden withdrawal. And now it hits me. Dominic's need to talk to her alone, to give her information she held... *He knew*.

Even earlier, he wouldn't give me information, but *he knew*. I don't know how, or whether there's more of a history between them than Violeta revealed, but the point is I've been fucking lied to, over and over and over again.

Because everything you're saying is part of the world we live in, and I need to understand where you're coming from. Her words, when we'd talked about my past. Her insistency that the royals had done nothing wrong.

Here I was, worrying that she was dying faster, that I would lose her, the light in my empty life. And all along, I was a useful pawn. It *hurts*. My chest aches with something I can only describe as consuming. My throat feels ashy, recalling everything I'd told her. Everything I believed from her lips.

Well, more fool me.

Violeta takes a step back as I advance once, twice, and then I'm on her. My hand is on her throat, clenching, same as I just pulled off those vampiri's heads. It was so easy, with them. Let the anger take me over, release the frustration onto those who would do me harm.

But with her... I can't make myself carry it out. And at the back of my mind, I know she's more powerful, that she could easily throw me off. Royals are the crème de la crème, the upper echelon of our society. The psychos who've started wars and used vampiri like me to accomplish their deeds. To carry out all the killings so they wouldn't have to get their precious hands dirty.

I know she has the power to shove me off her. Whether this disease of hers was a lie or not, she has shown time and time again that she is more than capable of taking care of herself.

So why isn't she pushing me off? Why isn't she doing to me what she's done to the rest of them?

Instead, she lets me hold her. She watches me even as my fingers tighten on her throat, her eyes filled with tears. *Fake* tears. No way I believe any emotions coming from her now.

"A royal." I growl, moving closer, my face in hers, nose to nose. "You're a fucking *royal.* And you didn't think it proper to tell me?"

"Marcus, I—"

I clench my fingers just enough to stop her words, but she still pushes past the uncomfortable feeling.

"I meant to. I was going to, and then you told me about the wars, and I couldn't. I knew you'd hate me."

"Damn right!" I punch the tree above her head with my other hand, and bits of the bark fly around her. "You *lied* to me. How much is even true, out of everything you said? Hmm? *How much?*"

A single tear rolls down her cheek, followed by another, and another.

A part of me hurts at that. At the trembling of her lips, the wavering in her voice, the picture we've been reduced to. But a bigger part of me, an *angrier* part, is filled with loathing.

She shuts her eyes, and a half-sob escapes her. Fool that I am, it's enough to make me release her and step back. Violeta slides to the ground, looking at me with a tear-stained face. She makes no attempt to get up, to retaliate.

It doesn't fit my mental picture of the royals. None of this does. Not her tears, not her hunched over body, not the guilt in her eyes. I'd expected calm, cool and collected. Majestic. Snobbish and imperial. Not...this.

"I'm so sorry. You have no idea, Marcus."

"Don't. I want nothing to do with you, or with your lies, or with your so-called disease. For all I know, you lied about that, too."

"I didn't!"

"Well, I wouldn't know, would I?" I shake my head. "I thought I could trust you. Especially after all that bullshit with the mates. Or did you pay the wolves to say all that, to wrap me around your little finger that much more?"

"What! No!"

Her horrified expression could be real enough. Then again, it could be another trick. I've no way of knowing. This is not the woman I've been spending weeks with, it's a complete stranger. An enemy stranger. And while I may be unable to kill her, it doesn't mean I have to remain in her presence any longer.

Violeta scrambles to her feet, reaching for my hand. I yank it out of her way, but it doesn't stop her from trying again.

"I didn't lie about my disease. Or anything else. And I do care about you. And the wolves, I've only ever met them now!"

"You seemed pretty chummy with them."

"Only because they were friendly! And because their leader showed up at our castle, to let us know he was in the area."

Castle. Of course. While the rest of us live in poverty, they're living it large. Not even caring what happens in this world. Not even caring of the damage they've caused.

Then the rest of her words sink in and a snort escapes me. "So you *did* meet them before. See, you can't even help yourself from lying."

"No! I– Marcus, the *only* lie I've told you is about who I am. I swear it. Everything else was real."

"How am I supposed to take that for fact, hmm? When you've lied so much, changed your story so many times? From the moment you stepped into my life, all you've done is lie, and lie again. And then you *omitted*. As if that's any better."

"Some of it was to protect you!"

"Protect me!" I snarl, clenching my fists so I don't wrap my fingers around her throat again. "Is that why you bullshitted me about whatever it is Kalla told you?" My eyes narrow on her. "Was that a play, too? Atop Poenari Fortress, when I thought you'd take your own life?"

Another sob leaves her, this one more gut-wrenching. "I swear it wasn't a play. It was all real. Kalla told me about the bloodlust, I didn't lie about that and about the fear coursing through me. She also told me Father—Țepeș—that his death wasn't just by his own hand. She said rumors were flying in the area of our return, and that vampiri were mobilizing against us. That's what I didn't tell you!"

I shake my head, sneering. "Poor you. That's the least you deserve after all the shit you pulled."

She only stares at me in horror, as if my words were the least she'd expected. More tears bathe her face, and *why the fuck do I feel guilty seeing them?*

A bitter laugh escapes me. "You really have been playing me, Vi. Well, congratulations. But that's all over now. I want nothing to do with you or with your kind."

"Marcus, please! Listen to me. Just once."

"No. I'm done listening to your poisoned lies. You can damn well fuck off."

Without waiting for more, I take off. Running through the trees, letting their branches beat at my face, trying to ignore the pain in my chest. If I'd had a beating heart left, it would be utterly destroyed by now.

I enter my house, hating how the first thing I smell is her scent. I stomp to the bedsheets and tear them off the bed, tossing them into the fire. Acrid smoke fills the room. Good. At least it'll wash off her smell.

Memories assail my senses as I go on a rampage to destroy every trace of her presence here. Memories of her waking up the first time here. Of making me hot chocolate. Of pretending to be human, only for both of us to find out neither one is.

Her hesitation to tell me what Kalla had said—now I know why. It would've given me information about her real identity. And her delays with finding the wolves, after we had all the information—also because Dominic could've given her away.

I've been such a fool.

And I can continue berating myself for all eternity, but for now, it's time to erase every trace of Violeta Dracul from my life.

Chapter 16

Violeta

"Marcus, wait!"

No, no, no! Dammit, this isn't how he was supposed to find out.

He ignores me, only a blur ahead of me as he heads back home. He must be heading there, after all there's nowhere else he'd feel safe, I would think? Maybe I'm wrong. I don't know him that well, surely. And what the wolves said, I can't let that get to me.

Vampiri don't have mates.

Royals don't have mates.

I ignore the pang in my chest. There's no heart there, it makes no sense I would feel this phantom pain. But no amount of rationalization will stop me from rushing after him, stumbling. Fighting those vampiri took more out of me than I'd like to admit. Or is it the fact that seeing his hate was more of a blow than I'd expected?

I know nothing about consorts other than what Father deigned to say. And Dominic and Lucrezia seem pretty close together. If Marcus and I... If he's my consort... Is it possible his rejection could hurt this much?

If Dominic is right and I do have a mate—consort—Marcus would be it. No one else has come close to making me feel what I feel for him, and I've been around long enough to know that no one else will.

I keep rushing through trees in bursts, only stopping when I'm back at the cabin. I drop my bag at the entrance and knock on his door. And when he doesn't answer, I storm inside. "Marcus!"

He turns from the sink, his knuckles white, features drawn. "What do you want?"

This isn't the man I slept with. It's not even the man who took me in, caring for me. This is the soldier, the hardened criminal, the one who doesn't care. The pain of centuries is etched on his features, a pain that, once again, reverberates in my very bones.

It's the agony of all the innocent lives he'd taken on orders from us—or that he thinks were orders from us. The raw anger at having been a puppet shines in his eyes, along with the disdain for all the lies I've told him.

"Marcus..."

"Leave."

I shake my head, taking a step towards him. Then he's there, grabbing my arms, slamming me into the door.

"I said—*leave*."

"No." I meet his eyes, reaching for his cheeks, but he lets me go and moves backwards. He doesn't want my touch—that realization stings. Too much.

I know I have to get through to him. The pain in my chest only becomes heavier. I've only ever had my siblings, my family, and myself. And since I met Marcus, he's been something else. Something I never would've thought I'd reach. A utopia of love.

And now I've lost it.

My own fault. Lying to him. I shouldn't have done it. I knew it would bite me in the ass. I should've come clean a long, long time ago.

But how was I supposed to tell the man I fell for, that I was part of the reason for his hurt, for everything that went wrong in his existence, for… argh.

"Marcus, please."

"I don't want to hear it." He points to the door. "Leave."

"No!" I advance on him, shoving him into the counter. It cracks behind him, but I pay it no mind. "Hear me out, at least."

His gaze is lost when it lands on mine. There's a chaos to his behavior, something I'm unused to in someone so versed in control. "You—do you have any idea—" He shakes his head, holding on to the counter with white knuckles. "I don't want to talk to you."

"Too bad. Because I'm not going anywhere."

"You don't deserve to be here."

Ouch. That stings even more, but I try to steel myself against it.

"You don't understand. I had nothing to do with your wars, or anything else."

A bitter laugh escapes him. "Were you, or were you not, with House of Dracul in the last centuries?"

"I was but—"

"And did you live in castles? With pretty things? Surrounded by your precious family?"

"I—"

He snarls. "Then don't *fucking* tell me you know what's going on. Don't *fucking* pretend like you know any of this. Because you don't. At all. You..." He shakes his head, running a hand over his face. "You're everything I've always hated. And I *bedded* you."

I move my hand to my chest, rubbing it in hopes to take away some of the ache. The memory of our limbs entangled is something I don't want tainted, least of all by his bitterness.

"Marcus, I didn't know of your suffering! And worse, I don't think it's true." At his scowl, I try to backtrack. "I don't mean it like that. I do believe you, but—"

He snorts. "What, there's another side of the story? Something that justifies what the House of Dracul did? Don't make me laugh. There is *nothing* that could justify the hell you people have put me, and others like me, through."

"I'm not saying there is, but all I'm saying is the signature you saw was fake!"

He frowns, trying to see where I'm going with it. Then his confusion clears. "And I suppose your proof of that is gone?"

"No. Not gone. It's just..." I take a step closer, wanting to hold him, wanting to bridge this distance between us, but unable to. "Marcus, the House of Dracul isn't the evil spawn you think it is. We're—"

Words fail me. How do I describe my siblings, how do I describe myself? How can I show him there's something redeemable about us, and that we're not the villains he's painted in his story?

"We're not what you picture," I end, weakly. I can't stand his cold gaze. Not when those same eyes have warmed with heat, with desire, with love and admiration for me. With care.

"No, of course not," he says. "You're much, much worse." He moves closer, finally closing the distance between us. "Because you're the monsters nightmares are made of."

Marcus

Violeta physically jerks back at my words, putting more distance between us. It's just as well. I can't deal with this. With her, in my house, her scent, her presence, her body nearby. When I've had her, bedded her, and now she's... she's.... exactly the worst of my nightmares.

I turn away, forcing myself to care less. "I can't. I can't look at you, or talk to you. Please leave."

"Marcus, *please!*"

It strikes me, at the worst possible moment, that she's my princess. My sole existence in this world is at her mercy. I may not belong to a clan or to an army any longer, but I do still serve her. And if she wanted to, she could technically be able to *make* me listen to her. Royal glamour is powerful, taking over anyone's mind—including older vampiri like me. Yet she hasn't done any of that.

Or, has she?

I whirl on her, jabbing a finger in her chest. "The human, in that cabin. When he died. You did something to me, didn't you? You compelled me, as royals are allowed to?"

Regret flashes across her expression. "I did, but I had to, Marcus!"

I'm thankful for the counter behind me as it takes my weight when I sag against it. I'd been thinking of ways to express my care for her, and meanwhile she was lying to me about what happened. Because she'd taken away my free will—after I'd told her how important it was to me—and reduced me to a puppet.

"You're no better than my old masters," I hiss.

"Marcus, please," she says on a sob. "I *had* to. You were going to kill that man, *for me*. I knew how much killing for others had cut at you and—"

"You know nothing! Not. A. Fucking. Thing. You haven't been around to witness the shit that's been happening. You've been too busy taking care of yourselves." I run a hand over my face. "I'm such a goddamned idiot."

"Marcus... It was for your own good. I felt sick glamouring you, but it had to be done so you wouldn't kill for me."

"Sure, that's why you did it. You removed my free will because you simply had to. And there were no selfish motives involved, hmm?"

She says nothing, and that's answer enough.

"I'm sure most dictatorial humans had the same reasoning," I shoot at her.

She scowls. Seeing her as something less than the simpering idiot she's been since I clued in is almost satisfying. Almost. I want her undone and gutted over this as much as I am.

"If I'd wanted to, I could have done it over and over again. Made you do things you would hate yourself for."

"I already do!"

She doesn't take the bait this time, and instead continues, "But I didn't. I only compelled you that one time, not before, not since. I swear it on my siblings' lives. And I've made sure such a thing can't be used against you again!"

Doesn't matter. Doesn't mean she's any better than the rest of them. Just that she's better at hiding it.

"I was turned by Vlad—Father—in the 15th century," she says. "Right after Nico. I didn't lie about him being my brother."

I try to block out her words, but part of me wants to hear it. Needs to. I need to know why she lied to me, why she pretended all along. Why the fuck I opened my heart to her, when I should've known better.

"I... We were rogue, sure, but we were trained by him. He explained our roles. That we were to keep the vampir world from shattering on itself."

"Great job you did at that."

She ignores me, instead waving a hand towards me. "I didn't know about you. About the soldiers. But I can promise you, we didn't ask people to give up their lives for us."

"No? So, what, my sacrifice was in vain?"

"No!" She seems horrified. "That's not what I'm saying. All I mean is what you were saying, about the letters and the orders, we never sent those."

"So you've said. But I've *lived* through that. I saw the seal with my own eyes."

"Seals can be forged!" She stomps her foot in frustration. "And someone is lying, most probably your clan."

"I don't belong to any clan."

"But you did, not that long ago. And every clan has a leader. And those leaders hate us."

"Because all you've done is rule us in complete selfishness and start wars that make life harder for regular vampiri."

She's shaking her head before I'm even done speaking. "Nu. It's because we're more than they could ever be. And because a god's influencing them to rise up against us, to destroy Father's legacy."

"A god?" I snort. "I thought I said to stop with your lies."

"I'm not lying… Please." She closes her eyes, then opens them again. Those brilliant blues land on me. "I swear I'm not. This disease of mine isn't a disease, it's a curse thrust upon Father's lineage by the same god."

"I'm never going to believe this shit, so you might as well move on to whatever your next point is. And hurry the fuck up, I don't have all day."

She stares at me, and something like pain crosses her expression. She doesn't try to shield it, but it hurts me to see it. I look away.

"Believe what you will, Marcus," she says in the end. "But the vampiri clan leaders have always had it in for us, because we represent a time of the past."

"Yes. Of slavery."

"No. Of guidance!"

I shake my head. I've heard the spiel before. That having masters is better than being on my own. Not knowing where I'm going. Being without purpose. Being without a life. Being…lost. It was what attracted me to the army in the first place. I finally belonged. I had a purpose. And I wasn't alone. Until I was…

"Some guidance. You ran off and cowered away at the first hint of danger."

"Marcus, you don't understand. We didn't leave without a reason! My father forced us to. He was losing his mind, and the only way we could get him to stay with us was to go with him. We told him someone needed to remain behind and keep things on track, but he refused to listen. We had no choice. Please...look at me. See that I'm not lying. There's so much more to this story, if only you'd let me tell it."

I avoid looking at her. The pleading in her voice is enough to undo me. I have to actively remind myself that royals have the power to compel us all, and regardless of Violeta's reasons, she's already done it to me. And she can do it again, deciding with a tilt of her head what's on and what's not in my head. And I can't allow her to do that. Whether she lied or not about it before, now's my chance to stand my ground. And it's the only thing I have left.

I face her briefly. "No." My tone is firm, even as I clench my fists to avoid reaching for her. "I've heard all that you wanted to tell me. I need you to leave."

Violeta stands, staring at me. Her eyes are dulled by emotions. Her lower lip is trembling. Her body— I avert my gaze.

"*Leave.*"

I can't think with her around. I can't breathe with her around.

For so long, I've cared for no one. And now I've come to care for someone who is part of the same family that's been my undoing, for all my existence. The same people who are just as responsible for the blood on my hands as I am. The two sides can't live together. Can't cohabitate.

Leave. Please leave. Please.

Silence only answers me, then a gust of wind. When I glance at the spot she'd been in, she's gone. And I don't... I don't know what to think.

I know what I've seen. I know what I've been made to do. But is it possible there's another explanation? No. Every fiber of my being denies it. Every fiber demands the truth, which is not what she just told me.

It can't be. She's a royal, born and bred to lie. To deceive. And I'm probably her crowning glory at this stage. I was there when she was weak, and she's been able to twist me and wrap me around her little finger in ways I never have been. Part of me wonders if that was compelled, too, but I push aside the notion.

Despite everything else Violeta has done, compelling me to have sex with her was unnecessary, given I already wanted it. Desperately. And still do.

"Damn her and her entire family!" The curse leaves my lips harshly.

I glance out the window. At Violeta's tracks in the snow. Dmitri's vampiri will follow her soon. They'll want her. They'll want vengeance over what happened, I have no doubt about it.

And I should be there.

I want to be there.

To protect her, or to destroy her? I want to say the latter. That I want to see her blood spilled, her head decapitated, and live in the knowledge that I've had my vengeance. But there are too many doubts, too many conflicting emotions. And that's not the full truth. Because, it's not to destroy her that I want to be there. It's to protect her.

The realization is even more jarring than knowing Violeta's history. It makes me angry at myself, at my inner desires. I shouldn't want to. I shouldn't... I should be in complete aversion about her. And her family. And everything they represent.

I've just heard more than I needed to in order to make up my mind about them. And I should be hating them. Hating *her*.

So why am I not?

They've sent tons of us into wars. They've made us do their

bidding. They've stripped us of identity and purpose, and molded us to fit their needs. In short, they made us their puppets.

So how can I, *still*, care for this vampir? Especially given her lineage?

None of it makes sense. None at all.

I could blame it on the shock of learning it all. Or on the stupid mate bullshit the wolves told us. Or better yet, I could blame it on Violeta and her compelling ways. But no matter which way I throw the blame out, the truth is there, plain for me to recognize.

I've come to care for her. For the way she laughs, the way she moans, the way she feels in my arms. The way she fights like a Valkyrie, all vengeful and goddess-like. The way she tries to be the better part of herself. There are so many facets, all now split up by the lies she's told me. But they are nonetheless facets of Violeta's that I've come to love.

And it'll take more than a day for me to get over that stupid impulse.

For the first time in my existence, or at least the first time in a few hundred years, I do what I haven't done and open the cupboards in my kitchen until I land on some old, old liquor. I take the cap off. The smell of alcohol makes me cough.

I'm a vampir. Hangovers aren't part of who I am, nor do they remotely work the way I expect them to. But still, the drink burns down my throat, making me cough. And forget. And forget some more.

Chapter 17

Marcus

A shrill ring brings me back from the fog. I stumble around in my cabin, trying to see where the noise is coming from. It's a cellphone—mine. I barely use the damn thing. The last time I remember seeing it in use was when Violeta had called her brother.

I pick it up, staring at the unknown number dialing me. After a beat, I answer. A man's voice immediately blasts through.

"Vi? Where are you? You said you'd get back in touch but you haven't, and everyone at the castle realized you were gone. Tassa's phone been blowing up non-stop, so we're heading back. *Where the hell are you*?"

My fingers tremble on the phone, and a plastic creak warns me before it sizzles in my hand. I toss it to a corner, it hits some dishes, and the whole pile explodes. Something like a grunt escapes me, soon turning into a roar of rage.

Is that her brother, or her lover? Or both? After centuries spent together, who's to say they didn't develop some messed up relationship?

I've heard the caring in her voice, now it's there in his. And it may just be my mind playing tricks, but what else am I supposed to think? There have been rumors around for centuries that the royals inbreed. For all I know, they could be true.

My mind unwillingly goes to such images—her, in the arms of another—and bile rises in my throat. I haven't felt the urge to hunt, to *hurt* in a long time, but now it's there, all too present. I need to release this coiled, raw anger inside me before it burns me up from the inside out.

What else has she lied about?

She said she cares for me, but all along she's only told me exactly what she needed to, to keep me playing to her tune. I've been her play toy, her puppet. The toy of a royal. One of the same ones who are guilty of my current state of mind and where my life has ended.

But I know there's more to my reaction than that.

It's not just that she lied.

It's what she lied about.

Because at the end of the day, the thought of Violeta in the hands of another... I don't want to feel a thing. Not right now. Not ever again. For the first time in forever I opened my heart, and it's only gotten stomped on.

Destroyed.

Betrayed.

Shattered.

I sense a trickle of something go down my arm and glance down. Blood is seeping from a wound—the plastic from the phone must've cut me. I don't bother licking it to heal it. Instead, I slide down to the ground and lean my head back against the cupboard.

Unwelcome thoughts continue to intrude. Of Violeta here, of her hands on me, of the time we'd spent together. Short as it was, it felt like it had been so much longer.

Because she's not just a royal, a voice whispers in my mind. *She's your mate—your consort. Your other half. The one meant for you and you alone.*

I muzzle that voice and shove it into a compartment of my mind I never visit. The same one I've shoved hope into.

Violeta Dracul is nothing to me. The sooner I get that through my mind and body, the better.

I take a deep breath and close my eyes, praying I never have to open them again.

Violeta

The first night, I don't go too far. It's like I'm tethered to Marcus by an invisible string, one I can't just snap in two. So I stick around, keeping far enough that he can't smell me. I sleep leaning against a tree trunk, and wake up weaker than before.

I don't know what I'd expected.

That maybe he'd get over his anger miraculously and come after me? Forgive me easily? Forget everything? Nu...What I expected was that love conquers all. When I knew all along it doesn't, because if it had, well, we wouldn't be here in the first place.

Of course, he doesn't come to find me.

Because he hates me.

The realization hits me well into the night. I've always been a slow processor of information, but this pain guts me, sending me to my knees. It's my own fault, I know it is. But it also hurts. And despite everything I've been taught about forming attachments, about how impossible it is for us, I know I can't just let this be...

He was meant for me, and me for him. That part feels even more truthful now, with it all coming together. Dominic hadn't been lying, and Father did omit things. Which means my disease is truly the work of a god's curse. And it won't stop nor reverse unless my consort and I end up together.

I close my eyes against the trunk, refusing to let more tears fall. Everything happens for a reason, meaning the best thing I can do for now is...let Marcus go.

When dawn pokes its rays on the horizon, I edge close to his cabin again. Everything is dark—he must be asleep. I think of him in bed, of his kindness, of his touch on me, and I hit my chest in the hopes of taking away some of the ache.

I stare at the lights in his cabin, remembering the good times we'd had there, the way he'd looked at me like I was his everything. I'll miss him. It's going to tear me apart, not being with him. But if it's what I have to do...then so be it.

Turning my back on it, I hoist my backpack on my shoulder and let my feet carry me through the woods.

I've run as far as I can from Marcus' house. Put as much distance between us as I could, though I know it won't be enough. Not by a long shot.

I can't erase what I've just done. I might've potentially been able to avoid it, if it hadn't been for my own stupidity. My own stubbornness. And for my own experiences that have shaped me into the person I am now. A betrayer. A destroyer. A liar.

Which is why I've ended up all alone. And losing strength once more, with no way to contact my siblings or ask for the help they'll readily offer.

I clasp my fist and bring it to my mouth, biting hard on it. And then I scream, and scream, and scream. Crows in the trees fly off. A hawk cries in the distance. And still I scream, and scream, and scream.

I scream my anger, my pain, my guilt, my agony, my heart breaking in two. Because I can't keep it inside, not if I'm to survive this.

And then, like a good little princess, I pull myself back together. After all, I've been taught to keep my shit together. And while I've screwed everything else up, I won't do that. If I'm on my own, then so be it.

What do I know, so far?

That my disease isn't random.

That my family isn't spot-free of guilt.

And more shit is going on than anyone knows.

And, da, somewhere in there I fell in love with a vampir I probably won't see ever again.

I have to focus on what I can affect, and right now, that's not Marcus.

Forget him. Just like any other. You can return to him later, if you get a chance to.

If I survive this.

But even if I don't have my consort, I have to tell my siblings everything about the curse. They need to know, because it affects us all. And while we're a backstabbing bunch that drives each other crazy, in this, I know they'll have my back.

So I force myself to walk. And keep walking. And with every painful step, with every dizzy spin of my head, I remind myself that I was strong before I met Marcus, and I will be strong again even with his rejection. For however long it lasts. Nico did it, Mirabela did it, there's no reason I can't.

Lost in my thoughts, I don't pay attention where I'm going. Which is how I walk smack into another scene of vampiri feeding.

Glazed pairs of eyes turn to me, blood dripping down the corners of their mouths.

"Ah, fuck."

Marcus

Returning to my life *before* her should be easy. Smooth. Transitionless.

Instead, it's anything but.

As if to drive this point home, by the second day my land is invaded once more by unwelcome visitors. Only this time, it's not vampiri. Rather, wolves.

I smell them first, then step around the house and watch with wariness as three approach. Dominic, if I recognize his fur correctly, and two others. One looks like a younger copy of him, but with a smut of red fur around his neck. *Must be his son.*

Once they're out of the woods, Dominic looks right and left, then shifts to human. The third wolf—a vrykolakas judging by the yellow eyes—drags a pair of jeans to him and he gets dressed.

A moment later, Dominic approaches me, running a hand through his hair. His gaze scans the area, as if seeking someone. I tense even before he speaks.

"Vi around here?"

"I didn't know you two were on such good terms."

He narrows his eyes on me. "What are you, jealous?"

An odd sort of anger runs through me. Not jealousy, not even close. More like I want to throttle him. Because he helped her hide her lie, and he gave her information I wasn't privy to. If there's a camp of me and her, Dominic's obviously on Violeta's side. And that doesn't endear him to me in the least.

"Not even close," I growl and step closer. "You must've had fun, laughing behind my back, huh?"

"What the fuck are you on about, man?" He glances around again, dismissing me. "Where's Violeta?' He moves past me, his shoulder purposefully bumping mine. "Hey, Vi! Come out here before I teach your vamp boytoy a lesson."

I snap, shoving him out of the way. Dominic jumps backwards and lands on his feet as sleek as a cat. His other two wolves growl and jump between us, but he *tsks* them away.

Then he glances between me and the house, sniffs the air, and bursts out laughing. "Oh, shit. I came at the wrong time, didn't I?"

His abrupt change of demeanor disarms me. "What?"

"You and Violeta. She finally told you who she is, didn't she? And took off to visit her family, tell them about Dracul's curse?"

"Dracul's… What the *fuck* are you on about, wolf?"

Dominic's expression falters again, and darkens. "All right, let's start from the beginning. 'cause obviously we're getting our wires crossed here or something. I came here to see Violeta. Is she, or isn't she, here?"

"She's not."

He takes note of my gritted tone and nods. "O-kay, then. And where can I find her?"

"Beats me."

Dominic's eyes narrow again. "I'm trying to play nice here, but you're making it fucking hard. Are you seriously telling me you let your mate leave here, angry and unprotected?"

"*She* has no right to be angry. Not after hiding everything from me!" I purposefully ignore the other bit about mates. As if I'll fall for that shit again.

He shakes his head. "Buddy—"

"I'm not your buddy. Keep your Americanizations at bay."

Dominic growls. "I'm Romanian first, dumbass. And you'd better watch your tone, I'm not exactly known for being diplomatic."

"You don't say?"

He pinches the bridge of his nose, muttering something. Out loud, he adds, "You're some kind of stupid, you know that?"

I clench my fists, moving forward. Growls from the other wolves warn me to stay away, but I'm not interested in paying attention. Right now, shoving my fist through Dominic's smug face sounds good, regardless of the consequences.

"Whatever her reason for hiding from you, maybe you contributed to that. Ever thought of it?" he adds.

I pause in my march onwards, fists still clenched. He has no right to speak to me this way, no right to intervene. It's not *his* consort this affects. And then I realize the trap I've fallen into, thinking of her exactly the way he wants me to.

"Yeah, I see you didn't. Well, maybe take a look in the mirror. And regardless of what horrible deed you think she did – she's your mate. A bond like that is incredibly rare to come upon. In vampiri, damn near impossible. Don't go fucking squandering it away for pride."

He stares me a moment later, then at my fists. A smirk curls his lips. "Not that long ago, I would've taken you up on your offer for a brawl. But I have other priorities." The smirk turns into a self-deprecating smile. "Damn. Guess I got some diplomacy trained in me, after all."

He whistles to his wolves and turns his back on me, then the moment after he's shifting back to wolf, disappearing into the woods once more. And leaving me with too many conflicting thoughts.

Chief among them is his mention of the consort bond, and it being rare.

It's true that until he'd mentioned it, in relation to me and Violeta, I'd never thought it possible. I've never even seen it, or heard of it through our kin. So yes, it must be as rare as he says it is.

But if that's so true, then shouldn't *both* consorts be treating it with respect? Or does the onus fall on one alone, while the other gets to do whatever? That doesn't seem fair.

At the back of my mind, a nagging little voice tells me I'm being spiteful. I ignore it, instead heading to the back to cut some more wood.

It's only as I pick up the axe that something else hits me. *What the fuck is Dracul's curse?*

Violeta

I shouldn't be fighting. The last thing I should be doing is going against my own kin, and leaving more dead bodies behind to alert Dmitri's crew to my being here. But if they're going to attack – fuck this.

I drop in a crouch, my eyes settled on them. When they move, I'm already there. My hands lash out, nails sharp as claws, tearing their skin off. It's taking the rest of my energy, but luckily there's a flesh supply of blood for me.

Howls. Growls. Blood. Guts.

I impale them, I pull out their guts, and still it doesn't satisfy this lust. It burns through me, demanding destruction and the complete annihilation of everyone around me. It's more than survival instinct, more powerful than anything I've felt before.

Nico used to talk about a rage inside him.

Now I know what he means.

But in complete contrast, my mind is a sea of calm. Utter, complete, calm. No chaos. No thoughts. Nothing but—bloodlust.

By the time I stand, the area around me is filled with bodies. Vampir bodies, sprawled about, tainting the snow with their blood. It's nothing short of a massacre, a disaster.

Fuck.

I grab one vampir who's closest to me and bend my head to his neck. My fangs come out, tearing his flesh. There's nothing sweet about this. I tear into the neck and the blood gushes out, warm and heady on my tongue. He must've fed recently. There's a faint flutter as he struggles, then he goes limp in my arms, and I drink my fill.

He's no match for me. I'm the master here, the ultimate conqueror, the ultimate predator, the ultimate survivor. The ultimate *ruler*.

For too long now, our power has been contested. And I've let my siblings make the choices around it, because I didn't want innocent humans caught in the midst of our wars. I also didn't want to lose any of my dysfunctional siblings, since they're all I have left.

But enough is enough.

Father trained us to never take any prisoners, and to always impose our will. He was great at that—the best. No matter what else he hid from me, I cannot turn around and hate him, because without him, I'd be nothing. Less than nothing.

He turned me, gave me a purpose. And somewhere, amid all this craziness, amid my fear of giving in to the bloodlust, I've forgotten that purpose. I've become a shadow of myself. It has taken this curse to coax out of me that which has been hidden for so long—my true nature.

I'm not meant to be some fragile princess in an ivory tower. I'm meant to be here, asserting my rule, and ensuring peace and quiet in the vampir world. We're *all* meant to be here, not cowering away in a castle that's seen better times.

I let go of the vampir, and his drained body falls on the snow, joining the others. For a brief moment, I close my eyes, breathing in deeply. Then I stand, rolling my shoulders. I feel pleasantly full, and the weakness that had threatened is gone once again.

How long will this work for, when the times in between my feedings are getting shorter and shorter? I can't say. But at least I won't be cowering away waiting for death to find me—which it will, now that Marcus has rejected me.

When I walk away, filled with blood both inside and out, I don't even bother cleaning up behind me.

Let them see what I did.

Let them know my rage.

And let's see if they'll come after me now...

Because when they do, it'll be my pleasure to deliver some of Father's best punishments.

I've never been a bloody one. But today, this battle, and too many things converged into one, have made me realize one thing. *Anyone* can be a savage if given half the chance.

Including a princess like me.

Chapter 18

Violeta

After the vampiri, I wander aimlessly through the woods. I sleep in a cave for the night, then move onwards. Recent events have me feeling calmer, more at peace with my nature, but also worried.

If I head straight back to the castle, will I then be leading Dmitri's troops to our doorstep? I'd much prefer keeping them here, acting as bait, and trying to reach my siblings instead to warn them so we can come up with an offense strategy.

The wolves... *I wonder if Dominic has a cellphone.* Such a simple thought, I wonder why I didn't think of it right after leaving Marcus. Resolving to find their encampment again the next day, I find a cave to sleep in for the night.

Growls outside greet me at the same time as dawn.

I creep out, ready to attack and defend myself. The vampiri shouldn't have tracked me down so easily, but who knows?

The moment I'm outside, I know I'm screwed. Royally. Because it's not vampiri I'm faced with, it's a pack of wolves. For a moment, I think it's Dom's wolves, but it's not. These are lankier, thinner, but there's a definitive un-animal glint in their eyes.

There's about ten of them in a semi-circle, blocking my way out of the cave. The head one takes a step forward and in the most fluid transformation I've ever seen, shifts to a woman. A *familiar* woman.

"Kalla?" Something like hope spreads through me. Could Marcus have sent her after all? "Thank the fates, I—"

When I try to step forward, a growl rises out of the wolves. A warning growl. I stare between them and Kalla, recalling with stark accuracy how my siblings always said I trust too easily.

And I have. Because she was Marcus' friend, I never stopped to think twice. Her warnings had all come true, so seeing her here, I immediately assumed she had come to warn me some more.

I should've known better. Muroni aren't known for being helpful.

"I see the truth dawns on you," she says.

"What truth?"

"That I am not here to help." She gives me a cool smile. "Nor will you fight us."

"Why not?"

"Because if you do, the muroni I have watching Marcus will decide they're done waiting for my orders and kill him."

Whatever calm I'd been trying to force within me evaporates at her words. *If not being with him is causing the curse to make me sick, what will him dying do to me?*

"He's your friend! How can you be so callous?"

A flicker of some emotion runs across her features. "Friends do not supersede duty."

"Funny. I learned the opposite is true."

A shoulder lifts in a shrug. "To each their own. Now stop wasting time and come with me."

I survey the wolves again. It's still amazing to me that one of our kind can actually turn shapes like this. And to think that we used to be able to do so as well. Now, the best I could summon—on a good day—is dark shadows.

"Where?" I finally ask.

Her eyes narrow on me. "You know where. I intend to sacrifice you to our god."

The ground feels wobbly under my feet, and I allow myself to lean against the cave wall. "Your...god?"

Centuries ago, I wouldn't have given a shit about gods. But since the curse Dominic mentioned is very much real, now the mention draws my attention at every turn.

"Da. The one who made it possible for us to achieve our current state." She purses her lips. "You may believe *your* line is the purest, but ours is so much more."

I shake my head. She's speaking, but her words make no sense. "I don't get it. What current state? You're a muroni. You have to live in caves, avoid sunlight, and every myth humans have about us is thanks to you. What, of that, is enviable?"

She smirks. "You forget that I can shapeshift and Darkness sees in me a friend."

I arch an eyebrow. "Huh. Didn't think that held such weight."

"That's because you no longer live in these times. You live in the past, and that has been your demise, as he has planned all along."

My bravado leaves me along with my breath. If it's sacrifice to a god she's aiming for, there's only one *he* she could be referring to.

"Zalmoxis?"

"Do not say his name!"

I grab her clawed fingers as she reaches for my throat, tossing her hand to the side. "And don't *you* touch me. Remember who it is you're facing off against. I am Violeta of House of Dracul, and I will not be bullied by a lesser being than I."

One moment she's there, the next I feel the cut of metal on my skin. I gasp, and Kalla's back to her original spot. But blood pools at my feet. I glance down—the witch slit my wrist. I bring it to my mouth and lick the wound closed, only to have the cut burn my tongue. Blood keeps pooling, and a familiar dizziness takes hold of me.

"W-what did you just...do?" My mouth feels pasty.

"A little trick of the trade to make sure you're not at your peak. Even I wouldn't be stupid enough to fight you then." She scowls at me. "Move. Or my wolves *will* attack your beloved."

I glance around them, already more weakened. If I fight them and lose, I'm screwed and so is Marcus. I won't have that be my legacy. So I'll follow them, if only momentarily.

Head held high, I move past her. "Show me the way, then."

I shouldn't be surprised. My first instinct did warn me Kalla's a crazy witch, but I chose to ignore it because Marcus had vouched for her. What a stupid, silly mistake. One I'll pay for with my life now, it seems. *On the bright side, I won't have to wonder how the curse will continue.*

The wolves speed through the trees, Kalla leading them and me trailing behind. "What will this sacrifice achieve, exactly?"

I know she can hear me. She chooses to ignore me. Which brings me to my taunts.

"Are you sure you're even doing this for the greater good?"

Nothing.

"Or is it more that just like any other vampir out there, you envy us for everything we have? It wouldn't be surprising, really. But if that's the case, we can give you money. You don't have to kidnap me."

Kalla whirls on me, and this time she doesn't hold back. She slams against me, her fingers going for my throat. My reflexes are half-assed, so I barely duck out of her way in time.

The second time, I don't. She cuts through the skin of my neck and watches the blood flow out of me. Leans in closer, takes a whiff and licks at it. Then she sighs in bliss as the wolves behind her whine.

This will only weaken me even further. Shit.

"You can fight me all you want," she hisses. "But before the moon is high tonight, you *will* be sacrificed to him. Your blood, your death, will ensure the fall of the House of Dracul. And your siblings with it."

"That's what it's all about, then? Speeding things along?"

I can't even muster the energy to tell her to fuck off. My body fills with such a mind-numbing energy, I know I'm beyond screwed. And alone.

We finally stop moving somewhere atop a mountain. Kalla signals the wolves to fan out, and she grabs my bleeding wrist to tug me along the way. There's another cave hidden behind a boulder, and we go inside. And then farther and farther in. She walks with purpose, as if she's been here a million times before.

And she probably has. We finally emerge out of a tunnel into a massive, circular room. Torches are set up everywhere and they burst with fire the moment we enter.

"What is this place?"

Kalla throws me a look, then walks to the middle of the chamber. Her tattered robe sways around her. Judging by the fact she's showing me her back, she's perfectly sure I won't be doing anything to harm her or escape.

A moment later, I figure out why.

Because when I try to move, I can't. My entire body is immobilized, and I'm only able to move my lips.

"What did you do to me?"

Kalla glances over her shoulder at me. I'm stunned to see her eyes are completely black now, no whiteness left. "Only a little spell."

"Vampiri can't do spells."

She laughs, muttering something I can't catch, and continues to her target in the middle of the chamber. More light appears around it, illuminating a massive effigy of what I'm guessing is Zalmoxis. All I can see of it is the massive torso, the long, shaggy hair and beard—similar to depictions of Zeus in Greek mythology, weirdly. But then, looking closer, it almost seems as if the hair is made of...snakes.

Kalla faces me again. Her voice carries easily over the distance. "Vampiri cannot do spells, you are correct. But I was a Dacian long before I was a vampir. And my master allowed me to keep those powers, in exchange for my eternal loyalty."

Dacians... Dominic had said they were warlocks who'd worshipped Zalmoxis. Fuck, fuck, fuckity fuck.

When she starts chanting, the vibrations in the earth really do start freaking me out. I can't deny the power here. But it's not coming from this puny vampir, no... it's already been here.

In an effort to stall, I ask, "You knew more about my disease, didn't you? You knew it was his curse on my bloodline."

"Da."

"Then why not tell me?"

She's on me with a knife, extending the slash from my wrist all the way up to my elbow before I can even move. "Because I wanted you exactly where you are. And I knew if I gave you enough rope to hang yourself, you would."

The minutes the knife touches my skin, I sway. Blood pours and I watch as it undulates, like snakes. "What's...happening?"

If I didn't know better, I'd say I'm drugged. But I can't be. Vampiri don't get drugged. Not in my family. But the way I can't move, I... crumple to the ground, unable to hold myself up.

"Don't worry," she says. "He's on his way."

And then the effigy doesn't seem made of stone anymore. It seems like it's moving. Like it's rising. Like...

There's a sudden movement, a rush of new bodies. I can't keep my eyes open to see them, but I hear them. Snarling. Biting. Fighting with the other wolves, with the muroni masquerading as such.

Who...

I don't have time to voice the thought, or even complete it in my head. Darkness pulls me under, just as I feel human hands picking me up.

But I don't slip into unconsciousness. Not right away, anyway. Instead, the oddest thing happens to my mind. I...fly. I can see mist and clouds everywhere I go, and woods underneath me. Then I lose altitude, sucked towards something at a faster, and faster rate, speeding through—until I hurtle into them.

And then I'm standing over a tree stump, putting up new blocks to chop. In my hand, there's an axe that weighs heavy. My muscles are strained, but I enjoy the burn. I *feel* the enjoyment, the satisfaction at cutting things up. With each swing of the axe onto a new piece of wood, with each splinter of it, I revel in the movement. In the control it gives me. In the sound of the metal slicing through, and the wood thumping on the ground.

Because it calms me down, cools the anger inside me, anger directed at someone who's hurt me. Who's made my heart bleed. Someone I feel for dearly, deeply, in a consuming sort of way I've never felt. The emotions scare me, but it's better not to feel them, better to focus on the axe and the wood and the slicing and the thumping. Nothing else. Just the coolness of the breeze on my face, in contrast to the anger boiling in my blood.

Then I turn sideways, and my vision changes. It's now encompassed by a cabin—one I'm all too familiar with.

And then it hits me. I'm in *Marcus'* head.

The realization is so jarring, it breaks the link—or whatever the hell that was—and I'm cast out into nothingness. Untethered, I fall into sweet oblivion.

Marcus

I'm busy cutting wood when I feel it. At first, it's an odd sensation, like the wind's been knocked out of me. It might concern me if I was human, but as a vampir? I don't need to breathe. I do it out of habit, because breaking the habit would make me stand out among humans otherwise.

But this odd sensation is unlike anything I've ever felt before. And then it gets worse, like my mind's in a confused mesh of something. Learning. Feeling. Analyzing.

Before I can catch on to all of that, the bone weariness hits me. My legs sway and the axe slips out of my hands, falling into the snow with a heavy thud.

"What the fu—"

Then my head starts. A pounding like nothing I've ever felt before, barreling into my mind, into my very brain. Everything else disappears except for that, and its intensity drives up a notch with each passing second. Is this punishment for all I've done? Punishment from somewhere high up above? I don't know. But it feels like it.

I cover my head and stumble back to the house, trying to avoid the light that's suddenly making everything worse. Once inside, I slam the door behind me, then slide to the ground, resting my head on my knees with a shaky breath.

What the fuck was that?

It takes me the better part of an hour to pull myself back together.

And for the longest part, all I want to do is ignore what just happened. But I can't. Because something tells me that what I felt, it wasn't mine to feel. I'm pretty sure it was Violeta's.

Which makes no sense. I don't want it to make sense. I want it to all go away, her included, so I can forget her and move on with my life.

I want anger to burst through me, to obliterate these thoughts and the feel of her in my head. I *need* anger, because crawling into bed and letting the sadness consume me would make me a wreck.

But Violeta's pain had been so intense. And now that I've felt it, it makes me wonder...

Dominic's words. About the consort bond, and allowing my consort to leave in anger. Me being too stubborn to listen. To give her a chance. The consort bond being rare among vampiri. Almost as if it's my duty to be there for her, no matter what.

I'd denied it from the beginning, but is there any way to continue doing so now? If I'm feeling her emotions, and my entire being acts as if it's missing its second half... I don't want to believe it. But I've also never been one to bury my head in the sand and ignore the signs.

Yet if Violeta is my consort, if that's a fact I have to accept—that this treacherous royal is the one fate had intended for me—it only makes her betrayal that much worse. Because she'd also been ignoring all the signs, and instead lying to me. Tainting a bond that's meant to be so pure, nothing can break it.

Unless she didn't lie about the hurt they've caused.

Violeta did seem intent that her family didn't do all the bad I thought they did. And I didn't listen. I didn't want to listen. I don't know what it is about feeling her pain that's making me want to listen, now when it might be too late.

Did Dmitri's vampiri catch up to her? Is that what's going on?

If they did, it's not my problem. Not my job to rescue her. Not my problem to fix. Not my...anything.

Except for the fact even my new bedsheets smell like her and I want nothing more than to lose myself in her still, that is.

Except for the fact that I'm pretty sure the goddamned wolf was right and she's meant for me.

Except for the fact I'm annoyingly unable to get her out of my mind, no matter how much I try to. And now I'm wondering about her safety.

Fuck.

Before I've even fully grasped the extent of what I'm doing, I've grabbed a hunting knife, my axe, and I'm out the door.

I have to reason with myself. I'm going to the vampiri, my old clan, to iron out some history. To find out if there's truth to what Violeta said. Because knowing said truth is in my best interest, and might put my mind at ease after everything I've done.

And if Violeta just happens to be there against her own will and I can rescue her, well, there's no harm in that. She'll go on her merry way, back to her siblings, and that'll be that. Doesn't mean I have to accept her back in my bed. All it means is I'll have peace of mind, finally.

Dominic implied that the consort bond means I should be protecting her. All my life I've been a dutiful soldier in the royals' army, so yes, technically I should be protecting her, even if it's from her own delusions. Once Dmitri confirms that what she said is a lie, I'll just take her and bring her back to her family, so they can figure out Dracul's curse—whatever the fuck that is—together and leave the rest of us alone, same as they've done for centuries on end.

So no, there's no harm at all.

I'll go, get my answers, and get out. Maybe even find out what the hell this Dracul curse is, so I can be prepared if it affects me in any way. Then I'll get back to my regular life, without feeling like I owe any obsolete princess anything.

If nothing else, the truth will put me at ease.

Unless, of course, I don't get the truth I'm after.

Chapter 19

Violeta

I jerk up, expecting to see that crazy witch around me pumping me for more blood. Instead, I'm alone in some kind of room. A quaint, clean room, with light from the waning moon shining through.

I get off the bed and to my feet, swaying a little. To be expected. I was already weak before Kalla, and now that all that blood is gone... My eyes fall on my bag, at the bottom of the bed. And a very familiar-looking carpet.

"Oh, you're awake."

Hang on. I know that musical voice, it's—

I turn my head, meeting blue eyes and red hair. "Lucrezia?"

She smiles, holding a tray of food and drinks towards me, including sweets. Something that smells wonderfully fresh and chocolatey. And a decanter of that blood again…

"Thought you might need to replenish your strength. Wasn't sure if it was a human-food type of situation or both, so I brought plenty for either."

"I… thank you."

She places the food on the small bed and gestures for me to have some, while she takes a seat on a chair.

I go for the chocolatey loaf first—it's cozonac. One of many favorite Romanian desserts, this one's especially popular around Easter and Christmas. I break apart the loaf, and am soon surrounded by a citrus-scented smell. The dough is twisted around a nutty filling, this one made with additional chocolate. Tender as all sinful things should be, it separates perfectly, and melts in my mouth.

Manners fly out the window as I practically inhale it, then gulp down the too hot tea and continue eating in mindless abandon until everything is gone. Then I gulp down two full glasses of the vrykolakas blood.

"Sorry," I say as I wipe my mouth. "I didn't realize…"

Lucrezia waves my apology away. "Don't even think about it. That's why I brought it over. How are you feeling?"

I shrug. "Better, I guess. But.. What happened?"

"Bad shit." Dominic steps in then, his hair a little shaggier than before, his jaw a lot more unshaven. He places a hand on Lucrezia's shoulder and smiles at her, before turning his gaze on me. "We smelled your blood, leaving a trail behind. Too many people were hunting you, we decided to investigate and landed on… I don't even know what the fuck that was. So, care to explain?"

Images of Kalla calling upon Zalmoxis batter me, and I shudder. "I'll try. Before you found us, Marcus had brought me to a muroni, a friend of his. He said she was different than his kind, that she could perhaps help me because she'd been around for a long time." I gulp. "I don't think he realized for how long, exactly. Nor did I. When I met her, all I saw was my preconceived notions about muroni, and didn't look past anything. If I had, maybe I wouldn't have been so blindsided."

I toy with the bedsheet, biting my lip. How many times did Father warn us not to underestimate anyone? How many times did he say to be careful? And I'd failed at all of that.

"What did she say to you?" Lucrezia asks.

"Um, she talked about the bloodlust in me. She talked about Father—Țepeș—and how his death hadn't been…" My eyes widen at the realization and I smack my palm against my forehead. "Goddamn, it was right there in front of me. She said Father's death hadn't been a simple thing, and then started talking about rumors the royals were back, and how I'd be hunted, and how I should stay away from Marcus." My eyes seek Dominic's. "She knew all along about the curse, and tried to keep us apart. When that didn't seem possible—presumably because she didn't witness our showdown—and she kept sensing my scent around his place, she decided to speed things along for her god."

"Her god?" Dominic's jaw twitches. "Please tell me it's not where my mind is going."

"It is. She said she was a Dacian long before she was a vampir, and then she found her way back to Zalmoxis through becoming a muroni." I shudder again. "What she did, in that cave, she shouldn't be able to… But she is." I sigh. "She forced me there saying Marcus would be attacked by her wolves otherwise."

It still hurts to say his name, but it hurts even more to think he might've had something to do with this. Would he have, in truth? I don't doubt he hates me right now, but there's goodness in him. I refuse to believe he would... It might make me a fool, but no. He wouldn't.

"What happened to Kalla?" I ask.

Dominic shrugs. "We killed most of her shifters. A few survived and took off. I didn't see the point in having my wolves hunt them down, but we've set up guards here just in case. As for the witch... She's gone."

I clench the bedsheets tighter. "Killed or...?"

"Vanished. Used magic. Sorry."

I shake my head. "Not your fault. Thank you for saving me."

Another shudder racks through my body and Lucrezia hands me a blanket. I take it, wrapping it around my shoulders, and burrow deep in its warmth. Despite the vrykolakas blood, my body is acting human. The blood I drink lasts less. Almost as if.... as if Marcus' rejection has sped things along. More and more, I'm losing my grip, and I'm worried what it'll do to me.

Maybe, just maybe, it's time for me to accept my fate. That death is at my door, and it'll eventually end this cursed immortality, and free me.

Lucrezia clears her throat. "And Marcus, he's..."

Tears fill my eyes. "Gone."

Dom nods. "He found out you were lying to him."

"Dom!" Lucrezia elbows him in the gut.

"Draga mea, you can elbow me all you want. But Violeta knows I'm right because I warned her."

"Da, you did." A sigh escapes me. "And you were right. It was worse than it could've been—maybe—if I'd told him the truth from the beginning."

"No point thinking on the past," he says. "And for what it's worth, your mate's surviving. I saw him the other day."

I cringe. "And?"

"He was angry, understandably. But he'll get over it."

I shake my head. "Not so sure about that, Dominic. I've seen his rage, I've felt it. It's... He has every right to it."

Lucrezia leans forward. "You can try talking to him."

"No, not now. I... He needs space. And I have to reach my siblings, warn them that rumors are spreading of our presence, and warn them of the hunters."

"I can get a wolf to them," Dominic says and hands me a notebook. "They'll be there by nightfall. Write them a note, and I'll make sure it's delivered."

More tears hit the back of my eyes. "Thank you. I don't know how to repay your kindness."

"Start by not dragging us into your feuds," Dominic says, ignoring an exasperated look from Lucrezia. "That'll be enough."

"What do you plan on doing now?" Lucrezia asks.

"I'm not sure. Make my way slowly back home? I'd left because I wanted to experience things, to live life before I died but... I dare say I have. All I want now is to be back with my siblings and enjoy whatever time I have left with them."

Lucrezia shares a look with her mate, then smiles at me. "Stay here then, for a bit. Have a breather, and then we can help you get back home."

I glance at the notebook. It would be easy, to write the letter, then relax here. After all, what's the harm?

I shake my head, amazed at their kindness. Definitely a family here. One that stands united, despite their differences. I suppose in some ways, so do we, but...differently.

And in the end, what do I have to lose? It's my life at risk here, not my siblings'. Well, not yet. I doubt the curse has hit any of them yet, and another day won't change anything. Besides, it wouldn't do to repay kindness by sending them in Alex's direction.

"Thank you. I think I'd like to take you up on your offer."

Marcus

What is it with clan leaders and manors?

When I'd been in the army, working for various masters, the strongholds we'd visited were always manors, old Victorian villas, or smaller castles. It seems to be a disease of the hierarchy that they always want something so ostentatious.

The thought of disease swims in my mind unwelcomingly, reminding me once more of Violeta. I shove it away and instead make my way to Dmitri's gates.

Made of thick, black metal, they block the way to the old manor beyond them, ending on spikes. Dangerous-looking, one could say. In the distance, the manor doesn't look any more welcoming. Thin windows bathed in darkness, dark brick layout, and what I know will be acres and acres of land beyond it. Some are filled with cellars underneath which Dmitri loves using as prisons, and others are storage space for their weapons.

But from out here? Looks like a perfectly normal—albeit dark—human abode.

As I near the gates, two vampiri appear out of nowhere dressed in black suits. Similar to the ones who'd sought me back home, the brooches on their left breast pocket indicate their allegiance to Dmitri.

"What is your business here?" one asks.

They're new, these two. And dangerously so. The younger ones always have that arrogance coupled with the fact they're now immortal.

"I request an audience with Dmitri Ardelean."

One of the guards scoffs. "Just like that? Go through proper channels, buddy."

I take a step closer to the gates, wrapping my hands around the metal bars and scowling.

"Da, just like that. Tell him Marcus is here. He'll see me."

The same vampir scoffs but his companion, uneasy, decides to follow my orders and disappears.

A moment later he's back, his expression wary. "Dmitri will see you now."

Some of the bravado escapes the other one's features. They open the gates and I pass through. With a smirk, I walk beyond them and head into the area I know well.

Tall ceilings, sunny-filled rooms on one side, darkness-coated on the other. The carpet is velvet-smooth, and brand new by the looks of it. *Money must be good.* Unsurprising, really, given from the tabs I've managed to keep, Dmitri has continued his father's shady dealings.

Everything in here screams of opulence, of luxury. Violeta would be right at home, I'd imagine.

I try to push thoughts of her to the back of my mind, if only so I can focus on this task without losing my shit. Tough as it is, there are other things that draw my attention. Like the fact I'm walking these walls as a free man, instead of glamoured or otherwise forced into serving the Ardelean clan.

Let's not get too cocky. In, get the info, then get the fuck out before he gets any ideas.

When I finally find him, Dmitri is seated behind a mahogany desk. He's the epitome of our Roman ancestry, with his dark olive skin, equally dark hair and eyes, and aquiline nose.

"Ah, Marcus. A pleasure seeing you again."

I sit in the armchair opposite him, not waiting for him to invite me. Old habits die hard.

"What brings you here?"

Despite all the shit he's done—constantly sent his men on my land, tried to ruin my reputation—here he's acting like we're old friends.

Might as well play along. "Was hoping you'd be able to help me out."

"With?" He does a good job masking his annoyance, I'll give him that. Leaning back against his chair, folding his hands and waiting with rapt attention. If I hadn't known him that well, I might've missed the glint of warning in his dark eyes.

I tap my chin. "It seems... Hmm, with history."

A faint flicker of uncertainty crosses his expression, one I would've missed if I hadn't been watching him closely.

"What history?" he asks.

"The wars. The ones I was in. The ones I spilled my blood and other innocents' in."

He turns his attention back to the papers laid out in front of him. "What of them, exactly?"

Violeta's words keep echoing in my mind. I need to not ignore them. "Who gave the orders? For everything that happened. I thought it was the royals."

"It was."

I wait until he looks at me. "I know it wasn't." It's a bluff, nothing else. I didn't even expect to say what I just did. Didn't really believe Violeta's words. But something in me warned me to try, to at least push past the limits of what I've always seen as the social constructs of my life.

Kill. Drink. Repeat. Survive. But what good is survival, when it's all for a lie?

Dmitri laces his fingers and stares at me. "What, exactly, do you think you know?"

I lean forward, lips curled in a snarl. "I don't *think*. You've just confirmed it. My god, but how stupid have we all been? So the entire army, everyone under your thumb, you've been using for your own good haven't you? Has everyone else? Are we all just puppets?"

Dmitri narrows his eyes. "When have you never been puppets?'

"I...what?"

He scoffs and gets up from the table, contouring it to walk to the window. He stares out for a moment, then turns back to me, his expression cool. "You've always been a puppet, Marcus. And not just you, but all of you good little soldiers."

I lunge from the chair but before I can attack him, two guards have entered, restraining me.

"This isn't right!"

He laughs. "None of it is. I gave you a chance, allowing your little cabin in the woods and your little freedom you thought you'd earned. But like with most of you, all I have to do is give you enough rope to hang yourself with. And you just have, Marcus. Truth is, your righteous kind need to be disposed of. The way of the world depends on it."

"And, what, you'll continue to have royals blamed for all this?"

"Why not? They're not around to defend themselves, are they?" He smirks. "Except for the one you've been harboring. But no worries, my men have found her trace and will soon bring her to me."

Violeta.

Guilt racks me even as they drag me away, readying me for whatever it is they have planned. But my thoughts aren't with them. Instead, they're with her. And with the last words I'd said to her, with everything I accused her of.

Chapter 20

Violeta

As I exit the house, I run into Luca—Dominic and Lucrezia's son.

"Is it true?" he asks point blank. "You're a vampir?"

I laugh, leaning against the wall. He's acting all tough, just like his dad, but he's not stupid enough to get too close to me. Smart kid.

"I am."

"And you're a princess?"

"Mhmm."

"So, where's your crown?"

I burst out laughing, hard enough that I attract his father. "I wish I knew, kid." I ruffle his head and move away, ignoring his muttering.

He's not too happy about being called a kid.

"I see you met my hot-blooded punk," Dominic says.

"I wouldn't say hot-blooded."

"That's because you haven't been around him enough," he mutters. Then he gestures to the path ahead and I fall in line with him. "So, how are you feeling?"

"Pretty good, considering."

"I hate to be the bearer of bad news, but we've been keeping an eye on the vamps in the area. And it seems they're on the hunt. My guess is, for you?"

"Probably." A sigh escapes me. "I won't stay in your hair for too long. You've been so kind, the last thing I want is to drag more shit to your door."

"Believe me, we can handle them. And Luz would kill me if I kick you out." He turns on me, his expression losing its laughing ways. "Though, I have to say this. If anything does happen, she will be my priority, followed by Luca. First and foremost. And my pack will follow."

"I understand. And I wouldn't expect it to be otherwise."

"That being said—"

I don't hear the last of his words. Maybe it's because of the fresh vrykolakas blood I had this morning, but my senses are even more alert than ever. It's that which picks up on a twig snapping miles away from us. And then another.

I turn that way, my eyes narrowing into the trees. And like before, I'm not here, but I'm farther into them, as if my mind is able to move into the distance and see what's there. Humans, with weapons. And not just any humans. Their blood-red eyes hint they've consumed muroni blood. Their weapons, though, are very much anti-vampir.

Dominic's hand on my shoulder snaps me out of it. "You looked like you were having a seizure. What is it?"

"You have to get your wolves out of here, and Lucrezia and your son. Vampiri hunters are coming this way, and I think they're coming for me."

Dominic glances around, nostrils flaring as he tries to pick up a scent. He meets my gaze again.

"I'll go meet them, try to buy you time," I whisper. "I'm sorry for this."

Before he can say anything, I rush out of the encampment, and into the trees. No sense of self-preservation holds me back, not this time. Perhaps it's because I've cowered for too long from other vampir clans, and now that I'm no longer afraid of what's inside me, I'm not going to hold back.

Whatever the reason is, an odd sense of calm descends on me as I move forward, blazing past the trees. I hurtle into their midst like a boulder, taking two humans with me, slamming them against the trees.

Then I turn to face the rest—four more. And they're all hunters.

I thought they were solitary creatures. Why the hell would they be hunting together?

Crossbows are aimed at me, and arrows are released. I evade a few—and feel the jolt in my body as two nail me, one in a thigh, the other in my hip.

Growling, I yank both out and force myself to move onward. I slide back into the fighting moves Father drilled into me, and Nico practiced with me over and over. Using the palm of my hand, I slam my entire force into their chests, propelling them backward. It's not enough to render them unconscious when they're high on muroni blood, but it's enough to buy me time.

I get up close and personal with one of the two left standing, and use that brief moment to pull out his stakes, tossing them away. Then I grab a hunting knife he'd had lodged in his belt, and use it to gut him, twisting the blade to ensure the most damage is done.

Then I turn to the other, blocking his knife's hits with my own, until I slash at his wrist. He hisses, pulling back and trying to hold his arm against his chest. I move against him, shoving him into a tree—its broken branch impales him.

Another one comes up behind me, putting me in a chokehold. I take the knife and shove it into his side, but he doesn't let go. If anything, his hold on me grows tighter. It wouldn't do anything because I don't need to breathe, but there's something on his sleeve—some kind of poison—that's burning through my throat and chin.

A few weeks ago, Nico and Vlad found a hunter. They thought he'd been responsible for some of what was happening to me, but it hadn't turned out to be true. Still, he'd tried to attack Tassa and in a fit of rage, Nico killed him. I remember Tassa saying there had been many poisons in the man's cabin, poisons he'd indicated he was using to kill vampiri in the area.

If this is one such poison, I'm utterly screwed. Because the way it's burning through my throat, the agony—

A growl echoes around us. A moment later, the hunter holding me relinquishes his hold, instead yelling in agony. I whirl on him, panting, and pull the knife out of him, only to stab him in the neck. Blood spurts out and he collapses on the ground.

I turn my gaze to the wolf panting a few feet away. Dominic's son.

"Dammit, Luca, what are you doing here? Go back to your parents!"

He wags his tail as if to show me just how much he'll ignore me, and instead lunges on another vampir.

Shit. Dominic will have my hide for this.

That's three hunters done and eliminated, three more left. With Luca on one of them, I focus on the other, while trying to figure out where the last one disappeared.

Unfortunately, this particular one proves to be tricky. He flicks his wrist towards me and I don't feel it right away—then the lash of a whip cuts across my skin, slashing my clothes. It's made of metal spikes, and before I can even recover, he's whipping me again.

I curl into myself, trying to back away from him. Then the agony worsens as the cuts start burning. In a rational corner of my mind, I realize it must've been the same poison as the other one. But it doesn't help me control my scream of pain.

It draws Luca's attention, distracting him for a moment—enough for the other hunter to whip out his own. Even as I'm curled in pain, I scream, "Luca, *back away*!"

He listens right in the nick of time, evading the whip. But the second time he's not so lucky, and it hits his fur, removing a few sections where it hits skin.

My senses pick up a snap—like a crossbow being set. I glance around, noticing the third hunter, the one I hadn't been able to find, hidden in the shadow of a tree. His bow is aimed at me, but then he turns it to Luca.

No, no, no!

I pull deep within myself for the resilience I've been blessed with and grab the whip lashing at me with both hands. I pull—my strength is no match against the fucker who's been shredding my back. He loses his balance and is dragged to my feet. I lean down and whip out a knife, shooting it towards the hidden hunter, ignoring the agony in my shoulder as I do so.

A grunt is my sweet answer, but it's short-lived. He releases the arrow as he falls backward, and it goes straight for Luca. I don't even think, I just step straight in its path. A vampir's speed versus an arrow—never thought I'd be trying to win that particular race.

But I do.

Because the arrow embeds itself in my chest instead of Luca's. I stagger, stumble, and then I'm on my knees. A red haze descends on me, and all I can focus on is the need for blood. To heal myself, to pull myself together.

But the only blood appealing to me here is Luca's, and that's a no-go.

A whimper behind me distracts me. I hear the rip of flesh from flesh, followed by grunts of exertion. Then Luca's kneeling next to me, naked from his shift.

"Violeta!"

"I'm fine," I say through gritted teeth. "Kill the other one. And...woods. Tree. There's a wounded one there."

Luca hesitates, then seems to understand my pain is not the priority, but our survival is. He walks to the vampir, and through blurry eyes I see him snap the man's neck. Then he walks into the woods, and my ears faintly pick up the sound of a knife slashing through flesh, and a last man's dying words.

Luca emerges moments later and helps me up. "I got them both. But what that last one said makes no damn sense."

"Doesn't...have to. Let's just...go."

We make our way back to the encampment, Luca supporting most of my weight. Every step brings more agony until darkness overtakes me and I feel nothing.

I wake up into the guest house I'd been in with Marcus. Once I realize where I am, I close my eyes, and I swear I can smell him. Tears slip past my eyelids as I try to shove the hurt, the pain of his rejection away—the same way I've been doing for days.

"Violeta."

I open my eyes. The low voice isn't the one I'd been hoping for, but it's still a welcome sight.

"Luca. How are… Your wounds?"

He grins and pulls up his shirt. I ignore the six-pack he's flashing me and instead focus on the unmarred skin. "Good as new. Mom helped with some healing."

I nod.

"She helped you, too."

Now that he mentions it…

I warily move a shoulder, preparing myself for the agony on my back. But there's nothing. When I move my thighs under the blanket, a similar lack of pain answers me.

"I'll have to thank her," I whisper. "But that was idiotic, following me into the woods."

Lucrezia walks in then, shoving a lock of hair out of her face. Her features seem more drawn, but her eyes are blazing with the same lightning as when she'd warned Alex off. "I told him much the same. But it's not you who should be thanking me, it's the opposite." She reaches the bed and takes my hand in hers, squeezing. "Thank you for protecting my son. He told us what happened."

"It was nothing. I wasn't about to let him get hurt when all he tried to do was help me."

"Even so... thank you."

I nod, unsure what else to say.

Luca helps me out. "That last hunter's words. He said, *you can stop me, but you can't stop the others*. What do you think he meant? That there are more coming?"

"Da," I whisper. "And I think I know where they're going. Lucrezia, have you heard back from the wolf who went to warn my siblings?"

She nods. "Yeah, they sent back a letter and a phone number to reach them."

A smile tugs at my lips. Mirabela had been so against those contraptions, I'm surprised she allowed this. They must be really worried.

Lucrezia digs into her jeans and pulls out a folded paper. Tears fill my eyes again when I recognize Mirabela's handwriting. Hard to miss, when it looks like it could belong on fancy wedding stationary.

"What will you do?" Lucrezia asks.

I glance up. Luca's gone, presumably off to rest.

"I guess, warn them. It makes no sense to keep staying away, right?"

Lucrezia smiles, understanding in her eyes. "Yeah. But sometimes family is hard on you."

"Da..."

Dominic barges in then. "You may have to decide sooner rather than later. We just got word the vamps hunting you have Marcus."

Dread runs through me as my eyes fall on the bloody cellphone he's holding.

I need to protect Marcus, don't I? Even if he told me to leave him alone, I love him, I care for him, and despite our issues I need to be there for him. And if that means saving him...

"Take me to him."

"Are you sure? This isn't going to be easy."

I think of his features, of his gentleness, of the man who'd been there for me. Who taught me to keep in touch with myself. The same man who thinks it was my orders—my family's—that are responsible for the worst moments of his existence.

Does it matter, that he doesn't believe me?

Does it matter, that he won't listen to me?

The answer is as clear as the need inside me to save.

No, it doesn't. Because at the end of the day, what's between us is stronger than anything else. I'm not just meant to be by his side when things are easy. When he's sweet, or giving me the best sex ever. I'm not just meant to be there when it's convenient.

I'm meant to be there when it's hard, when it's a constant battle, and when it tears at my insides. Those moments, those *hard* moments, are what'll make or break our relationship. And I'm not about to run away from a fight. Especially not when it's one meant to save him.

"Da, I'm sure. He needs me, and I plan to be there for him."

Chapter 21

Marcus

Violeta was right. I was wrong.

It's as simple as that.

How many men, vampir or human, have thought those same words to themselves? Beats me. But they're the truth, and I've got to stop fooling myself.

Violeta didn't lie to me when she said the royals had no hand in the orders I'd received. They had no guilt to bear for the innocents I'd killed. They had nothing to be responsible for, except for not being around at the time to stop it.

And to think, I held her responsible for something she wasn't even at fault for.

I glance at my raw knuckles. I might've used them to pound the walls a bit too much, and now they're still healing. The pain is a welcome distraction from beating myself up.

A sigh leaves my lips and I return to my pacing.

Dmitri didn't lock me up in the cellars. No, his imprisonment is more luxurious—a guest room on the far end of his mansion. It's nestled in the coolest part of the house, meaning it's freezing in here, but the cold doesn't bother me.

On the contrary, listening to the wind outside as it beats against the worn window frame is almost soothing. Not soothing enough, though. Thoughts of what I'd said to Violeta, what I accused her of, everything I didn't listen to assail me, forcing me to admit I've truly been an asshole.

She deserved better. While I had a right to be angry, I should've listened to her, eventually. But there's no point thinking in *should've* right now.

Now, how to get the fuck out of here and find her to apologize... that's another story.

Plus, why would she listen? She's my ruler, not my lover. No matter how much I want her to be. No matter what Dominic said about the consort bond, I don't think he truly took into account the royalty bit. He couldn't have. He doesn't know our world enough.

Vampiri like her, if they were to *mate*, wouldn't do so with someone like me. I'm unworthy in all the worst ways, and we all know this isn't a fairytale. But if this bond isn't something we can choose, is there any hope in having her back in my arms?

The door opens behind me and I turn slowly, coming face to face with Dmitri. He's accompanied by two vampiri guards, both of whom line the wall on either side of him, ready to stop me from leaving if I attempt it.

Little do they know I wouldn't even try, for the same reason I haven't yet. Because I need Dmitri to tell me everything he knows. And now I have a better purpose—to see what his plans are concerning the royals.

I quickly scan the guards, more out of habit than any intention of disarming them. Instead of swords at their hips, I see the outlines of stakes and human guns.

Wonderful. Talk about evolution.

"Came to gloat at my captivity?" I ask Dmitri.

"Not quite, no. More to find out where your little bitch is hiding."

A growl tears out of my throat and I take a few steps closer. "Watch your tone. That's our princess you're talking about."

"Funny. A few hours ago, you were in my face and practically loathing her." He smirks. "I see. She's that good a fuck, hmm?"

I lunge for him—or, try to. One of the vampiri is at my throat with a stake the moment after, his gaze cold and inscrutable. Like mine used to be, long ago when all I used to do was take orders.

Since any extra movement on my part will only lead to my death, I settle for being as still as I possibly can be and glare at Dmitri instead.

"Now, now, Marcus. We used to be friends, remember?"

"You were never my friend. Only a master I saw from afar, one who's been responsible for atrocity after atrocity committed in the name of survival." I jerk my head out of the vampir's hands enough to spit at his feet. "So don't fucking talk about friendship."

He gives a theatrical sigh. "Must you be so obstinate?"

"I guess I must." Focusing on my initial goal for this confrontation, I sneer. "Let me guess. You need information on Violeta so you can feed it to your other buddy clans, right?"

His eyes narrow on me. "What do you know of them? You've been a hermit since way before I made any political moves."

"Ah, but you forget how well I know you, Dmitri. I was always a little too observant. It's how I knew why you killed Maria—and why it backfired with the Cazacu clan. Tell me, are they still *friends* with you?"

"They have no choice." He smirks. "What you seem to forget is the clan leaders have a *scratch my back and I'll scratch yours* type of philosophy, my dear Marcus. And right now, they have a pest they can't get rid of—vampiri hunters." He tilts his head to the side. "Surely even *you* heard of them."

"Da, I have. Fought a few these last days, too. What of them?"

"Something is moving them, causing them to act...oddly." He frowns, glancing away as if talking more to himself. "The Cazacu don't know how to handle them. The Eder clan have lost their major generals to them, and the Hatmanu and Munteanu clans are equally perplexed. And worried, given their territories encompass large lands and, well, these pests do seem to love the cover of woods." He shrugs, tapping his chin. "Only the Lazarescu clan has remained silent. And I was planning to ask them *why*, before your little bitch ruined my plans and started killing my men."

The scowl is back full force now. Dmitri steps closer, only a few inches from my face. His eyes shine brightly, but whatever he tries to do, it seems to only make him angry.

"Why aren't you susceptible to my glamour anymore? What did she do?"

Ah, so that's what it was. He's trying his old mind control trick.

I think back to the human, to Violeta admitting she'd glamoured me. Could it be that when Violeta removed that glamour, she removed my ability to be glamoured by anyone else, too?

It wouldn't be unheard of. Royals have powers that exceed ours, and it makes sense that their influence would leave a mark. It only makes me that much more stupid for raging against her, for something that has ended up benefitting me in the end.

Her words from before echo in my mind. *I've made sure such a thing can't be used against you again!*

I'd been too angry to listen, but now? Gratitude rushes through me. She might've used the same power against me, but she put in place something to ensure she would be the last one to do so.

A grin stretches my lips. "Guess I won't be playing to your tune after all."

"We'll see about that."

Dmitri steps back and nods to the guard. The moment after, he punches me. At first, it's just his fist. But once I'm bent over, the next punch becomes a stab as the stake is driven into my gut. I can almost feel the pieces of wood breaking apart in me, then he withdraws it. And does it again. And again.

I drop to the ground, groaning in pain as blood seeps out of the wounds and onto the carpet. In a dim corner of my mind, I realize these wounds are not enough to kill me. If I'd been a human, yes. As a vampir, all they're doing is weakening me. Dmitri isn't trying to kill me, not in the least. He's trying to torture whatever information out of me, the sick fuck. And probably hoping that once I'm weak enough, his glamour will work on me.

Instead of giving in, I spit out a glob of blood and look up. "That the best you got?"

The guard moves forward again. This time he kicks, and his boots have nasty little wooden spikes on them that dig into my skin over and over as he hits. Each one feels like a sting, followed by fire blazing across my skin, almost like acid. They must be coated with something for maximum effect.

I lose track of how many hits I endure. All I'm aware of is my body rolling on the carpet every few hits, and those spikes finding new, unharmed areas to hit.

"Enough," Dmitri finally calls out. The floor creaks as he walks over and crouches over me. "Tell me where Violeta Dracul is. And I'll give you enough blood to heal you, then send you on your merry way."

Through a swollen eye, I glance at him. His expression is intent on me, his lips curled up in distaste, his jaw clenched. But underneath it all, his eyes are filled with desperation.

That's when it hits me. Despite his best efforts, Violeta must have eluded him. Which means she's either back with her family, or with Dominic's wolves. My hope is the former. They'll protect her better than any furry creatures.

Either way, that means he doesn't have the one thing he could use as leverage for me. Too damn bad, because her well-being alone would've been enough to make me talk.

I lift my head off the floor enough to spit in his face, and a spatter of blood decorates his otherwise clean face. He scowls and wipes it away with his hand.

"Tsk. I would've thought you knew better, camarade. Especially given she's touched by Dracul's curse." Something in my expression must've given me away, because he chuckles. "She didn't tell you all, then? So you have no idea about their inability to form armies, nor the fact they're slowly dying—all six of them?"

Everything freezes around me.

Inability to form armies, nor the fact they're slowly dying.

The words dance in my head like a song on repeat, not making sense at all. Until they finally do. That's what Dominic told Violeta, the last time we'd been there. It's what she was hiding from me, and why she seemed so wrecked. All along she'd thought her symptoms were from a disease, but they were a curse.

And instead of being there for her, like a fool, I let her walk out. Not just *let her*, I actively pushed her.

If that doesn't make me the biggest jackass on the planet, I don't know what does.

I don't give Dmitri the satisfaction of revealing more, schooling my face in an expressionless mask.

"Still won't talk? And here I thought you were smarter. At least smarter than Kalla."

I can't hold back the jerk of my body. "What did you..."

"Tsk, tsk. Don't worry your head with it. Kalla was useful, up to a point. Unfortunately, she didn't achieve what I needed her to. Not when it came to your precious princess."

I wait. Knowing him, his narcissistic personality, he's bound to want to brag.

"I thought it would be enough to kidnap our precious princess. See, Kalla intended to sacrifice her to Zalmoxis. As for me, well..." He leans in closer, as if about to tell me a secret. "I don't care either way. I just wanted her out of my way, *after* I'd learned all her secrets." He pulls back. "And then the damned wolves saved her."

Thank the gods.

Dmitri scowls at my relieved expression. "Kalla and her leftover sprites disappeared, otherwise I'd have had her head on a spike. And while Her Majesty is off into hiding again, don't go thinking she's out of the woods. Sooner or later, I'll get her. So you might as well make it easier on yourself and tell me what I want to know."

My only answer is to clench my jaw, biting the inside of my cheek to avoid cussing him out.

"Well, no matter." He smirks. "If she cared enough to fuck you, she'll care enough to rescue you once she receives my message." He gets up and in true modern fashion, snaps a picture of me beaten up with his cellphone, then turns and walks away.

I wait until the guards have disappeared before dragging myself to the window and letting the cool breeze wafting through reinvigorate me. It'll take me a bit to heal, but none of the injuries are fatal.

What worries me more than my beat-up state and current predicament is how much Dmitri knows about the royals. It explains why he's been able to impersonate them and create this mess in the first place. But then again, how many others also know, and have done the same thing?

Don't come for me, Violeta. I don't deserve it, and you'll be walking straight into a trap.

I can only hope she hears me. If this bond thing is as strong as Dominic makes it to be, then hopefully she will.

Violeta

Dom turns to me. We're on the edge of the woods, close to the vampir hideout. The manor rises out of the darkness, surrounded by mist and metal gates. A shiver runs up my spine. There should be guards there, there should be something warning others not to go in.

Instead, the gate is wide open, as if inviting the unsuspecting lambs—us—in for the slaughter.

Dominic touches my shoulder. "Thank you. I didn't get a chance to say, earlier, but for Luca."

"You should be angry with me, not offering to help me out. Luca was only in danger because he got dragged in with my own shit."

Dominic chuckles. "My son was there because he has the same reckless and hotshot streak I had in me at his age. He'll smarten up eventually. But make no mistake, it was his fault as much as yours."

I face him, arching an eyebrow. "So why are you helping? I could just call my siblings."

He shrugs. "Hunters who attack my own is one thing. They're humans, and I'll find the rest of them eventually. But this?" His gaze darkens as it lands on the manor. "I won't let you go in alone, and I owe you for saving him. Plus, if this guy and others like him are threatening your rule, that means it'll eventually trickle down to us."

"Ah. So you're forming alliances with the strongest pack, then?"

A smile tugs at his lips. "Something like that."

I nod, and turn my attention back to the manor. I try to do what I did in the woods—look beyond the gates—but all I see is darkness. Not a soul moves. And I definitely can't sense anything of Marcus.

"Are you sure about this?" Dominic asks. "There's no going back once you get in."

"I know." I straighten my back. "But it's what I have to do. If no one's going to keep them in check, then I'll have to."

He reaches in his back pocket and tosses me a cell phone. "Then do me a favor. Call your siblings, just in case. It'll take them a bit, but at least it's a backup we sorely need. You and I both know this shit's just for show."

I stare at his phone for a long moment, then grab it and dial the number. There's a dull ring, then another, and Alex answers.

"Da?"

"It's me." There's a long silence and I go on before I lose my nerve. "I don't really have time to explain everything, but I need you. I need *all* of you."

A beat of silence follows. "Where are you?"

I give him the rough coordinates, trusting that he'll be there for me.

"I have only one question," he says when I'm done.

"Yeah?"

"Did you find the answers you were seeking? The ones that made you leave?"

Tears sting my eyes at the hurt in his voice. I wouldn't have expected it from my most psychotic brother, but this is the light I'd always hoped still lived in him. "I did. And they affect all of us, Alex. I'll tell you everything, but first—"

"We'll be there," he interrupts me, and hangs up.

I give the phone back to Dom. Only as I do it do I realize that I didn't tell Alex about the wolves. *Shit. I'll deal with that when it comes to it.* And hopefully my silence won't turn this situation into an even bigger mess than it is.

"All good?" Dominic asks.

I nod. "All good. They're coming."

"Cool." He turns away and the moment after, he's back to wolf form, and charging at the gates.

His vrykolakas follow him—perfectly trained soldiers. They're like a dark shadow moving down the hill, through the trees, aiming straight for the gates. There's no contesting, no arguing with him. No questioning why he's putting their lives in danger for someone who's not even part of their pack. There's just obedience, and loyalty.

And for the first time, it hits me—was this how Marcus felt, part of a whole? At someone else's command?

When I think of the power someone like Dominic wields, and how that same power was used on Marcus, something in me clenches, making me unbearably sad.

Is it any wonder he'd had the reaction he did when he discovered my lies?

I pull myself together and follow them. Unlike whoever had control of Marcus, I intend to protect these guys as much as possible.

The entrance goes by as smooth as can be. Dominic and his wolves spread up to cover more ground, and he leaves three of them with me. I figure if Dmitri's holding Marcus anywhere, it'll be in the manor itself, so I head straight for it.

No sooner do I enter, that I feel my legs wobble.

Worst possible fucking time for me to get dizzy. I lean against the wall, trying to pull myself together, and that's when two guards come around the corner. Followed by two more. Dressed in black, they both sport matching cropped haircuts, dark suits, and a brooch pinned over their left breast pocket.

They're on me in unison. One of the vrykolakas jumps on a vampir, but the other evades him and comes for me. I slam him against the wall and before I know it, I'm sinking my teeth in his neck, his blood spilling in my mouth like the best of whiskeys. It tastes fucking amazing. And I enjoy it a little too much, forgetting about the other two.

A stab in my back reminds me, and I pull back with a roar. Blindly, I reach for the stake embedded in my flesh and yank it out.

Then I whirl on the vampir, my claws on his throat, tearing it apart and overpowering him within seconds. Three more come around the corner, and this time I face them, no longer overpowered. Blood sloshes in my stomach, fueling me with the strength I need. I'm ready for my fight.

I glance over my shoulder. Two of the vrykolakas are still with me. The third is lying in a puddle of his own blood. *Dammit.* I realize there's no way to stop casualties, but I'd hoped.

I'll do better with these two.

When the guards attack, we move in unison. And this time, I watch their backs as much as they watch mine. Everything's going smoothly until another squadron comes around the corner.

Goddamn, did I pick the worst spot to infiltrate or what?

Then it hits me. Rather than pick more weapons from the dead vampiri lying at my feet, I walk ahead to face the new ones. My eyes land on theirs and I exert the full force of my glamour.

"You will not hurt your princess. Lower your weapons and kneel."

There's a faint resistance from one of them—must be an older one—but a black wolf jumps from behind and rips his throat out before I can do anything.

"Thanks, Dominic," I mutter.

The other two vampiri kneel, blank expressions on their faces. I walk to them and snap their necks, then rip their heads off. Father always said never to take any chances in a fight, and now's not the time to start.

I turn to the black wolf, whose fur is now matted with blood. "Thanks."

He nods and then runs to the side. He turns a few feet farther down, then points his nose in a specific direction.

This time, when I follow, it's on unsteady feet. But it has nothing to do with being weak, rather, with the fact I've finally understood.

My body knew it before my mind registered it. And with each step in the direction of what I'm guessing is an office, I feel that tug, the one in me, pull me stronger. Faster. harder. Towards him. Hurtling like a wave ready to meet the beach.

"Marcus?"

Dominic nods, and I pass him, ridiculously eager now.

Unbeating heart in my throat, I can't stop. Not now, not when I'm so close. I don't know what I'll find, I don't expect he'll be happy to see me. But he'll be alive.

The smell of blood only has me moving faster, until I stop right at the edge of the door. Waiting. Holding my breath.

I push it open.

Chapter 22

Marcus

I've been a fool, trusting in those I shouldn't have. Giving my life for those I shouldn't have. Serving masters that only cared to use me for their nefarious goals. Goals I helped achieve. Goals I spilled blood for... so much blood.

And all for what?

To end up alone, holed up in a damp room and awaiting my execution.

Without hope for a future. Without hope for more. Without... Violeta.

I shut my eyes against the wave of agony that spreads in my

body, but it's too late. It hits me in the gut with all the force of a well-packed punch and I fall to my knees, hiding my face in my hands.

I owe her an apology I'll never get to. Something I...

The door opens and Dmitri walks in.

"What do you want again?"

His expression is too intense, too focused. He walks straight for me and clasps me by the throat, lifting me off the ground and shoving me into the wall behind me. Either he's here to kill me, or he wants to torture me some more. Only, he doesn't have guards this time.

So after the moment of surprise is gone, I retaliate.

I bunch against his hold, and shove him off me. He staggers, eyes widening as if not having expected me to do so.

"What, thought I'd take it like a good little soldier? A *puppet*?" I laugh and advance on him, cracking my knuckles. "Nah, Dmitri. This time, it's you and me."

My fist meets his jaw, and a crack echoes in the room as he stumbles backwards. He soon recovers, and crouches towards me. "You don't want to do this."

"Try me. I've been itching to wipe that smug grin off your face."

He ignores my mutters, already searching for a way to destabilize me. Only, the joke's on him. He might've taught me everything, but I've picked up things along the way. When he attacks, we clash together, two opposing forces, each wishing to destabilize the other. It's not long before he grabs my arm and with a sickening crunch, breaks it on a wood table.

But I get up, wiping at my mouth and ready for more.

I remember the grueling exercises he'd forced upon us. Every. Damn. Morning. He'd been relentless, and when any of us showed weakness, he'd only doubled down on the intensity, making all of us suffer.

But thanks to those exact exercises, I'm able to see his blows coming. I duck, hitting him in the gut instead. I pull my fist back only to have it hit his jaw. Dmitri stumbles back.

"Gone soft, have you? That's what happens when you have too many soldiers around. You think yourself invincible, until you're one on one."

Though I'm still weakened, I dig deep for the leftover of my strength and blur in front of his eyes—hitting him from the side, instead. He doesn't see me coming this time. I ignore my broken arm and instead go straight for the jugular. My fingers clench around his throat, and I snarl in his face.

"*What* do you have on her?"

His eyes widen. I don't think he really expected me to be doing all this for the sake of someone else.

Then he coughs a laugh. "You...are only trading...one master...for another."

"Fuck you. She's not my master, she's my consort, you fool."

This time, the expression on his features isn't surprise. It's something else, something I can't quite put my finger on, but that looks eerily like fear.

"*Imposibil*!"

"Sorry to disappoint, but it's damn possible." I shake him a little and he chokes. "Now tell me. What do you have on her? What's this curse you're talking about?"

He chokes some more, and finally, I toss him to the ground. As I loom over him, it hits me—for the first time in centuries, I'm making decisions of my own volition. I'm choosing who to protect, who to go against, and it's more freeing than I'd have thought.

Dmitri coughs. "The curse is on their entire family."

"And what does it *do*? Give me something useful, or I swear you'll wish you weren't immortal with the amount of pain I'll inflict on you."

He holds up a hand. "Okay, okay. Stop. He—Țepeș. It all started with him. He *made* us." He looks up at me. "Don't you see? He made us, then abandoned us. Turned his attention to only six favorites."

"They were his chosen ones, of course he'd care more for them."

Dmitri shakes his head. "You don't understand. We were left to our own devices, no one to enact the decrees he pushed out. And then rumors started—that he was sick, that he was planning to die. Then they all went into hiding. The rumors got worse, almost as if fueled by someone."

He coughs again and leans back on his haunches, meeting my gaze. "I'll admit, I took charge. But I wasn't alone. Many were the clans who chose to take control, to rearrange their territories as they saw fit. Some feared Țepeș would come after us. But when he didn't—" He shrugs, as if that alone explains his duplicity.

I spit at his feet. "You are an embarrassment to our kind and to what we stand for. You, and everyone else like you, including the other clans."

"What we stand for?" he laughs. "Don't make me laugh, Marcus. What do you think we stand for, exactly? Love and peace? Helping humans? I've got news for you. Our existence was and always has been meant to destroy humanity."

I shake my head. "No. You're twisting it."

"I'm not. Ask anyone. Ask the clans—Cazacu, Eder, Hatmanu, Lazarescu, Munteanu—they'll tell you the exact same thing. Our purpose is survival, and to do so, we have to make do without the monarchy."

"No, we don't," I growl. "*You* want to do so, and you've probably twisted their minds. And other clans, outside of Romania." I give him a little shake. "Haven't you?"

Dmitri's eyes shine, a glassy hue coming over them. "Perhaps we've sent a few letters, same as we received some. *But there's a reason for this.* I've done a lot of research these last centuries, while they were in hiding. And I know. I know all about the curse that's tearing them apart, forcing them into the light, into seeking help. Kalla did, too."

I take another step towards him, clenching my fists in evident intent. Dmitri looks at them, then at me.

"You don't have to torture me. I'll tell you, gladly. Then you'll understand. See, when Țepeș' first wife died, everyone thought it was the Turks' fault. Everyone but Țepeș—he blamed himself. And so did another. Her father. His father-in-law. The god Zalmoxis."

"Zalmoxis?" A snort escapes me. "I've had time to read, too, and I don't have time for fables and myths."

"It's not a fable! He's as real as they come, believe me. I've...I've spoken to him."

My eyes narrow. "Dmitri, don't fucking lie to me to save your ass. It won't work."

"I'm *not.* Zalmoxis has it in for the House of Dracul. He intends them to die a painful death, paying for Țepeș' mistake. This consort thing? That's part of it."

"What part, exactly?"

"It's meant to save them. If they all find their mate and make a blood sacrifice to Zalmoxis, it will save their sorry asses from atrocious deaths."

I think back to Violeta and her disease. How it has no heads or tails, how no one's been able to actually find something to fix it. Least of all myself.

"It makes no sense. Why would a god be involved?"

"Because it's he who created us."

My frown deepens. "All of us?"

"He gave Țepeș the first blood. Probably some other vampiri, as old as Țepeș himself and in other corners of the world. Either way, Țepeș, in turn, created the rest of us."

I shake my head. "This is insane. Why would I even believe you?"

"Because you know I'm right. You've been with her, you must've seen something. My men said her scent was weird. That she wasn't as strong as they expected." His eyes take on a feverish glint. "It's started, hasn't it?"

I don't want to admit it, but he must see it in my expression. Slowly, he stands.

"I can help, you know. I have information. Things that could help her. Make things easier."

Why would he be back here, without guards, and trying to change his tune? It strikes me then that this is weird. Even for Dmitri. Unless this is a different ploy to get me to admit Violeta's whereabouts. And if it is, it failed horribly.

"I don't think so. You've done enough. The only thing you're going to do now is sit quietly so they can administer their judgment on you." I move on him, my intent more than clear.

He holds up a hand, backing away. "Wait. This isn't what I came here for."

"Yeah, then what?"

"The House of Dracul, they—"

He turns to the side, as if hearing something I can't. Then he stares at me, and this time his expression gives away his eagerness. The moment after, he's run out of the room. I rush after him, hitting my fists against the wood and making it shake. But he's barred the door shut behind him, locking me in once more.

Violeta

He's not here.

The office is completely empty—or so I think. Then someone roars, jumping from behind the large desk, and I move out of the way just in time. A stake misses me by millimeters only.

Then the vampir who'd thrown it comes out of the shadows, running straight at me. I evade her attack—barely—by stepping out of the office and into the hallway.

"Is he—"

Dominic's question's cut off when the vampir comes out after me. He shifts again to wolf form, ready to help out, but I shake my head at him. "Go! Find Marcus' trace, and come get me after."

When he's gone, I turn to the female. I'm faster than her, and older. It doesn't take me long to overpower her. I grab a handful of her hair and yank her head to the side, exposing her neck. The few dizzy spells I've had have been a few too many, and I don't want to take any more chances. Since she's my closest snack... I sink my fangs into her, enjoying the sweetness of her blood.

Too late, I hear the whoosh of an arrow behind me. It catches me in the shoulder, and I let go of the dead vampir with a groan. She crumples to the ground, and I whirl to face my attacker.

Dark hair, slicked back. Sharp, black eyes. An aquiline nose. Something about his expression isn't quite right. His eyes glint feverish, but his hand on the bow trembles. A complete contradiction.

"You can call me Dmitri." He advances on me. "Your Royal Highness."

He knows who I am. This can't be good—it must be Marcus' old *master*.

I back away, out through an archway and into the courtyard beyond. And still I don't like how close that bow is getting to me.

I should rip his head off for aiming a weapon at a royal, but this is my chance to find out Marcus' whereabouts—and maybe more. Only, instead of my feet being as strong as I would've expected them to be, I stumble.

My shaking hand reaches for the arrow. There's an odd burning reverberating from it into my flesh. When I yank it out, I have to do everything in my power to hold back a cry of pain.

Was it poisoned? Normal poisons don't work on vampiri, at least not on us. The tip doesn't seem coated with anything other than my blood. But already I'm feeling the same fire in my stomach. Could it, whatever it was, have moved in my system so fast?

The vulnerability of my position hits me hard. Dominic's gone, his vrykolakas somewhere around here, and I'm weakened by whatever the hell Dmitri put in the arrow. My body was already fighting against me but now my chances of holding my ground are diminished.

Shit. Didn't think this through properly.

Another wave of dizziness hits me, stronger than all the rest. I close my eyes for a millisecond. Hear Father's voice in my ears. *Don't show weakness. Don't show weakness.*

It takes all my willpower to straighten and school my expression, but I do it anyway. I may not be able to disguise all the pain I'm in, but I can do some.

"What did you do?" I ask, forcing an imperious tone.

Dmitri shrugs. "We discovered a while ago this poison works only against old vampiri. Well, not us. I really should give credit to where it's due—the hunters have come in handy every once in a while." He purses his lips. "I thought it was enough to give this to the muroni female, but it seems she was unable to hold you captive long enough for me to collect you." He takes another arrow and notches it on the bow. "A pity, really. She had her uses."

I remember Kalla's fevered tone, her words while I was unconscious—*he's on his way*. I'd thought she meant Zalmoxis. But the *he* she was referring to was Dmitri. He's been making plays long before this, then, and she used him as much as he used her.

"You—were behind that?"

I blink a few times, trying to fight off against the stupid dizziness. This isn't the time. Not again. But it's not dizziness because of the...usual... It's... Too much, too fast. No way an arrow had that much poison in it.

I glance at the female vampir.

Dmitri chuckles. "Yes, I had her drink plenty of it, too. It made her a bit, hmm, raging, and uncontrollable, but it was worth it in the end, I'd say. Pawns, and all."

I've backed up as far as I can, literally into a corner.

"W-why?"

He laughs darkly, towering over me as I slide to the ground, unable to hold myself up. Best intentions go out the window as my feet can't hold me up and I'm wrecked by shivers I can't control. Whatever this is, it's worse than my disease. It's—hell.

"Because it's time for new rulers in these lands. Your Marcus may have refused to give me your location, but at least you walked right into my trap." He grins. "And I'll make sure to tell him goodbye, don't worry." He raises the bow and aims straight for my heart. Just as he's about to release it, I hear a familiar voice behind him.

"That's my sister you're fucking with, fool."

The hand holding the bow disappears—wrenched from its socket. Blood gushes out, the bone protrudes, and suddenly it's all I can see. Dmitri's mouth opens in a silent scream, but a pale, slender hand wraps around it and silences him.

An auburn head of wavy hair peeks around his shoulder. "Hey, Vi. Alex said you needed us?"

Chapter 23

Violeta

I stare at Liza in shock. She grins, ever the buoyant sister despite the scar on her cheek.

Dmitri is frozen in fear. Maybe on some level he realizes she's the worst possible royal he could've landed upon. That she has no ounce of mercy in her.

For once, I'm thankful of that. Because without her, I would've been kissing my immortal existence goodbye. And while I've been saying I'm ready to die, clearly, that's not even remotely the case.

Then, to make matters worse, Liza glances to the side and none other than Alex shows up. In a smooth transition they're all too used to, he takes the vampir off her hands. "Kneel the fuck down and shut up, would you?"

With the way he towers over him, it's no wonder Dmitri listens. His face scrunches in pain as blood continues gushing out of his wound, tainting the area all around us. We can heal many wounds, but dismemberments? Not possible.

Dmitri kneels obediently, bowing his head as trembles cover him head to toe.

"Are you okay, Vi?" Liza says, and moves on me, pulling me in a hug. Her auburn locks tickle my nose, and I return her hug, trying to mask my surprise.

Liza's never been one for shows of affection, and lately she's been more prickly than, well, sisterly.

Don't look a gift horse in the mouth, a nagging voice warns at the back of my mind.

"You're so bad, leaving the way you did. Had us all worried." Liza steps back and shares a look with Alex. "Is it me, or does she look even worse for wear?"

My blond brother narrows his eyes on me, then grips my chin and tilts my head left and right. There's relief in his gaze—at me being okay?—but I soon lose track of it. The tilting movement he's forcing has stars dancing around my vision, and makes my head ache in a very unpleasant way.

Alex must see that, and more. He lets go with a grunt. The moment after, he's marched off to Dmitri and grabbed hold of his other arm, yanking it in warning. "What did you give her? She's obviously drugged and in pain. *How* do I undo it?"

Dmitri looks like he wants to argue. On some level, perhaps he still thinks he has a chance. But then Vlad comes out of the mansion.

Dmitri may not know what all our faces look like, but the cape he's wearing with the House of Dracul crest over his human clothing—same as Liza and Alex—is enough to tip him off.

That, and the fact he's not alone. A large fraction of Dmitri's soldiers are accompanying him, glamoured and silent as puppies.

All fight goes out of him, and his shoulders hunch inwards. "Poison."

"Nice try," Liza says, also giving him her full attention. "Now tell the truth before I rip your other arm off."

"I'm not lying!"

Alex smacks him over the head like a child. "Do you think us stupid? Poison doesn't affect vampiri. Not in this way."

"I swear I'm not lying. I—there's a special brand. For vampiri as old as yourselves."

"Really?" Alex leans into him. Dmitri cowers even more. "What is it?"

"Vervain mixed with silver," he says.

I hear the words, but they're an echo. Like they come to me in waves, all too slow and not easy to understand. Or retain. Vervain is an herb many used against us in the past, one that was worse than holy water for us. But it lost its effectiveness—we grew immune to it, one could say.

"That's not enough to cause this reaction," Alex growls. "It never has been, many have tried."

"Not this silver!" Dmitri defends himself. "It disturbs the energy, the balance in your bodies. It—it *works*, believe me."

"Alex!" Liza cries. Her fingers on my shoulder tighten—she must be trying to hold me upright, but I find all I want is the sweet comfort of the snow against my cheek.

"Tell me how to fix it!"

Alex's snarl has me blinking. He's got Dmitri by the lapels of his shirt, shaking him like a loose leaf.

"B-blood," he says.

Alex lets him go and snorts. "Do you see a human around here? Nice try." He looms closer, more dangerously, and Dmitri actually starts shaking.

Is it possible he feels Alex's darkness, or has he heard of the atrocities he's specifically committed? Out of all us, him and Liza have the biggest reputation.

"N-not h-human," he adds quickly. "S-she n-needs v-vampir b-blood. To restore the b-balance of D-Darkness."

Alex freezes, glancing at me. I'd expect revulsion or incomprehension in his eyes. Instead, he walks to me and pushes Liza out of the way, then offers me his wrist. "Go on."

I would resist it, if only for the sake of my other siblings. Vlad and Liza are keeping an eye on the other soldiers, but their concerned gazes are on me. I don't have time to explain—I can feel the essence of whatever's keeping me alive, leaving me in hordes.

I look at Alex through blurry eyes, then his wrist. Lick my lips, knowing too well I'll give in. I'm too far gone. So far gone, in fact, that I don't even bother questioning Alex's quick acceptance of Dmitri's words. My fangs sink into his wrist and his blood pours into my mouth, fresh and inexplicably rich.

Maybe because of the connection, or maybe because I'd half-expected it, I sense it the moment Alex tenses. A rush of anger runs through him and I break my hold on his wrist, turning every which way to identify what's gotten him so agitated.

Already, the blood I've had is coursing through my veins,

destroying the poison in its path, restoring my focus, my senses. First my vision, then my hearing, and, finally, the use of my limbs.

And then I see them—wolves. They're escorting another bunch of Dmitri's men to the courtyard, all of them in various states of disarray. Dominic's at their head, fully human and dressed in a pair of slacks he must've taken off a dead one.

Alex growls and makes a move to head towards them, but I grip his arm. With his blood, I'm now restrengthened, the poison seeped out of my system. He meets my gaze after a beat.

"They're with me."

His lip curls. "Please tell me they're not the reason we're here to rescue you."

"No." I frown, looking around. "They came to help me, actually. They've *been* helping me."

"We could've done that, if you'd let us," Liza shoots back.

My gaze shifts to her. I can't remember the last time I heard hurt her in her tone. Even a few weeks ago, with her little tantrum with Nico, she'd been cool and collected. I had almost gotten to the point of believing nothing could faze her. But looking in her eyes, I realize that's not true.

She turns away, crossing her arms over her chest as if annoyed she's let me see too much. I allow her the moment, instead turning towards the wolves.

Vlad's already joined them, conversing with Dominic. At least I have another mediator to help me keep the interspecies peace.

That makes three of my siblings, but where are the other two?

"I didn't want your help," I admit in a low voice. "I wanted to live freely and then die in peace, instead of continuing the rest of my existence in seclusion."

"You wanted to die?" Liza's shocked gaze collides with me. "Like Tata did?" A glint of fear runs through those irises, one that makes me feel even shittier than before. We all had our nicknames for Father. *Tata* was hers.

I sigh and admit my shame with a bow of my head. "Yes. But then I learned there's another way, a way to fix me, and... yeah. That's, actually, why we're here."

Alex scoffs. "And the *wolves* told you all this?"

"We did," Dominic says, now only a few feet away. "We have no quarrel with you. On the contrary, what happens to you will affect this entire region, meaning my mate, son and pack as well. It's in my best interests to help you."

Alex has nothing to say to that, but I know by the way he's standing that he's silently seething.

In the midst of the awkwardness between him and the wolves, Vlad comes and hugs me. Whispers in my ear he's glad I'm ok, then pulls back.

"Where are Nico and Mirabela?" I ask, knowing he's likely to give me more straight answers than the other two ever would.

"Mirabela stayed with Tassa. They only returned from Marea Neagră this morning. Nico's hunting for the one you're seeking here. Dominic filled us in." His eyes are filled with questions, and I gulp as my other two siblings stand to attention.

"Filled you in on what?" Liza asks. "What's going on here?"

I glance at Dmitri, then at the rest of them. In the end, he won't live to see the sun rising, so I might as well. "This thing, this disease in me, it's not random. And it's curable. But for it to be curable, we all need to do our part, and be what we've actually never been—a family. Care for each other."

I'm met with frowns and confused gazes. As concisely as I can, I explain to them the full convoluted story Dominic had shared with me. When I'm done, the air pulsates with incredulity and anger.

"In a weird way, that all makes sense," Vlad says.

"Sense? *Sense?*" Liza shouts. "There's no damn sense in this! Vampiri, with a consort? *Royals* with a consort? Are you fucking kidding me?"

She marches on Dominic, glaring at him from all her tiny frame. "You're a liar and a vagrant."

He bursts out laughing. "Haven't quite heard that before. But believe me, everything I've told your sister is the truth."

"You have no proof," Alex says. His tone is cool, weirdly calm, but underneath it I sense the same anger as in Liza.

"Show him, Vi."

Sighing, I pull the notebook out of my back pocket. "I have Father's journal. He's not lying, believe me. All of it is true, in as much as I've been able to retrace."

Alex withdraws within himself, Liza scoffs and stomps some more, and Vlad just watches me.

"So what you're saying is we can save you? If we all don't fight falling in love."

"And don't mind tying our existences to someone for the rest of our lives!" Liza snorts. "Nu, mersi. I enjoy my promiscuity."

I roll my eyes. "Liza...."

"I don't want to hear it."

Well, that's a closed conversation there.

Vlad smiles and says, "We'll talk when we get back home. There's no point getting into it here and now."

I sigh. "No, no point at all."

As I look away from him, I meet Dmitri's gaze. The calculating glint in it is hard to miss. He's heard everything, as I knew he would, and thinks he'll be able to use it against us. Fool. Father trained me better than that.

A second later, I'm in front of Dmitri. "And you. I hope you're not making plans with everything you've heard, because you're not going to live to see them."

Everyone freezes behind me, and I sense their attention on me. Even Dominic. None of them think I'll do it, none of them expect me to. I'm not sure what Dominic's plans were for these vampiri, but in my gut I know we have to send a message. One that can't be contested, one that will reverberate across the mountains into every vampir clan that owes us allegiance.

"W-what?" Dmitri asks.

"You could spare yourself a few precious seconds. Where did you get this new silver for this poison? And how did you know it would affect me like that?"

Dmitri clenches his jaw. Ah, so this is one piece of information he's not so willing to give. I'd hoped as much.

I shift to the side and shove my hand into his open wound, twisting. He tosses his head back in pure agony and screams, for long, long moments. Everyone's gazes burn on my back, but to their credit, none of them stop me.

Calmly, I remove my hand and wipe the blood off on my jeans. Then I lean down to whisper in his ear. "Speak. While you still can."

Panting, he meets my gaze. Rage burns in them, and pure hatred. "I'm not telling you fuck all."

I straighten from my bent position, looming over him. Every other death before this, I've done it in self-defense. The vampiri in the woods, each and every time they found me. Even the human, back in the cabin. Definitely the vampir hunters. But this will be cold-blooded murder. Can I do it? Do I have it in me, after all these years spent fighting my darker impulses?

The answer is simple. For my family, I'll do anything.

Even if they won't return it when the time comes.

Marcus

Dmitri left so fast, I didn't think much of it. Now that my ears pick up the noise outside, I'm reminded that without the royals, our clans are very much a free for all. There is no law, not really. Only survival.

And it sounds like someone's definitely attacking Dmitri's clan. And I'm here, unarmed, practically a prisoner of war and at their mercy.

Well, if they come for me, I'll make them pay. There won't be any second guessing. I've been a soldier all my life and I'll be one until the day I die.

Even if I die alone.

But when the door opens and I stand, ready to attack, it's not Dmitri. It's not even a stranger vampir. Instead, I'm faced with someone that looks very much like Violeta—only, as a male. Dark hair, same piercing blue eyes.

I lower my hands and straighten from my crouch, assessing the newcomer.

"Are you Marcus?" he asks.

The voice from the phone... The one who'd called, asking after Violeta. Is this her brother?

I nod. "And you?"

"Nicolae. Most people call me Nico." He looks me up and down. "I take it you can walk?"

"I… yeah."

"Good. Cause shit's turning ugly here and the sooner we can leave, the better."

I follow him out of the shack and onto the grounds of Dmitri's palace. We stop under an archway, right on the edge of the courtyard, with only half a view. We come upon some of Dominic's wolves, and some other vampiri I don't recognize.

I silently count them. Notice the faint resemblances in their clothing, the richness of it, the way they hold themselves. The way even the wolves keep their distance.

Are these…

I stand straighter next to my companion. "You really are Violeta's brother, aren't you?"

Nico sends me an amused glance. "Guilty as charged."

Royalty. He's royalty. The same kind of royal I've been hating all these centuries for no reason. And Violeta's brother. The same Violeta I shunned after finding out her lineage, the same woman I refused to listen to despite her being my consort.

Another jolt runs through me. My consort. Do they know? Will they fight it? Are they here to finish me off instead of Dmitri?

"But—" I glance around. "And the other vampiri, they're—?"

"My siblings." He runs a hand through his hair, and shrugs as if to say *what the hell*. "We're the royals. The ones, I'm told, you've been thinking are behind all this."

"I…" No other words escape me.

Nico peers at me closer. "If you're wondering how I know, let's just say we didn't find you here by luck alone. My sister called Alex for help. And before that, the wolves sent my other siblings a message. It seems she's been busy while I was off enjoying a short vacation with my consort."

Consort. So he has one, too.

My eyes immediately start seeking Violeta out. "She's here?"

Nico nods. "Somewhere. We split up so I could find you first. Explain that what you think you know about us isn't really the truth. Not by a long shot."

"Why is that any of your business?" I cringe the moment the words are out. It's not how I'd meant them, but it's too late to take them back.

Luckily, Nico doesn't seem to get offended. Instead, he simply watches me for a long moment, as if taking my measure. "To be frank, it's not. But Violeta is, and I don't want her hurt because of preconceived notions around us. Also, I'm the first turned among us six, meaning what happens in our little family is always my mess to fix." He tilts his head. "Thus, this is also on my shoulders."

What can I say, really? That I changed my mind? That I've been confronted with the truth? All of that seems so...less. Less than they deserve.

Nico seems to take pity on me, as he clasps my shoulder. "I had a best friend, once. He was also a soldier, and he gave his life to protect mine. All of ours. His name was Silva, and I've never forgotten him." The hand on my shoulder squeezes. "We aren't monsters, Marcus. We aren't perfect, either. This will be a longer conversation at some point, but for now, I want you to know I do appreciate your service. We all do. And you have our deepest apologies for not being around to stop your suffering. We didn't know things were so bad—for any vampiri."

His words are the apology I never knew I needed. And the moment they're out, lingering between us, it's like the heaviest of burdens leaves my shoulders. Because I haven't been hating for no reason. And he has taken accountability for the part they've played. But I also know the truth now.

"And now that you know how bad things are, will you do something?"

Nico frowns, then opens his mouth to speak, but a cry from the side distracts him.

"Nico, come talk her off the ledge. Before she does something she might regret."

Chapter 24

Marcus

The auburn-haired vampir who spoke soon becomes entangled with one of the Guards who slips out of the shadows. She rips off the vampir's head like it's nothing—this despite him being almost two heads taller than her—and urges Nico to move faster. I'm on his heels. Technically, I should be running away from here, away from anything and anyone. After all, he gave me that choice, even if it wasn't really voiced.

But something tells me my role to play isn't done. And as we round off the corner of the mausoleum, we come into another courtyard. And all breath leaves my body.

"Violeta."

Nico speaks her name before I can, but she doesn't move. She's standing over the last remaining vampiri, including Dmitri. They're all kneeling, most of them beaten up and some with limbs missing. Dominic's wolves are behind her, two of them, and the rest are off into the shadows. Only their yellow eyes are visible.

At first, I don't understand what's the hold up. Then Violeta moves, her hands curling round Dmitri's throat. Her soft voice carries to all of us.

"Tell me again how you did nothing wrong, vermin. How I should spare you even though you'd never do the same to us."

I've never heard her use this tone. Granted, I've only known her for the better part of a few weeks, though it feels like longer. But the shock I see on the other vampiri, on her siblings' faces, mirrors my own.

Nico's the only one who takes another step closer, his tone even. "Vi, this isn't you."

"Why not?"

"Because you don't kill in cold blood. Never have."

She laughs. "I have now. Ask this guy. I've killed hordes of his vampiri as they hunted me down."

"That's different, it was in self-defense," the other one says, looking at her nails like the sole factor of being here is boring her out of existence.

"Save your words, Liza," Violeta retorts. "Your wisdom isn't needed here. And you're the worst one to give me advice in this."

Dmitri chokes as her nails dig further into his throat. Without thinking, I rush until I'm right by her side. A foot away, enough to smell the blood coming off her, but also, underneath it all, her sweet scent.

"Vi, don't do this."

She glances at me for the barest of seconds before focusing her attention on the vampir.

"Marcus. You're all right."

Her eyes flick to me again, take me in, my slowly healing battered self, and I see the resolution dawning on her further. The hands around his throat clench.

Before she can kill him in retaliation, I whisper, "Don't do this."

"Why not? He's heard us. He knows about the curse, about the consorts. He'll use it against us. Vermin like him should be exterminated. All they do is cause chaos in an otherwise perfectly normal society."

I slowly let my hand make contact with her shoulder. "He planned all this. He was behind Kalla taking you, too. I'm sorry about this—about all of it."

"And he tried to poison me. As if this goddamned curse wasn't enough, he had to add poison next to it." Under her breath, she adds, "They all know, now. About everything."

"And he deserves punishment. He's done much worse to others, I'm not denying it. He's worthless and deserves to die."

"Then you, of all of them, shouldn't be trying to stop me."

"You're right." I put my hand over hers, both our fingers now pressing on him. "Let me do this. Not you."

She stares at me with so much to read in her eyes. So much to decipher.

Does she realize why I'm standing here, by her side? Does she understand what I'm trying to express, without words? Or does she only think I'm doing this to placate her, to stop her from taking a life?

Because I'm not. I just don't want this death on her conscience, not when she's so—good. Better than me, better than her siblings, better than all of us. When she could've turned into a psychopath, she's learned to forgive. Learned to live. To understand, to keep her humanity. Something not all of us have been able to do, at least not to the same extent.

It's not fair that out of all of us, she'll be the one paying the price for this. Not for someone like Dmitri, someone who doesn't even deserve it. I've seen the good in Violeta, and I don't want that good extinguished over someone so…unworthy.

Dmitri gurgles something, and Violeta's fingers reflexively tighten on him. Mine move over hers.

"He did this to you," she says, "and to countless other soldiers. Condemned them to a life of loathing. Of loathing themselves, and us. *He was going to attack us.* And if we hadn't come, he would've imprisoned you, used you again."

"His glamour didn't work on me. Thanks to you. He wouldn't have won, Vi."

"He has to pay," she continues as if my words didn't even register.

"And he will. But not by your hand."

"Why not?"

"Because you don't have it in you. Nor should you, not when you—"

A louder gurgle distracts me, and I glance at Dmitri, only to notice his body slumping over. And another vampir, behind him, pulls out his hand from his chest, along with his heart and lungs. He grins manically.

Violeta's hand, and mine, drop to our sides in shock.

Blood drips from the vampir's hand, and still, I'm aware of

Dmitri slowly shriveling into himself. This vampir—he has to be one, no one else would've gotten the drop on us as he did—barely lifted a finger, and now my former commander, my superior, is gone. Extinguished from the world like he'd never existed.

I wish I could say I feel something, but there's only emptiness where there should have been something. Instead, another sentiment altogether takes over me. Something I've only recently become accustomed to.

Out of sheer instinct, I move in front of Violeta. Intending to defend her, to stand by her side as I should have before.

But as it turns out, that's not even remotely necessary.

Blondie says, "He's right, sis. You really don't have it in you."

I turn to Violeta, my eyes wide as I repeat the moniker. "Sis?"

Violeta

I ignore Marcus and his wide eyes, instead moving around him and slapping Alex's hand. Dmitri's heart and lungs fall to the ground with a yucky squelch.

"I had him!" I yell at him.

"You were taking too long." He shrugs, glances around. "And I'm a bit done with this place, don't you think?"

"Alex—" My growl falls on deaf ears as he simply turns and walks away.

I gape after him, unable to reconcile this version of him with the brother who'd come to my rescue. At least not until I remember his reaction to my revelation, his offhandness... What in all hells is going on with him?

Whatever had him in a bunch after feeding me his blood, it's now gone. Instead, his usual superior expression is back, and I know there's no talking to him. Not now. Maybe once we're home, but definitely not now.

Dominic's wolves follow his movements, plainly not knowing what to do with him. Neither do I. Nor does Marcus, judging by his reaction.

I turn to the other vampiri. They were soldiers under Dmitri. Same as Marcus was, once ago. Do they deserve to die, to be exterminated? If we're to send a message, they should be. Father always said it's better to wipe out your enemies, to leave nothing coming back to haunt you. It's one of his lessons I never truly agreed with.

Nico moves closer. He'd been near me, but Marcus had moved first. I still don't understand why. Even now, the way he's positioned as if to defend me... Does he realize what he's doing? Is this the consort bond at play, or something more? Should I even be hoping, when I've seen loathing in his gaze before?

But there's no loathing now. There's just—I turn away, unwilling to see his emotions so naked on his features. They'll make my decision much harder.

My gaze lands on Nico. Despite his nearness to me, he'd allowed Marcus to try to talk me out of killing Dmitri. Out of all my siblings, Nico's the only one without knowledge of the bond. He wasn't here when I explained everything. Yet he trusted another vampir whom he'd just met to get through to me?

He inches closer and wraps an arm around my shoulders. Looks at the vampiri with me. Drops his mouth to my ear. "I know why you want to kill them." I shouldn't be surprised. There was a time, not too long ago, when he knew everything I was thinking. "I know about Marcus and what he is to you. What Tassa is to me. It's what we found out on our little trip to Marea Neagră." He pauses, resting his forehead against me for a moment. "I swear to you, we'll protect them both."

I jerk my head to meet his gaze, but he's already turning to our siblings, speaking louder. "We have two choices here. We can either kill them all, leave a bloody massacre as a message. Or..." He moves to Dmitri and rips his shriveled head off the corpse. "We can be smarter, the way Father would want us to be."

"Father would *want* the massacre," Alex mutters.

Vlad's reaction is much more subdued. "What are you on about?"

Like me, he's always hated bloody displays. But the way he's staring at Nico clearly shows his fear.

And I know why. Our father loved one thing above all—psychological warfare. While we all took mandatory lessons, not all of us liked them.

Already, Liza has caught on. She cackles gleefully then sprints in the air, a ballerina sprite, and rips a flagpole off one of the windows. It'd previously had Dmitri's signage on it, the same one worn by all the guards. It's gone in a second and in Liza's hand, removed as if it had never existed. Liza lands softly down, and I catch Marcus' sharp intake of breath.

Da, my siblings are something. Away from humans, where they have to hide their true nature, they're a force to be reckoned with. And whether he wants to or not, Marcus is about to witness the full, unrepentant side of royals.

If my lies sent him running, this is probably going to do even worse.

Liza throws the pole to Nico, who catches it mid-air. He

positions it on the ground then lifts Dmitri's head and...impales it. I stare in awe and shock and a fair amount of revulsion as he takes the spike and jumps to the metal gate. Perched on it like a monkey, he places the head so it's in full view of anyone who'd come near. He even bends the bottom of the pole around the metal bars of the gate to keep it in place.

Then he falls back down and wipes his hands on his pants, facing us. The gory display behind him drips whatever blood it has left all over the gate. Soon, it'll be coated in it.

Even the wolves are quiet, watching on. I glance at Dominic, but his expression is poker-smooth.

"*This* is our message," Nico announces. "For too long, we've cowered and hidden away. And behind our backs, these fuckers have done the unimaginable. Not only have they lied and cheated and overlooked our rules, but they've taken our very name and used it to hide their duplicity. This has to stop, and it has to stop now." He gestures to the head behind him. "The message is simple—that we're back. And no one should fight us, lest they end up like Dmitri. Impaled, and with their army becoming ours." His gaze lands on Dominic. "Thank you for helping our sister. For that, you have our eternal gratitude—and I do mean eternal. Anything you need, ask for it."

Dominic glances around, his gaze lands on mine, then he meets my brother's again. "We're good for now. Just get your shit together."

"That's the plan," Nico says. "But it might be best you bow out now. Vampir glamour can be unpredictable to those in the area, and the last thing I need is your wolves becoming victims of it."

Dominic nods and with a whistle to his wolves, he marches out the gate.

Nico then strides over leisurely to the first of the vampiri who's kneeling. "Stand, soldier."

The vampir does as ordered, trembling all over. Nico grips his chin and forces him to stare at him. A moment later, his eyes glaze over.

I glance at Marcus, fear and trepidation running through me. Will this bring back memories? Not only of his time as a soldier, but of my own betrayal?

Instead of seeing revulsion on his features, I'm surprised to find him frozen, watching carefully. His gaze collides with mine, but it's too much—too intense—and I can't hold it more than a few seconds before breaking it.

Nico speaks to the vampiri he's glamoured. "From now on, you forget all allegiances. All but to one. The House of Dracul is your only family. Your only duty is to protect its members. Look around." The man's gaze falls on me, Vlad, Liza, Alex, then back to Nico. "*We* are your family. You protect us, we will protect you in turn. Are we understood?"

"Da, prințul meu."

Nico nods, then moves on to the next. Liza joins him, then Alex, and finally Vlad. As they go about glamouring everyone, I face Marcus.

Behind, all I hear are repeated choruses of the first answer, all delivered in firm tones. Not one has escaped the massive glamour, not one has contested it. Almost as if somewhere deep down, they knew all along who their allegiance belonged to.

I force myself to meet Marcus' intent gaze. An apology is on the tip of my tongue, for lying to him, but it simply won't fall. Pride, perhaps. Or something else. Fear that he'll forgive me, only so he can turn his back on me when things get tough.

"The clan is done for in these parts," I finally say. "As you can see, they've now become ours."

He looks around, then back at me, his gaze inscrutable. "You didn't kill them."

"No."

"Why not?"

A sigh escapes me. "Because Alex is right. I don't have it in me. And because...Father taught us better. He would have preferred we'd massacre them all, it's true. But every once in a while, he also taught us mercy. Everyone has its uses, if you know how to look at a situation."

"And what use are they to you?"

I glance at my siblings, and at the vampiri slowly leaving one by one after they've been glamoured. They move through the gates like robots, then disappear in a blur of movement.

"They'll spread the word that the House of Dracul is alive and well," I whisper. "That we're done hiding and are coming for all dissenters. Hopefully, that'll be enough to keep anyone from outright attacking us, as they came for me. It won't stop the hunters, but those we can deal with."

A muscle ticks in his jaw. "Hunters? More attacked you?"

I bite my lip, hating that I'd slipped up. Then I nod. There's no point in lying or omitting things from him anymore. "Da, they did. When I took refuge with Dominic, after...leaving your cabin. Hunters came for me there, and Dominic's son helped me fight them."

He steps closer, lifts a hand as if to touch me, then lets it drop by his side. "I should've been there."

"You have nothing to feel guilty over, Marcus. Everything you hated me for, in a way, you had every right to. Especially once I didn't tell you the truth." I glance around again. "I'll be fine. This message will help slow the attacks."

"And if it doesn't? Who'll protect you?"

"My siblings." I smile faintly. "If nothing else, this has given us a reason to be stronger together." I draw in a deep breath, though I don't need to, and release it even slower. Saying words that weigh heavily on my heart, but that need to be said anyway. "You can return to your hermit life, and I dare say no one will bother you."

"If they do, feel free to give us a call," Nico says.

Marcus glances at him, then at the rest of my siblings minus Alex, and finally his gaze lands back on me. "And you?"

"What about me?"

"Where are you going?"

It takes all my strength to speak normally and hide the tumult inside me. The storm raging like a tornado, threatening with waterworks and a hell of a lot more.

"Home. I'm...going back home."

"Why?"

Those green eyes shine with something—hurt?—but I shake my head, forcing myself to unsee it.

"There's nothing here for me."

"There's me," he whispers, so low that it hits me somewhere deep in the chest.

It takes all my willpower to keep a cool expression. "There's not, though. I've hurt you too much, and even if I hadn't, the perils of having me around are not worth it. I won't risk your life, not when you could have an easier one. I... It's better this way, Marcus."

He takes a step closer. "I know about the curse, too. I know you need me."

Tears fill my eyes. "Not because you feel obligated, though. That was never my intent." I touch his cheek, enjoying the rough stubble against my hand one last time. "Remember, this was only supposed to be something easy, and fun." Before he can say anything else, I add, "Now that we know what the vampiri clan are doing, it'll involve some cleaning on our end. Thank you for bringing it to our attention, truly." He frowns at my formal tone, no doubt, but it's the only way I can keep a hold of myself. "But while this has been educating, it's high time we return home." I pause, draw in a deeper breath, and let it out. "Goodbye, Marcus."

I turn before he can say anything and start making my way out, my siblings in tow. At least none of them ask me for an explanation now. And, for once, their aloof natures are a comfort.

It's our turn to disappear in a blur of movement, leaving Dmitri's manor behind—complete with Dmitri's impaled head.

And I do everything in my power not to turn around for Marcus.

Chapter 25

Marcus

Goodbye, Marcus.

For the longest time, I stare at the spot Violeta was in.

One moment she was there, the next she's gone. Out of my life. Leaving an emptiness behind that threatens to make me rip my undead organs from my chest and set them on fire. I thought my being here, my actions, would speak for themselves. Clearly, they didn't.

She's a princess. What did you expect, that she'd fall at your feet?

No. I never did. But...

I glance at everything around me. There's an odd silence now that everyone's gone. Dmitri's head continues dripping blood all over the gate. The snow underneath is slowly becoming tainted with the drops. In leaving, Liza left her cape with the House of Dracul crest hooked on the same gate.

No one can deny the truth of what happened here, if they come by.

And for the first time, I've witnessed for myself who the royals are. All my preconceived notions were flaunted in my face and destroyed.

They had a chance to massacre everyone. By all accounts, they should have. And yet they didn't.

That, if nothing else, is the final proof that everything Dmitri told me was a lie. A full-blown, hideous lie, designed to keep me under control of the clan. A control I snapped out of.

The Dracul siblings could've put me back under that control. They could've glamoured me, same as all the soldiers. But they didn't.

And I remember their words, as they did the glamouring. They could have said anything, could have literally wiped the vampiri's minds clean and inserted their own commands. Instead, their message had been simple. *We are your family. You protect us, we will protect you in turn.*

That was never the message while I was under Dmitri's rule. It was do this, do that—rules, regulations and orders. Commands. Every aspect of our life was his to do with as he pleased. But the royals, they've practically given free choice. None of the soldiers can go against them, ever, but if they choose to be loyal to them, they'll have protection for the entirety of their existence.

That's not the image I had expected.

To be perfectly honest, Alex was more what I'd expected. I was almost glad he and Liza were part of them, as they're closer to the ruthless beings I was trained to believe all royals were.

And even them... Their killing was centered around protecting Violeta. Around avoiding her the hardship of killing, of tainting the same personality I've come to love.

I clench my fists. Trembling runs over my entire body. It takes me a moment to realize it's me, fighting against myself, to stop myself from rushing after her.

Which is the most idiotic thing I could do, because what's keeping me away from her? Nothing.

Violeta thinks I'd be staying with her out of guilt, or a desire to keep her alive. I'm pretty sure the curse wouldn't work that way, but it's not me I have to convince. It's her.

Her family, I can deal with. If she'll have me, that's all I need.

I snap to and go vampir speed, following her scent. I end up intersecting her path when she's already halfway out of Dmitri's territory.

"Wait."

Violeta stares at me, but says nothing.

"I don't... I don't want you to leave."

A sad smile is my only answer. "We don't all get what we wish for."

Alex and Liza roll their eyes in tandem, while Vlad and Nico share a glance and simply step to the side, giving us a moment.

It would be an intimidating situation if they were normal. It's intimidating knowing they're vampiri, and older than me. But the fact they're royal on top of it?

You're not good enough is probably what they're all thinking right about now. But whatever may be the case, I can't let Violeta out of my life. Not when every molecule in my body demands I keep her in it.

I tear my gaze from them and focus on Violeta, taking a step closer. "I need you with me, Violeta. I'm sorry for all I said. I know a simple *sorry* isn't enough, but if you'll have me, I'll spend the rest of my existence defending you, protecting you with my life, making your existence easier."

She shakes her head. "That's just the thing, I don't want you to. I'm sick, Marcus. Temporarily, maybe. Reversible, maybe. But in the long run?"

I take her hand in mine. "In the long run, I'd rather have as long as I can get with you, than nothing at all. And this curse *can* fix you. Dominic said it himself, that if none of you reject your mates, then there's hope of breaking it. We'll have to find the ins and outs of the *how*, but it's more than possible."

While I might've thought my speech was worthy of a smile, all I get is a frown in return.

"I don't need you around me because you feel guilty. Or, worse, because you've been so trained into protecting others that you think I'm your new pet project."

A growl escapes me. I can tell I've attracted her siblings' attention again, but they're so far in my periphery I can't be bothered. Instead, I focus on Violeta and pull her a step closer.

"I'm not in this out of a guilt trip or hero complex, Violeta. Can't you understand being apart from you tears me apart from the inside out? I need you. Always."

"Is that really the truth?" She removes her hand, tapping her fingers against her leg.

The small tick doesn't escape my notice. It's similar to what she's seen me do when I'm nervous, anxious. Another manifestation of the consort bond, perhaps?

"Marcus, I don't think you understand," she whispers. "If anything, this whole debacle with Dmitri has put things into perspective."

This is what I'd been afraid of. That she'd use logic to back away from us. "How so?"

"My family's in danger. We have been for a while, but now, there are actual forces fighting against us. The clans are planning an offense, and they know where we live. The hunters seem to be acting completely unlike themselves... And now there's information about this curse. It's not just *one* thing, hell, it's not even things we can see sometimes!" She glances over my shoulder at her siblings, then meets my gaze again. "I see it with Nico—he's worried, he'll have to protect Tassa. I know it will be the same with us. And I can't have that." A tear slips down her cheek. "You—you'll end up hating me. This is a never-ending fight, and it'll drag you back in the folds of war."

Relief spreads through me and I break the distance between us, wrapping my arms around her shoulders instead. Giving her a gentle shake. "Do you think I care about that? I've fought before for something I gave no shits about. But you? I would lay down my life for you today, Violeta. Right now, in fact."

I let her go and drop at her feet, kneeling. The snow and damp earth underneath it soon soak my jeans, grounding me into what I'm doing. I look up, meeting her shocked gaze, and tilt my head to the side. Offering my neck, in the most vulnerable position I can.

"Marcus..." More tears slip down her face.

"I am yours, Violeta. My *life* is yours. Same as yours is mine.

We're each one part of a whole, and I won't allow your lineage, my pride, or anything else to come between us."

In the distance, I'm vaguely aware of her siblings' whispering. But I don't give in to the urge to yell at them to shut up. That won't help my case, and it'll only distract from the matter at hand when one of them loses their shit.

"What more do you need from me? Do you want me to cut my veins, offer you my blood? Because I'll gladly do it. I will feed your weakness, until you feel better. I will be your crutch, your everything. And I'll be there to love you, with my body, until the ends of time."

On a choked cry, Violeta falls to her knees before me, and cups my cheeks. "Stop. Please. You're making this harder than it should be."

"That's because it's not." I dig my hands in her hair, pulling her closer still, and brush my lips against hers. "I'm here. With you. For you. Never against you. Accept it, Vi. Please. Accept *me*."

"I do, I do, Marcus, but—"

I crush her mouth under mine, refusing to let the rest of the words out. And I don't stop at a regular peck. I push for more, until our tongues are battling for dominance, until she's panting against me, until I can clearly hear the cursing from the others.

"That's our *sister*—" Alex.

"And this is her moment. Shut it." Nico. I'll have to thank him after.

I pull back, if only so I can continue my argument before they fully interrupt us.

"There is no *but*, Violeta." I stare into her eyes. "There's only us. As long as you accept that."

Her eyes glint with more tears. Her mouth is red from my kisses. And it's all I can do not to return to it, to break away her resistance.

"I get it. I understand what it's like, to be a part of a larger whole. Your siblings, they're that. Your House, it's that. And I understand. All I ask, is that you let me take care of you. Let me be here, protect you. And let our bond slowly fight back at this curse taking hold of you."

Her lips part, and I brace myself. I don't want to hear a no. And if I do, I'll follow them home. Pester her, until I break down her resistance.

But Violeta only says, "All right."

A wave of relief so strong runs through me, my body threatens to sag under it. Instead, I get to my feet and pull her with me, crushing her in my arms the moment after.

Against her hair, I whisper, "Thank you. Thank you, for believing in us."

The air around us thickens, filled with something...electrifying. In my arms, Violeta gasps, as if getting a renewed sense of something. She pulls back and for a moment I see the color in her cheeks, and almost *feel* the strength in her bones. And then it's gone, as if it wasn't there.

"What was that?" I whisper.

"I think... I think it was the curse. We were...feeding it."

I think back to what Dmitri told me. "The acceptance. Yours and mine, it must've made it tangible."

Footsteps crunch in the snow as her siblings slowly approach us.

"Are we all done, yet?" Liza mutters. "I want to go *home.* Now."

Violeta tenses in my arms and pulls back.

Nico's frowning. "We all felt that. Was it the curse?"

She nods. "I think so. I think... My verbal and spiritual acceptance of the bond, of Marcus, might've fed it."

"And how do you feel?" Vlad asks.

"I..." She closes her eyes, then smiles, amazed. "Strong. I don't know how long it'll last, but it's the best I've felt."

Alex snorts. "Even better than after my blood?"

Violeta turns to him. Instead of anger, all I see in her expression is sadness. "I hope you never have to feel the effects of this, Alex. Though it may make you understand it more and get off your high horse, I wouldn't wish it on anyone."

Liza taps her foot impatiently. "No one answered *my* question."

Nico rolls his eyes. "Yeah, yeah. We'll go." He looks to Violeta. "But not you."

"What do you mean? I—"

A half-smile stretches his lips. "I think you know." And then he turns and looks at me, nodding.

Intertwining our fingers, I move closer still. "Stay. Stay with me, and I'll protect you. I swear it. I'll be here no matter what."

She stares at me for a long moment, then slowly nods. A breath of relief escapes me, and I pick her up in my arms, twirling her around.

Alex rolls his eyes. "Are we done yet with this fool? Vi, come on. You're not really staying."

She shakes her head in my arms. "I'm not coming, Alex. You guys go ahead."

He snorts. "Seriously? You're going to take a cabin in the woods over the comfort of our home?"

Though his words are meant to sting, something tells me they're coming from a place of hurt. I can't forget how he killed Dmitri, so she wouldn't have to. That tells me more about him than he'd like, I'd imagine.

"Vi, come *on*!" Liza says. "What about us?"

"You'll be fine without me. And plus, it's not forever. I just... It's for now. I think being with Marcus, cementing this bond, will help me. At least a few weeks."

They have nothing to say to any of that.

"Besides, it'll give you guys a chance to find your own consorts."

That gets Liza and Alex backing away immediately.

"Nu, mersi," she mutters.

"Same," Alex growls.

They're gone in the space of a breath, leaving behind a scorching trail in the snow.

Nico snorts, then glances between us. "You better take good care of her. I'm trusting her with you. This is her life, in your hands."

"I swear it."

Violeta reaches into her pocket and hands over something—a tattered notebook. "I've carried this with me for days, since Dominic gave it to me. I think you should all read it. Or, maybe we can do it together." It's not like her to ramble, but I immediately understand why when she adds, "It's Father's notebook."

Nico stares at it for a long time, then reaches for it. His fingers are trembling slightly, but the little black book soon disappears in his own pocket. Then he turns to Vlad. "Come on. Time to get home."

"One second." The quietest of them, he moves to Violeta and hugs her. When he pulls away, he says, "Watch your back. Father taught us well—and this won't be the last of the attacks."

"I know," she says. "I promise I'll be safe."

He looks to me then. "We're trusting you with our sister. You know what the punishment is if anything goes wrong."

A mirthless laugh escapes me. "Believe me—your punishment

would be nothing compared to what I would inflict upon myself if anything were to happen to her."

The answer seems to suit them both, as they're gone in the next breath, as well.

And then it's only me, and Violeta. I turn to her, cupping her cheek.

She tears her gaze from the spot her siblings were in and meets mine.

"Ready to go home?" I ask.

Chapter 26

Violeta

I follow Marcus home in silence, still thinking of that powerful burst of energy I'd felt. Blood—vampir, vrykolakas, muroni—has fed me and kept me sane for the last few weeks. But this was new, a different type of burst, one I still sense buzzing in me. Not even the pot I used to smoke has ever given me such an experience.

We reach Marcus' cabin about an hour later, and I pause on the edge of the woods, watching it. Remembering being here, wishing I was inside with him, while he was cursing my name.

Marcus stops by my side, intertwining our fingers. "Come on."

I follow him at a regular human pace, and we enter the cabin.

The moment we do, I push him against the wall, shutting the door behind us. Hands cupping his cheeks, I rise on tiptoes and kiss him like I've been meaning to since his sweet words earlier.

Marcus groans when my tongue touches his lips, and his hands come to my waist, then drop lower until they're on my hips, pulling me closer.

My hands are already fiddling with his belt, and before I've even succeeded, I'm shoving the jeans off him. Then the rest of his clothes. Marcus moves us inwards, past the kitchen, and to the back door, towards the outside shower.

Naked, laughing, we rush outside and he turns the water on, letting its heat fall over us. I face him, already reaching for him. He's on me in a moment, caressing my breasts, one hand sliding between my legs, already driving me crazy.

But I won't be the only one, this time. I fall to my knees, taking his length in my hand, and run my tongue over him. Marcus' hand settles on my hair, and at the next lick, he slides his fingers within my hair, holding on for dear life as I worship him with my mouth.

"Vi, stop, I—" He tugs on my hair, then pulls me up and crushes his mouth against mine with more intensity than before.

In one fell swoop, he picks me up and moves us against the wall, rattling it with the force of the movement.

A laugh escapes me. "Better watch it, we don't want to break down the house."

Marcus grins, and on my next chuckle, thrusts inside me—deep. A broken gasp escapes me, followed by another. And then he drops his mouth to my breast, tugging a nipple in his mouth as he continues to thrust inside me.

My moans, his groans, fill the air around us. Nothing else exists except him, and me, and this moment.

Much later, when we're dry and snuggling in his bed again, Marcus kisses the top of my head. "I meant what I'd said. You can feed on me whenever."

I look up at him, giving him a grateful smile. "Thank you. I'm hoping this new...burst...will continue for a bit longer. And besides, I may just visit Lucrezia a few times. That vrykolakas blood sure is tasty."

He hovers over me, hips rolling into mine. "Really?"

"Mm. Sure beats having mine taken."

That stops his teasing, and his expression sobers. "Is that what Kalla did? Dmitri said she'd kidnapped you on his orders."

I nod. "Said something about sacrificing me to Zalmoxis." A shudder escapes me. "I don't know, Marcus. I wanted to believe this curse shit is crazy, but it's not. None of it is."

His arms tighten around me. "I'm here, and I always will be. Curse or no curse, threats or no threats. You can always count on me."

His kisses erase my mind of anything but the primal need to have him back inside me. For now, at least, we have our little happy corner. It'll have to be enough. Most humans are only given one lifetime on this earth—it's about time I start making the most of mine.

Epilogue

Dominic returned to the encampment. A few vrykolakas shorter, but at least with an alliance in place. Lucrezia was already waiting for him, leaning against the opening of their house.

Her relieved gaze connected with his, but she made no move towards him. Instead, it was he who pulled her into his arms, burying his head in the crook of her neck.

"I missed you, draga mea."

"And I, you. What happened?"

He took another moment before pulling away from her hug, and walking inside the house. As concisely as possible, he ran her through what had happened. What the vampiri had done, and what the outcome had been.

Lucrezia was biting her lower lip by the time he was done. "That sounds like a right mess."

"It was, yeah. But at least that's one allegiance formed."

"An allegiance that won't be worthwhile unless they're all alive. This curse may soon take care of that."

He ran a hand over his face. "Tell me about it. Tytus couldn't have tossed us into a hotter pit of hell, I swear. When's your next meeting with him?"

"Not for another month, but I can take a few wolves and go earlier. I'm sure he won't mind."

Dominic mulled it over, then shook his head. "No. Either I come with you, or you don't go. Between the vampiri wars, the hunters, and that crazy goddamned Dacian running rampant, I'm not risking you or Luca." He tugged on her wrist until she was on his lap. "You're more important to me than anything else, and I won't put you in danger again."

"We need more answers. This was supposed to be an easy move, but it sounds like things are getting more...complicated."

"It's the damned vampiri. If they'd had their house in order, our arrival here would've been as easy as Tytus predicted. We could've just focused on the curse bit, like we were supposed to. Instead, there's everything else. A fucking distraction, if you ask me."

Lucrezia caressed his cheek. "And something tells me not all of the vampiri will take the curse seriously."

Dominic grunted. "Mm. You may be right, as always." He lifted his gaze to her. "I don't want you in danger. When I thought the hunters were coming here—"

She pulled away enough to meet his gaze, and caress his cheek. "The Underworld was a long time ago, Dom."

"Not long enough," he growled, before cutting off her protests with a searing kiss.

All he could do was wait and keep watch. The time to act would come, he had no doubt about it. The only question was who'd be left standing in the end.

Two have fallen. Four remain. And now these royals know a god's curse is demanding their submission...

Vlad has a dark secret. Silviana has a secret mission.

She'll test his every boundary.... break his every rule...and turn him inside out.

Can this vampire heir survive, or will he get lost in her deadly deceit?

Find out in the next Lost Royals of Transylvania installment, Deadly Deceit.

Available for pre-order today!

To be continued....

And if you enjoyed Violeta and Marcus' story, please consider leaving a review at your choice of retailer. Even a line or two makes a huge difference to an indie author!

ROGUES EXTENDED UNIVERSE – READING ORDER

Moonlight Rogues
Flaming Rogues
Immortal Rogues
Lost Royals of Transylvania
Vârcolac Legacy (coming 2022)

Love my books?

Want to get your hands on them and review them first, before anyone else?

Sign up for my ARC team now

And you'll get to read and review everything first....

Including the next *Lost Royals of Transylvania* novel!

Vampires, sibling rivalries and mysteries continue.

About the Author

Alexa Whitewolf is a fiction writer, newspaper columnist of daily issues and author of the critically acclaimed ***Moonlight Rogues*** shifter series.

Alexa has been a lifelong writer and first began creating other worlds and characters at the ripe age of 12. Growing up in the Transylvania region surrounded by epic mountains and a never-ending stream of legends and stories was bound to create an overactive imagination. This shines through Ms. Whitewolf's writing by creating worlds filled with unique folklore, life wisdom and plenty of furry creatures.

An avid traveler, Alexa writes under a penname and spends her days between an office job and writing in Canada's capital, when she's not flying somewhere with lush landscapes and plenty of hiking trails.

Her series focus on strong heroines, kind yet sexy men, fights of good and evil and the never-ending learning curve of humanity's strong—and weak—points. Romanian folklore is intertwined with her writing, more notably in her shifter romance series, the Moonlight Rogues. Her other series draw on world mythology, such as the Avalon myth and Arthurian legend (***The Avalon Chronicles***) and Ancient Egypt (***The Sage's Legacy***).

You can follow her blog at www.alexawhitewolf.com/blog or on social media. Her column in Observatorul also tackles various issues, including health, technology, and a writer's life.

If you want up to date releases, make sure you sign up for her newsletter. For new releases notifications, you can also follow her on Amazon and Bookbub.

Also by the Author

Rogues Extended Universe

Moonlight Rogues series

Moonlight Rogues: Origins

First to Fall

Second to Surrender

Third to Tumble

Last to Love

Flaming Rogues series

Fanning the Flames

Igniting the Ice

Immortal Rogues series

Secret Shadows

Archer's Arrow

Cat's Charms

Trickster's Trap

Fickle Fate

Lost Royals of Transylvania series

Immortal Illusion

Cracked Casualty

Deadly Deceit

Blind Burden

Angry Addiction

Primal Protection

Demoni Sancti Extended Universe

Standalone

Blazing Ashes

Demoni Sancti series

Fallen

Broken

Unshackled

Risen

Ascended

The Avalon Chronicles series

Avalon Dreams

Avalon Wishes

Avalon Nightmares

Atrox

The Sage's Legacy – YA series

The Dragon Medallion

The Dragon Manuscript

Relics of the Underworld

Standalone novels

Blood Ties, Love Binds

Unconditional Love

www.ingramcontent.com/pod-product-compliance
Lightning Source LLC
LaVergne TN
LVHW041924090826
845145LV00015B/293

* 9 7 8 1 9 8 9 3 8 4 1 5 2 *